NIC TATANO

I've always been a writer of some sort, having spent my career working as a reporter, anchor or producer in television news. Fiction is a lot more fun, since you don't have to deal with those pesky things known as facts.

I spent fifteen years as a television news reporter and anchor. My work has taken me from the floors of the Democratic and Republican National Conventions to Ground Zero in New York to Jay Leno's backyard. My stories have been seen on NBC, ABC and CNN. I still work as a freelance network field producer for FOX, NBC, CBS and ABC.

I grew up in the New York City metropolitan area and now live on the Gulf Coast where I will never shovel snow again. I'm happily married to a math teacher and we share our wonderful home with our tortoiseshell tabby cat, Gypsy.

Follow me on Twitter @NicTatano.

Twitter Girl

NIC TATANO

HarperImpulse an imprint of
HarperCollins*Publishers* Ltd
77–85 Fulham Palace Road
Hammersmith, London W6 8JB

www.harpercollins.co.uk

A Paperback Original 2014

First published in Great Britain in ebook format by HarperImpulse 2014

Copyright © Nic Tatano 2014

Cover Images © Shutterstock.com

Nic Tatano asserts the moral right to
be identified as the author of this work

A catalogue record for this book is
available from the British Library

ISBN: 9780008113124

Automatically produced by Atomik ePublisher from Easypress

For Myra, who always sets my heart atwitter...

CHAPTER ONE

@TwitterGirl
Tornado whips through Mississippi trailer park, causes three million dollars worth of improvements.

Yeah, that's the tweet which got me fired. Unless you've been living under a rock, you know that it made me America's most polarizing figure overnight. I, Cassidy Shea, former network reporter (handle: @TwitterGirl) whose stories included a snarky attitude that attracted more than one million followers, let her 200 IQ ass do the talking once too often. Who knew that one hundred and fourteen characters could sink my career like a stone, but, then again, when something goes viral on the Internet... well, the thing whipped around the country faster than the tornado that inspired it.

Oh, and before you think I'm some insensitive New York snob who makes fun of those less fortunate, let me remind you of the follow-up story that hardly anyone saw. That tornado only touched down for a minute and it wiped out an abandoned trailer park that was about to be bulldozed by the government for a pork barrel project. It actually saved the feds millions in demolition costs and enabled them to start construction early on the desperately needed Museum of American Macramé. (Slogan: 'Got

Knots?') Not one person was injured by the tornado, nothing else was damaged, nobody was left homeless. It simply whooshed a bunch of ramshackle mobile homes outta there and was done. But nooooo, you didn't pay attention to *that* story, did you? You had the same knee-jerk reaction as the network president, who was deluged by angry tweets from flyovers (a network term for people the airlines zip over between New York and Los Angeles.) So even though I got canned three days ago, Twitter Girl still gets bushels of nasty comments collected in one convenient location by a very genteel hashtag:

#FireTheRedheadBitch
Merry Christmas, Cassidy. Enjoy the pink slip in your stocking?

Most of these tweets contain lovely terms of endearment and suggest I perform various impossible anatomical acts that I won't share. Suffice it to say I will never be able to set foot in the State of Mississippi again, which won't exactly break my heart. Or, more importantly, a television station. Which will.

So for the first time in my professional career, I have absolutely no idea what to do with the rest of my life.

"Hey, Caz, come look at this!"

The voice you hear belongs to my twenty-five year old kid brother Sam, with whom I share a home here on Staten Island, often called the forgotten borough of New York City. He's been a saint through all this, compiling all the nice tweets and direct messages of support so that the redhead bitch might cheer up during the holidays. Every night after dinner he cuts and pastes them into one document, prints it out and makes me read them aloud. But with three days to go before Christmas, I'm unemployed and not in the mood. I shuffle down the hall and find him rolling toward me in his wheelchair, iPad in his lap. "Sam, you don't need to keep doing this. I'm okay, really."

He smiles, making the dimples in his lean face pop. His green eyes brighten as runs his fingers through his mop of black hair to get it out of his face and points at the screen. "Caz, you really need to read this."

I roll my eyes. "I just want to forget about it, Sam. Look, I appreciate what you're doing—"

"I think it's a job offer."

His words make my jaw drop. For the past few days I've been radioactive, so much so that my agent dropped me right after she told me my television career was toast and I had not only burned every bridge but napalmed them down to the molecular level. "Some television station wants to hire me? You're kidding."

He shakes his head. "It's not a station." He hands me the tablet and I read a direct message sent to @TwitterGirl:

Cassidy, your voice mailbox is full and need to talk. We have a position for you in the campaign. - Frank Delavan

My eyes widen and I feel myself smile for the first time in days.

Sam is wearing his eyebrows-up-I-told-you-so look, which I get a lot since he's much smarter than I am. "So, Twitter Girl, still pissed at me for reading your mail?"

I hand back his iPad, lean down and give him a hug, then muss up his hair like I did when he was little. "Hell, no. I owe you big time. You know who Frank Delavan is?"

He nods. "Duh, my sister works in the news business. Of course I do. He's Will Becker's point man. And apparently he wants you to be a part of the team."

Me. Twitter Girl.

Working for *the* Will Becker. And unless you've been living under that same neighborhood of rocks for a while, you know he's America's most eligible bachelor and odds-on favorite to be the next President of the United States.

My euphoria is interrupted by the doorbell. I run across the living room to answer it, as I already know it's my boyfriend

3

Jamison back from a long trip to China. I've barely been able to get in touch with him since I got canned and now I can't wait to share the good news. While Sam has been doing his best to comfort me, it's brotherly love, and I really need a hug from my significant other. (Well, okay, more than just a hug.)

When I open the door I see that he's carrying something other than a Christmas gift. It's a metaphorical box of relationship coal for my stocking as a peek inside tells me it's my stuff from his apartment. My smile disappears.

"Hi," he says, looking at the box he's holding instead of my face.

"What's this?" I ask, even though my romantic GPS has already told me.

Your relationship has hit… a dead end.

Recalculating…

He walks inside, accompanied by a blast of frigid December air and I close the door. "I'm… uh…"

I bite my lower lip and feel my emotions well up. He's still not looking at me and I've been around the block enough times to know why. "You're breaking up with me?"

"I'm sorry, Cassidy."

"This why you didn't get back to me?"

No response.

"Look at me, dammit."

He looks up and I see very little emotion in his eyes. "I've been doing a lot of thinking since… you know. The incident."

"And?"

"I… don't think I can be with someone who is disliked by so many people."

In a flash my emotions switch gears. Upset to pissed off. My blood pressure zips past *elevated*, leaves *dangerous* in the rear view mirror and goes directly to *Irish-girl-wanna-hit-someone* level. I see Sam wheel to the edge of the living room and peek around the wall as he's obviously heard the conversation and is standing by in case I need him, which I will shortly. I slowly nod and fold my arms. "Wow. And here I thought you came over to support me. Alas, I incorrectly assumed you had a spine."

"The people at the firm today…" He shakes his head as his face tightens. "God, it was just brutal what I went through."

"What *you* went through? Excuse me, but are you actually playing the victim card here?"

"Cassidy, my reputation is at stake. How many clients will want to hire me if I'm in a relationship with someone like you."

Like me? LIKE ME???

His words push me over the edge and send Sam heading in my direction. I yank the box from his arms, put it on the floor, open the door and point out at the street. "Get out."

He reaches out and takes my shoulders but I twist away like his hands are on fire. "Cassidy, don't take it personally—"

"You heard my sister," says Sam, rolling to a stop a few feet from Jamison and glaring at him. "Get the hell out of our house. Now."

My boyfriend looks at my brother, who was a six-foot-two black belt in karate before the accident and has tremendous upper body strength from life in the chair. Jamison knows Sam would have no qualms about kicking his ass. He nods and turns back to me. "Well, know that I wish you the best."

"Yeah, right," I say, as he heads out the door. When he's on the way to his car I turn to look at Sam who has a gleam in his eye. He cocks his head at the pile of snow on the porch.

"Do it, Caz."

I know exactly what he's thinking. I step outside, grab a handful of the white stuff which has almost turned to ice, pack it into a ball, rear back and fire. It nails Jamison in the head.

"Ow!" He turns around. "What the hell was that for?"

"That's for the snowball's chance you ever have of coming back to me!" I flip him the bird, throw in the Italian salute for good measure (that's the hand slapped in the crook of the opposite elbow, for those not versed in Sicilian sign language), step back inside, slam the door and get a high five from Sam.

"Feel better?" he asks.

"A little." I feel my eyes start to well up. "Not really."

Sam reaches his arms up, I lean down and accept his warm hug. When we break the embrace we start the rehab ritual, which, unfortunately, I have gone through too many times.

Like I said, I've been around the block known as Breakup Square.

He rolls into the kitchen, I follow him. He reaches into the freezer, grabs a pint of Haagen Dazs rum raisin and hands it to me, already sitting at the kitchen table with a spoon. He wheels his chair next to me and starts stroking my hair. I lean my head on his shoulder as I savor the rich ice cream.

Sam kisses the top of my head. "Hey, wait till he finds out you got another job."

And wait till he finds out who I'll be working with.

***

"Yo, Twitter Girl!"

The words from a young hardbodied bike messenger greet me as I emerge from the cab in Brooklyn. I smile and wave at him as he pedals by, slows down to check me out head to toe, and returns a sexy grin. (If I didn't have an important meeting I'd grab a CitiBike and go after him.)

I head into the seriously out of the way tavern and pause a minute so my eyes can adjust to the very dim light. I walk past the ancient oak bar, empty except for a burly bartender wheeling in a keg, and spot Frank Delavan at the last table near the kitchen door. He stands up, much shorter than he appears on television, maybe five-six, and extends a hand. "Cassidy, nice to meet you. Thank you for coming."

I return the handshake. "Thanks for inviting me." I take a seat and adjust my chair as I take a look at the New York sports photos that cover every inch of paneled wall space. "This place is a little off the beaten path for you, huh?"

"Well, I thought in light of the publicity you might want to keep a low profile."

"That's not really possible when you're a six foot tall redhead who's been on network television for seven years, but I appreciate the thought."

He laughs a bit. Delavan has a nice smile which goes well with his short and portly look, but I know his reputation as a gunslinger. He may look like a bald, middle-aged lawn gnome, but every politician wants him in a foxhole. "Well, the food's excellent here. I actually try to get by once a month. This is one of the city's best kept secrets. I grew up down the block. Used to come here as a kid for the cheeseburgers and never stopped."

A young waiter arrives at our table, hands me a menu, and his eyes light up with recognition. "Hey, you're Twitter Girl!"

I put my palms up and shrug. "See what I mean?" I say to Frank.

"Nice to have you in our restaurant," says the waiter. "For what it's worth, I thought you got a raw deal from the network. I sure miss those tweets. You're funny as hell."

"Thank you."

"Well, I wish you'd start again. Anyway, I'll give you guys a few minutes to decide." He turns and heads back to the kitchen.

"See," says Frank, dark eyes gleaming. "Not everyone is mad at you."

"Nah, only about four hundred thousand people. And everyone in the state of Mississippi."

"Well, I'm not one of those people. And neither is my candidate. He's a big fan."

"Really? Will Becker's on Twitter?"

"Yep."

"I thought politician's accounts were actually managed by staffers."

"Most are, but he actually likes being in touch with real people. He feels it's more accurate than an opinion poll and it's instant.

Anyway, he loved your television stories and your Internet sarcasm. That's why I asked you here today. You have a unique talent the campaign needs."

"Not sure I understand."

"Cassidy, I don't know where your political views lie…"

"Well, I'm one of those old school journalists who actually keeps my opinions private, so I'm not gonna tell you. I know it's fashionable to be biased, but that's not me."

"That's very admirable in this day and age and the Senator will respect that. But he's hoping you like him enough to join the campaign."

"Let's just say that considering his views I wouldn't mind working for you. But I'm not sure you need someone who's toxic with half the general public for your press office."

Frank leans back in his chair and folds his hands in his lap. "That's not the position we have in mind for you. And, as I said, it's your unique talent we need. In fact, it's a position that's never existed in a campaign, and you're the only person who could do the job. This new digital world offers interesting opportunities. If you don't accept our offer for this position, one will not be made to anyone else."

Now I'm getting confused. "I'm not sure where you're going, Frank. If you don't want me for your press office, what would I do? Produce videos?"

"We need Twitter Girl."

I furrow my brow. "Okayyyyyy…"

"We need your unique brand of snark. Those wicked, sarcastic one liners that can cut people down to size and go viral. You may have lost four hundred thousand followers the first day after that tweet but you've picked up a quarter million new people since. Sarcasm is a valuable currency on social media. We want to hire you to do what you did for the network, only your targets will be the people we're running against. We could spend millions on TV ads but 140 characters from you could be more effective, cheaper

8

and a lot faster. And let's face it, politicians are fair game. You couldn't possibly offend anyone."

"And those targets you mentioned would eventually include the current President."

He nods. "Assuming the Senator wins the party primary. But until he does, there are a host of candidates challenging him who need to be taken down a notch by Twitter Girl. And of course, the President will need constant tweaks along the way while we're going through primary season."

"Your candidate is a stone cold lock for the nomination."

"No such thing. You never know what sort of land mines will explode."

"C'mon, Frank. He's never had a scandal and just got named to a certain magazine's most beautiful people issue. Can't say I disagree with their judges."

His face turns serious for a moment. "Still, there are plenty of wild cards in the deck you can't anticipate in politics. A lot of people still might feel funny electing a President who's single."

"Yeah, but he's a widower. He didn't get divorced. Big difference. The man can't help it if his wife got sick and died. And plenty of women would want to vote for the country's most eligible bachelor. Or date him. Think about it, you go from dinner and a movie to First Lady. It's the American version of marrying a prince. The only thing we don't have is Buckingham Palace."

He smiles and nods. "So, you get that part, huh?"

"I'm a single woman, he's unattached, and, no offense, the man is smoking hot. Hell yeah, I get it."

I almost regret saying that but Frank laughs as he reaches for his water. "You're certainly not subtle."

"Hey, you want Twitter Girl, this is what you get."

"Good, because that's the attitude we want. But Becker doesn't need a girlfriend right now. He needs a Vice President of snark. Help get him elected and then you can take your best shot at the Lincoln Bedroom."

One hour, two beers and a killer cheeseburger later, I'm seriously intrigued. Frank has laid the cards on the table and they're all aces.

"There is, however, a catch," says Frank, as he leans forward.

"Ah, I *thought* this was too good to be true. What's the catch? I gotta pay for my own lunch today?"

"Cassidy, the campaign is a long, exhausting road. Even though our main campaign headquarters will be in Manhattan you'll be away from home a lot, sometimes for a week at a time. From now till November."

I shrug. "I figured as much. What's the big deal?"

"I say that because… I, uh… read about what happened with your brother. We didn't know if you could be away or if… you know. You needed to be here in town all the time."

I lean back. "Nah, Sam is more self-sufficient than I am. He drives, has a good job. He's an advertising copywriter. Does all the cooking, grocery shopping. The network already sends me out of town a lot. Or at least they did. Sam is fine when he's by himself. Honestly, I don't even notice the wheelchair anymore. He sure doesn't."

"Oh, I just thought since you two shared a home."

"I was twenty-five when my parents died in the accident and Sam became unable to walk. He was fifteen. He needed a legal guardian and extensive rehab so I moved back home. My boss was very understanding and gave me a leave of absence. But he doesn't need my help anymore for physical stuff. And he's got some girls he hangs out with if he misses female companionship."

"That's good to hear. So, you never wanted a place of your own after he got better?"

"I originally thought I would but the accident made us incredibly close. Before we were always on different wavelengths because of the ten year age difference. We don't even look alike, except for the green eyes. He got my mom's black hair and I got the red hair and freckles. But Sam's like an extra best friend and I wouldn't want to have any other roommate. Until I meet Mister Right, that is."

"It's great that you have such a good relationship with your brother. My sister is the devil's spawn. I think if you shaved her head you'd find three sixes."

I laugh, already on the same sarcastic wavelength with Frank. "It's funny, but originally I moved back home because he needed me. Now I can't leave because I need him."

"How so?"

"It not just that he's my emotional rock and in some ways older than me. Sam's got a built in bullshit detector. He meets the guys who come to pick me up on dates. Let's just say he's saved me from a lot of heartache. The man is an incredibly accurate judge of character."

"I see."

"And Sam's my hero. He went through a whole bunch of surgeries and I know he's occasionally in a lot of pain, but he never complains and hasn't let his situation hold him back. I admire him more than anyone I know."

"That's nice." Frank smiles and takes a sip of his beer. "Cassidy, one more thing. I know this is another personal question, and I apologize for asking, but a Presidential campaign is unique. We need your total commitment, so would this job cause any problems with a relationship?"

"It might if I had one. My boyfriend left skid marks last night. Apparently an attorney cannot have a girlfriend who has attained national redhead bitch status."

"My, how supportive."

"He shoulda just broken up with me on Twitter. I'm thinking of writing a book. *Dumping your significant other in 140 characters or less.*"

"Was this a serious relationship?"

"I thought it was. You would think a lawyer would have a set of brass ones and stand up for his girl. But I got even. The coward

11

forgot he'd left a whole bunch of legal documents at my house for some cases he was working on. It made wonderful kindling for the Yule log."

"I'd better not get on your bad side. Sounds like you're not exactly broken up over it."

"Hey, better I find out now than when I'm walking down the aisle. Sam had warned me about him and turned out to be right again. Anyway, that catch of yours is no problem. I am unattached and not ready for another relationship, even if it was Will Becker." (Yes, my fingers are crossed behind my back. Bless me, Father, for I have sinned. I lied through my teeth while thinking about having sex with my new boss.)

He nods and smiles.

C'mon, we've gotten all the details out of the way. Get to the good part. How much?

"You seriously want to pay me just to be sarcastic? Travel with the campaign and play on Twitter? That's all?"

He nods. "That's all. And we're prepared to pay you fifty percent more than you were making at the network." He reaches inside his jacket, pulls out an envelope and slides it across the table.

I open it, take out a small sheet of paper and my eyes bug out at the figure, which is exactly fifty percent more than I was making. "How the hell did you know what my salary was?"

He cocks his head to the side. "Really, Cassidy? I do work in politics. Your tax dollars at work. By the way, your return shows you're very generous with your charitable dollars."

"Right, I forgot Big Brother knows all." I pick up the ketchup bottle and look underneath it.

"Problem?"

"Just checking to make sure the condiments aren't bugged." I look at the slip of paper again, knowing this is the only lifeline I'm about to be thrown and someone actually wants to pay me a ton of money to be, well, my snarky self online. I can work for Will Becker. I agree on some of his issues and don't on others, but

I wouldn't have a problem if he were President. I like him better than the current reptilian occupant of the White House. And, of course, there's that little thing about him eventually needing a First Lady and perhaps he might like a skinny, spunky redhead for that position. "Okay."

"That mean you'll do it?"

"Yep. But I don't want to be VP of Snark. I want to be the CEO."

"Done." We shake and I pull out my cell.

"Calling your brother with the news?"

"Not yet. Right now Twitter Girl's gotta dish out some payback." I quickly tap the keys on my phone.

#FireTheRedheadBitch
@TwitterGirl The bitch is back. Stay tuned.

CHAPTER TWO

#FireTheRedheadBitch
@TwitterGirl
Returning to work in January! Details coming up!

@TwitterGirl
Eating lobster, shrimp, scallops, calamari, crab, sole and crawfish. Merry Christmas Eve!

"Can I be your intern?"

I knew the question was coming.

"It can be my Christmas gift. You don't even have to wrap it."

"That's because you simply want to *un*wrap it," I say.

"Hey, 'tis the season."

My best friend Ripley DeAngelo is drooling at the dinner table, and it's not over the massive amount of seafood available at her family's traditional Christmas Eve dinner.

She wants a shot at my new boss and the possibility of becoming the next First Lady.

Honey, take a number.

"Haven't even met the guy yet, but I'll see what I can do," I say, as I reach toward the middle of the table and ladle another round of shrimp scampi onto my plate. "Boy, I really love this

Italian tradition, Feast of the Seven Fishes."

"Don't change the subject," she says, her caramel eyes narrowing as they fill with lust. "All I want for Christmas is a chance at Will Becker. I'll work nights, weekends." She licks her lips and raises both eyebrows. "Overnights."

Her mother gently slaps her on the shoulder. "Young lady! It's Christmas Eve!" she says, busy clearing one empty dish and replacing it with another.

"Ma, I'm entitled to a Christmas list. Besides, I've been nice all year. I wanna be naughty for a change."

Ripley's mom rolls her eyes while her dad laughs. I really want to get back to stuffing my face with crustaceans, so I need to keep her at bay. I fold my arms like Barbara Eden in *I Dream of Jeannie* and snap my head down. "Poof, you're an intern!"

She shoves her hair behind her ears and smiles. "Thank you, dear friend."

And dear friend she is since high school. The girl with the booze and food heritage (half Irish, half Italian, one hundred percent Catholic) is named after Sigourney Weaver's kick-ass heroine and seriously has the balls to take on acid-bleeding aliens. And with her looks she might actually turn Will Becker's head. A five-nine stunner with chestnut tangles just past her shoulders, classic high cheekbones and a slender, stacked Barbie doll body that would put a twenty year old to shame, she's a girl who could have her pick of the litter. But Ripley is so damn particular, she remains, like me, unmarried at thirty-five. She spends more Saturday nights with me or a bottle of wine (or frequently, both) than out on a date, and I can tell it's getting to her.

Will Becker would be the ultimate catch for Ripley.

And for me as well. (Okay, so I've been daydreaming about giving a TV tour of the White House *a la* Jackie Kennedy. So sue me.) But I'm not even remotely in her league in the looks department. I'll have to bring my "A" game to a "B" (padded bra) to get the attention of the Senator around her.

15

For a brief moment I find myself flashing back to high school, with two girls fighting over the same guy. I quickly shove the thought away.

Until, right on cue, Sam thoughtfully brings it up. "I haven't seen you two look like this since I was eight."

"What are you talking about?" asks Ripley.

"Remember that crush you both had on the quarterback?"

Ripley blushes, my freckles light up. "Ancient history," she says.

"Really, dear brother, we've grown up since then. The Senator is just another guy. It's not like I'm practicing the signature *Cassidy Becker* on top of my homework."

"Yeah, right. You both have tells when it comes to men."

Ripley furrows her brow. "Tells? What are you talking about?"

"Rip, whenever you talk about a guy who interests you, your eyebrows do this little jump." He turns to me. "And you start twirling your hair. Like you're doing now."

I immediately drop my hand. "It's a nervous habit. I do it all the time."

"Hell," says Sam, "if Becker was here for dinner tonight, you'd end up with a perm."

***

Wednesday has been poker night for a few years, and I'm always the lone filly at the table. Since this particular Wednesday falls two days after Christmas, the usual beer and chips have been replaced with wine and enough leftover cookies and cakes to send anyone into a sugar coma.

Anyway, Sam always sits across from me, and despite the fact that he's my brother he turns into a gunslinger when we play cards and cuts me no slack. Two veteran fortysomething photographers from my (former) network, Kevin Frost and Jake Helper, take up two seats while the fifth chair belongs to fifty year old network correspondent and my mentor, Dale Carlin.

And while I don't have a poker tell, everyone has picked up on the fact that I'm upbeat about my new mystery job.

"Pot's right," says Sam, as he starts to deal. "Five card stud."

"I hate this game," says Kevin, leaning back and stretching out his lean frame while he smooths his thinning brown hair.

"That's because you never win," says Sam. He flips a card in front of me and I gently pull up the corner and see a king of hearts.

Dale turns to me as he runs his hand through his thick salt and pepper hair. "So, you're not even gonna tell your mentor about your new job?"

I shake my head. "I'm a vault. I'm not allowed to tell."

"I can tell," says Sam. "She got a gig as a celebrity greeter at Wal-Mart. She's going to enforce a strict four tattoo minimum."

I crinkle my nose at him. "Very funny, dear brother."

Kevin turns to Jake. "You watch. She's going to another network and gonna kick our asses every night." They turn and both look at me, their eyes widening as they study my face for any possible confirmation.

I shake my head again as my second card arrives, another king. "You're not getting anything from me. If you see me out on a story in January, you'll know you're right. If not, I'll be somewhere else."

"Wish you were coming with us this year," says Jake, as the huge teddy bear of a man takes a bite out of a peanut butter cookie with a Hershey kiss in the middle.

"Fifty cents," I say, as I toss two blue chips into the pot. (Real high stakes game, huh?) "Why, where are you guys going?"

"Eleven wonderful months on Air Hump One," says Kevin.

Both of my eyebrows shoot up. "You guys got the President's campaign?"

Both photogs nod while wearing a look of disgust. "I can hardly wait for next week," says Jake. "My travel agent tells me Iowa's lovely this time of year."

"And there's so much to see and do," says Kevin. He elbows

17

Jake in the ribs. "Look, Jake, another cornfield!"

Sam smiles as he adds to the pot. "They really call the President's plane Air Hump One?"

Everyone laughs as I turn to my brother. "Sweetie, our Commander-in-Chief makes Clinton look like an altar boy."

Dale tosses his cards into the center and folds. "Yeah, and thanks to your little tweet, I get to join them in lovely Dubuque next week."

"It was gonna be my assignment?" I ask.

He nods as his face turns red. "Sorry, kid, that slipped out. I know how much you wanted to cover a presidential campaign."

Sam shoots me a wide-eyed look like a parent that tells me not to react.

"Yeah," I say. "But the job I have is still going to be very enjoyable."

"Would have been fun to watch," says Jake. "President comb-over has a thing for redheads and he's a leg man. He woulda been all over you like a cheap suit."

My face twists like a dishrag at the thought of being groped by a sixty year old fireplug. "Guys, please, the thought of doing Jabba the President will make me throw up on the cards."

Then it hits me. I have three close friends who will be covering a President they can't stand.

Three close friends who wouldn't mind helping me out when they find out what I'm doing.

It will be better than bugging the Oval Office.

***

"So, are we gonna have any ground rules on our campaign to be the candidate's permanent running mate?" asks Ripley, as she refills my glass of champagne.

"Ah, so we really *are* back in high school." I glance at the living room clock and see it's five minutes till the new year. (Yep, dateless again as the Times Square ball gets ready to drop.) "What do you mean, rules?"

"Well, we both want him, and neither of us is the type to share. That's too creepy, even if the guy being shared is Will Becker."

"True. Though I think any final decision would be his. Let's put it this way. If I don't get him, I hope you do."

"Same here, dear friend. It just doesn't need to be like that time during senior year."

She's right. We were a couple of immature teenagers throwing ourselves at the star quarterback, and the competition strained our friendship for a short time. Of course, he ended up with the girl known as the head cheerleader anyway. (She wasn't even on the squad, so you can probably guess the origin of her nickname.) So the flaunting of our wares went for naught. By the way, I googled said quarterback after that Christmas Eve dinner, and he's now a bald, fat used car salesman. Gotta love it when the universe evens things up.

"He'll go for you anyway," says Ripley, "I don't stand a chance if you wear a short skirt with those legs up to your neck."

"Oh, bullshit. Have you forgotten you put yourself through college as a bikini model?"

"That was years ago."

"And I'll bet they still fit."

Ripley smiles and sticks her nose in the air. "Of course they do. But you've got that gorgeous red hair and those cute freckles that make you look like a little girl. And you haven't gained an ounce since high school either. You're still skinny."

"I needed to gain a few ounces above the waist. Just once I'd like to say *My eyes are up here*. Men never talk to my boobs. They have a complete conversation with yours."

"You may be thin but you got the perfect mile long legs, so don't complain. You can't have everything."

"You have everything."

She shrugs. "Don't have Mister Right. So are we going to spend

19

the rest of New Year's Eve arguing about how beautiful we are?"

"Don't think we have enough booze. Tell you what, how about we do the opposite of what we did back then?"

"What, ignore him?"

"Ripley, you know that men always want what they can't have. That's one thing we *have* learned since high school."

"Very true. So therefore he would have to make the first move."

"Exactly. And then there would be no hard feelings between us."

Ripley slowly nods and extends her glass. "Very well. May the lucky girl win."

I clink her glass as the ball starts to descend in Times Square. "Just hope it's one of us."

CHAPTER THREE

#FireTheRedheadBitch
@TwitterGirl
Say bye to this hashtag, cause the bitch is back, joining Senator Becker's campaign! #HIREtheRedheadBitch!

@TwitterGirl
About to meet my new boss, Senator (and next President) Will Becker...

"Welcome," says Frank Delavan, extending his hand as I get up from the couch in the sparsely furnished lobby. "Great to have you on board."

"Happy to be here," I say, as I shake hands.

"Great timing, as we just opened this office. The Senator is very excited about meeting you."

"The feeling is mutual."

Mutual, hell. I'll bet his heart isn't hung up on his tonsils.

Frank leads me out of the lobby, down a hallway and through the campaign headquarters, a beehive of activity filled with mostly twentysomethings on phones dressed in jeans, probably volunteers. A few people are busy hanging political posters while a couple of teenagers are stuffing envelopes. I see several men in shirts and ties and a few women in expensive dresses moving about and figure them for the paid staff. Every one of the women gives me the once-over as I walk through the office.

Well, more than a once-over. More like a glare.

They see me as competition. They want the same guy I do.

Fine. Bring it.

For my first impression I've chosen a conservative long sleeved emerald green dress that matches my eyes with a hemline that hits just above the knee. My shoes take me up to six-three. I know a lot of tall women try to minimize their height, but hey, why should I pass up on great shoes just because I'm an amazon? Had my hair done this morning, so my red tangles bounce as I power walk, dusting my shoulders. I didn't go overboard on the makeup as I don't really have cheekbones to be accented anyway and I don't like to cover up my freckles. Like Ripley says, they're handy when I wanna play the little innocent girl card. (Okay, maybe not so innocent, but you get my drift. Add a pout to the freckles and it's game over.)

The door to the corner office opens as we arrive and a thirtyish guy in khakis and a blue oxford shirt walks out, nodding at Frank as he passes. We walk into the office and find Will Becker leaning over a cluttered desk, talking on the phone as he makes a note on a yellow legal pad. He looks up and smiles at us. "I'll have to get back to you on that," he says. "Talk to you tomorrow." He hangs up the phone, moves around the desk and extends his hand. "So, I finally get to meet the famous Twitter Girl."

"Pleasure to meet you, Senator," I manage to get out while we shake hands. I'm blown away by the real life version of America's most eligible bachelor as photos and television don't do justice to this man. His deep-set powder blue eyes lock onto mine, and the rest of the world seems to disappear.

"You can call me Will when we're alone," he says, placing his other hand on top of mine and sending a bolt of electricity through my body like a defibrillator.

22

When we're alone...

"And you can call me anytime," I say, before my filter has a chance to catch those words by the tail. I feel my face flush and know my freckles are catching fire.

"There's that wit we need for the campaign!" he says, obviously not realizing I was being literal with one of the oldest bar pickup lines. He lets go of my hands and gestures to the chairs in front of his desk. "Please, Cassidy, have a seat."

I sit down next to Frank as I take in this forty-three year old vision of masculinity. Becker is about six-four, slender with broad shoulders revealed by a tailored white shirt, an angles and planes face framed by thick black hair, a lock of which cascades over his forehead. The rolled up sleeves reveal sinewy, buffed forearms. A warm smile makes me feel like I'm the only one in the room. That smile, I can see, could easily melt a heart. The twinkle in his eyes makes him somehow incredibly handsome and unbelievably cute at the same time. A quick look at his slacks as he sits down confirms my suspicion that you could probably bounce quarters off his ass. He'll probably moonlight as a Chippendale when he's done leading the free world.

"So," he says, as he adjusts his chair, "this is the woman with two hundred thousand more followers than I have. Maybe you should be running instead of me."

"Yeah, but you've probably got more support in Mississippi."

"Hey, six electoral votes aren't gonna kill us. Look, I thought your tweet about the tornado was funny as hell and it was bullshit that you got fired, especially considering what really happened. But the network's loss is our gain."

"I'm happy the way things worked out. I can't thank you enough for bringing me on board."

"You're going to be a unique asset, our secret weapon. Though after today it's not going to be much of a secret. Nothing stays quiet on the Internet for long."

"I've given her the basics of what we're looking for," says Frank.

"But I know you've got some ideas of your own."

"Right. Cassidy, you'll be here about half the time working with our strategy team, and the other half you'll be traveling with me. For instance, we've got the first debate in Iowa on Thursday and I want you in place with a laptop next to Frank. He knows the other candidates like the back of his hand and can help you push their buttons. It will be great to tweak the other guys during the debate the moment they make a gaffe or say anything that gives you an opportunity for a comeback."

"Well, I was blessed with a quick wit."

"Not just a quick wit, but a snarky one," says Becker. "Some of your tweets were downright wicked and devastating. What was that one you had about the New York City Mayor shoveling his own driveway?"

"Politicians are used to shoveling something of a different color."

Becker nods and smiles. "A classic. Anyway I want you to take the gloves off. Nothing is sacred."

"Well, I don't want to tweet anything that will come back to bite you. You guys need to let me know if I'm about to cross the line."

"You let me worry about that." He turns to Frank. "Did you tell her about the other part?"

Other part?

Frank shakes his head. "Figured it would be better coming from you."

Uh-oh. My smile fades as my face tightens. "There something I should know about?"

Becker notices my worried look. "Oh, it's nothing bad. Just that if I do become the next President, there will be a position for you in my administration."

I exhale my worry and my adrenaline spikes.

I could end up working at the White House.

Of course, there's one position I really want at 1600 Pennsylvania Avenue, and it's not a job.

By four o'clock I'd been introduced to nearly everyone in the campaign. "I saved the best of our office staff for last," says Frank as we walk past the Senator's office. "Get ready to meet the smartest guy in the building,"

"Shhhh!" I cock my head toward Will Becker's door. "The Senator—"

"Hell, even Becker will admit Tyler Garrity is the Stephen Hawking of politics. The Senator prides himself in hiring people who are brighter than he is. But Tyler is off the charts smart. We're talking genius territory."

"Sounds like a guy I wanna get to know."

"Well, brace yourself, he's quite a unique character." Frank stops at a closed door and turns to face me. "This is the war room. Now, one thing you need to know about Tyler. He has a medical condition, some sort of rare fatigue syndrome, that only allows him to work every other day. Monday, Wednesday and Friday. And traveling wipes him out, he gets horrible jet lag, so Becker keeps him fresh here in New York. But even working on a limited basis, what we get from him is pure gold. Anyway, he doesn't mind talking about his health, so you don't have to tiptoe around him."

"Sounds like my brother."

Frank opens the door and leads me into a long rectangular room without a single window but with light provided by about a dozen flat screens that take up one wall, each tuned to a different channel. I see a guy in his mid-thirties opposite the monitors totally focused on a laptop. "Tyler, someone I want you to meet."

The man is furiously typing something, locked in on the screen, and doesn't look up. "Give me ten seconds." He finishes banging the keyboard and hits one key with a flourish, then looks up and closes the laptop. "Done. Ah, I see Twitter Girl has arrived!"

He gets up and moves toward me bringing an incredibly bright smile. Tyler Garrity definitely has that boy-next-door thing going, with tousled dark brown hair and a matching two-day growth contrasted by deep-set olive green eyes. He sorta reminds me of Bradley Cooper. He extends his hand and I shake it. I tower over him as he's not very tall, maybe five-nine, and slender. Still, he's a seriously cute little thing. "Pleasure to meet you, Tyler."

"Pleasure's mine, T.G."

I furrow my brow. "Huh?"

"T.G. You know, Twitter Girl."

"Oh, right."

"Tyler likes calling people by initials. Or nicknames," says Frank.

"You got it, Viper," he says.

I turn to Frank and raise one eyebrow. "Viper?"

He shrugs. "What can I say? I'm not exactly the warm and fuzzy type."

Tyler pulls out the chair next to his. "Have a seat, T.G. You need coffee, soda, juice? I've got bagels, donuts, croissants, every kind of chocolate you can imagine—"

"I can always go for a chocolate bar," I say as I sit down and he pushes in the chair. *Hmmm. Gentleman. I usually only get this in an expensive restaurant.*

"I'll leave you two to get started," says Frank, who leaves the room and closes the door.

Tyler opens a drawer on a credenza, pulls out a candy bar and hands it to me. "You look like a Dove bar kinda girl."

"Very perceptive."

He sits down and shoves his laptop out of the way as he swivels his chair to face me, wide-eyed with a look of excitement. "Well, your reputation precedes you. I must say I absolutely loved your tweets and cannot tell you how excited I am to have you on the team. I've been a fan for a long time."

I start unwrapping the candy. "Well, that's very kind of you to say. I'm excited to be here."

"So, did Frank tell you what I do?"

"He basically told me you should be designing rockets for NASA

26

or building a time machine."

Tyler leans back and laughs as I take a bite of the candy and savor the smooth chocolate. "Actually the time machine is finished." He leans forward and whispers. "Don't tell anyone, but I'm from the future."

I lean toward him and drop my voice. "Okay, it'll be our little secret." For a guy with a fatigue problem, Tyler is incredibly animated and talks fast with a ton of energy in his voice. He's more full of life than anyone I've met in awhile. Frank's right, he's definitely a character.

"Seriously, I'm the chief strategist here. I try to keep my finger on the pulse of the general public and play devil's advocate. Top Dog likes me to point out things he might be doing wrong."

"Top Dog would be Senator Becker?"

"You catch on quick. Anyway, I'm only here Monday, Wednesday and Friday, but you can always reach me at home on Skype or Face Time. Or if you're old school like me, call me on the phone. But I warn you I never shut up and may talk your ear off."

"Yeah, I kinda get that."

"Or drop by if you're in the neighborhood. I'll take you for a ride in the time machine back to the seventies and we can hit a disco."

"Sounds like fun."

"Frank probably told you that my body can't handle work two days in a row, but thankfully God blessed me with a decent brain." He looks at the clock, grabs a television remote and fires it at the wall of flat screens.

"Well, if you'd like a little help when you're not here my best friend has her own ad agency and she's incredibly clever. She mentioned she wanted to volunteer for the campaign."

"I'd love someone to bounce ideas off. Bring her in." He looked at the television. "You ready?"

"For what?"

"Showtime, T.G. Time to pop your political cherry." I can't help but laugh. Tyler is a free spirit unlike anyone I've ever met, and newsrooms are loaded with quirky personalities. He opens up his laptop and slides it in front of me. "President has a press conference. Watch, wait for the usual gaffe, and send a sarcastic tweet his way."

"Right now?"

"No time like the present and you're on the clock."

He turns up the sound as I log into my Twitter account. I look up at the flat screen just as President Gavin Turner arrives at a podium. A graphic fills the bottom of the screen with *Dubuque, Iowa* while a diagonal red *Live* banner stretches across the upper left corner.

"Good face for radio," I say as the high-def television brings the President into uncomfortable clarity.

Tyler leans back and laughs. "Never heard that one. A TV term?"

"Uh-huh. Suppose he doesn't screw up?" I ask.

Tyler leans his head to the side as he gives me an incredulous look. "Seriously?"

"Yeah, you've got a point."

The President waits for applause to die down before he begins. "Thank you all for coming out on this very cold day." He looks to the side at two men seated next to the podium. "Nice to see my good friends, Governor Lovegood and Senator Bracken... two great public servants."

"Wait for it..." says Tyler.

The President goes through a laundry list of people to thank, then looks out at the crowd. "As always, it's great to be in the Buckeye State!" The crowd groans.

"There it is!" says Tyler, pointing at the screen. "Ohio is the Buckeye State. Iowa is the Hawkeye State." He points at the laptop. "Go!"

I pause for a few seconds, and then my snarky muse hits me with a gem.

@TwitterGirl The President got a GPS as a Christmas gift.

Obviously he returned it.

"Ha! That's terrific!"

"Thank you."

He points at the screen. "Look at him. He knows he screwed up. But he may not be done yet, so stand by."

***

Thirty minutes and two scathing tweets later, Tyler and I are whooping it up in the war room as the President wraps up a gaffe-filled speech.

"I'd say you had a great first day," he says.

"Well, most of what the President said were hanging curve balls over the middle of the plate."

"Ah, baseball fan. Mets or Yanks?"

"Long suffering Mets fan."

"Me too. We should catch a game sometime. Nothing but obnoxious Yankee fans around this office and the majority aren't even from the area. Damn bandwagoners."

Frank enters the room wearing a big smile. "Great job, Twitter Girl."

"Ah, you were monitoring."

"I wasn't the only one. Those little barbs of yours have already been re-tweeted hundreds of times. The one about the GPS will probably end up as a joke on a late night talk show."

"Glad you liked 'em," I say.

"Well, Tyler's got a conference call."

Tyler looks at his watch and nods as he gets up. "Yeah, need to hit the phone. Great working with you, T.G."

"You too, Tyler. See you tomorrow."

"Won't be here, remember? Besides, you'll be on your way to sunny Iowa. If you need me, I'll be in cyberspace. Operators are standing by."

***

Dinner is with Frank's Deputy Campaign Manager, Roberta Willis, a mid-thirties sharp looking gray-eyed dishwater blonde I've seen on a few talk shows. While Frank Delavan is running the show, Roberta is the face of the campaign, being a lot more telegenic with a sharp wit. We are quickly bonding, as she also has a background in broadcasting, though she had bailed out of a dysfunctional newsroom (somewhat redundant) five years ago. In two hours she's covered just about everything I need to know about the campaign.

Of course, I want to know about the candidate. Ripley has already texted me twice to remind me.

What's the 411 on our objective?

"So, what's he like?" I ask.

"What, you mean away from the campaign?"

"Yeah, you know. When he's not *the next President* is he a regular guy? What's he do when he lets his hair down?"

"You haven't been around national politics a lot, have you?"

"I follow it closely, but that wasn't my beat as a reporter. I've covered a bunch of state campaigns, but nothing like this. Ironically I was set to cover the President's campaign before I got the boot."

She nods slowly, then takes a sip of wine. "Well, I'll give you the quick Cliff Notes version of Washington politics 101. There's one thing that is the common denominator with Democrats and Republicans."

"Getting re-elected?"

"Very perceptive, Cassidy. They all talk a good game about being public servants, but that term is an absolute joke. They have no more interest in serving the public than we have in washing these

30

dishes after dinner. Most of them are incredible egomaniacs who are turned on more by power than everything else."

"But Becker's not like that, right?"

"In some ways he is, but in many ways he's different, and losing his wife changed him. Humbled him in a way. Most politicians think they're bulletproof and when his wife died that was a huge dose of reality. It softened him, but in a good way. Made him unsure of himself when before he was always dead certain he was in control. I mean, of course he has a huge political ego… you can't be shy and modest on the national stage. He desperately wants to be President and he does honestly want to make things better for the country. But he'll also do just about anything to get there."

"*Just about anything* meaning…"

"Very little is off the table in politics. Despite his reputation he can get down and dirty like anyone else. What makes Will Becker different is the *way* he does it. Or, in his case, how he has other people do it for him. He's very well insulated."

"What about his personal life now that he's single?"

Her face tightens slightly and I can tell I've pushed a bit too far. She looks at her watch and turns to wave at the waiter. "I think it's time for the check. Got some calls to make."

CHAPTER FOUR

@TwitterGirl
Boarding Air Becker for the Iowa debates. Hope someone told the Prez they're not in Ohio this year.

I wheel my suitcase toward the steps of the private jet that will carry Senator Becker and his staff to the wilds of Iowa, which is currently experiencing the effects of one of those dreaded polar vortexes. Or vortices. Or whatever the plural of vortex is. In other words, it's friggin' cold. The people in Iowa are freezing their asses off cause it's ten below. Luckily I won't be working outside as I would be if I were a reporter, so it's no big deal. Still, I wish the primaries were in the Caribbean.

A middle-aged white haired gentleman in a suit walks toward me and smiles. "I'll take that for you, Ms. Shea."

"Wow," I say, as I pass the handle over to him. "Beats flying commercial."

"Have a nice trip," he says, as he turns and takes my bag toward the rear of the plane.

"Thanks." I'm filled with energy as I bound up the steps and am greeted at the top by the first really attractive flight attendant I've seen in years, since these days most are people deemed not cheerful enough to work at the Department of Motor Vehicles.

And, she's the first one I've seen smiling in years. "Good morning."

"Welcome aboard, Ms. Shea. I'm Jessica. May I take your coat?"

"Thank you, and please call me Cassidy." I take two steps into the cabin and my jaw drops as I start to remove my coat. It's a private plane, all right, but it's seriously decked out. A half dozen staffers on cell phones fill huge reclining tan leather chairs and I see Frank Delavan sitting in the back, reading a newspaper. "Guess I'm not in a middle seat in coach."

"It's the only way to fly," she says, as she hangs my coat in a closet. The woman is an absolutely breathtaking brunette, early twenties if not younger, tall with a mound of gentle curls framing huge pale green eyes and a tight body wrapped in a short red dress. If I'm going to turn Becker's head on this flight, my "A" game just got graded on a curve and marked down to a C-minus. "I think Frank is waiting for you in the back. Can I get you something to drink before we take off?"

"If you've got coffee made, I'll take a cup. But don't go to any trouble on my account."

"We have almond amaretto, raspberry chocolate, and creme brulee."

"And this obviously isn't the drive-thru at Dunkin' Donuts. I'll take some of that amaretto concoction, cream and sugar."

"Coming right up, and we'll have eggs Benedict once we're airborne," she says, as she extends her hand toward the back like a game show hostess.

I want to tweet *I have died and gone to airline heaven.* But probably not a good idea to let the voters know we're traveling like kings. If anyone asks, I'll say I was stuck in a middle seat next to a crying baby. No parent, just a baby.

I head down the center aisle passing three incredibly attractive men who are all on cell phones and look up to smile at me. Frank Delavan has a laptop open and is looking serious while on the phone. Behind his seat is a wall with a door, so I assume there's a meeting room or something since this part of the cabin only

33

takes up half the plane. He wraps up the call as I arrive and plop into the soft leather seat next to him. "Morning, Frank."

"Cassidy, great to have you along with us. I'm really looking forward to breaking new ground in this campaign."

"Sarcasm is new ground? I thought that road got paved with the first television commercial."

"Not Twitter sarcasm and not your brand of it."

"So what's on the agenda today?"

"Soon as we're airborne we'll have something to eat, then have a planning session." He cocks his head toward the back wall.

"So the rest of the plane is a meeting room?"

"Just part of it. There's also a TV room where we can monitor stuff and a few beds and couches in the back if you ever need to crash for a bit."

"There are bedrooms on this plane?"

"It's a long haul, Cassidy. Trust me, by August you'll need a GPS to remind you what city we're in. Anyway, we'll do some brainstorming, then the Senator has a full agenda as soon as we land."

"So I'll be with him?"

"Not till tonight. I've got you down for lunch with our advance man, Andrew Shelton, before he heads out to our next stop. He's the guy who has his finger on the pulse of the local voters. You'll see him briefly each time we arrive at a new city."

"You sound incredibly organized, Frank."

"Trust me, one look at my desk and you wouldn't want me to do logistics. We have a seriously anal retentive person for that."

I hear the engines fire up as the flight attendant comes over the loudspeaker and tells everyone to buckle up.

"And buckle up is literal in a campaign," says Frank. "You also need to hold on tight. This is the world's wildest roller coaster."

**

34

Two hours later Jessica walks toward us carrying a coffee pot and smiles. "We'll be landing in about half an hour. Bundle up, Frank, it's twelve below."

"Whoever put the Iowa and New Hampshire primaries in the middle of the winter obviously flunked geography," says Frank.

Jessica taps on the door to the meeting room and I hear the Senator tell her to come in.

I assume she's bringing him a cup of java. But she doesn't return.

Five minutes go by, no Jessica.

Ten minutes, no Jessica. Now I'm starting to worry about what's going on behind that door between the probable next president and a seriously hot babe young enough to be his daughter. Sure, he's single and entitled to have a relationship, but this doesn't look good.

Twenty minutes later she comes out.

My eyes widen as I watch her move to the front of the plane, smooth her dress, grab her purse from a shelf and touch up her lipstick.

The Senator then emerges from the back room, buttoning his shirt and tying his necktie as he heads for his seat at the front of the plane.

No one says a word or even gives this a second look.

And now I'm wondering what's really true about the guy I'm now working for.

Is Will Becker simply a product?

And is the race over before Ripley and I have even left the starting gate?

***

As I have lunch with advance man Andrew Shelton, I'm beginning to see a pattern.

This campaign, with the exception of Frank Delavan, is loaded with seriously cute guys.

And after what I saw on the airplane with our flight attendant, Becker may be off the table, so I may as well lay the groundwork for Plan B.

Andrew is probably in his early forties, maybe six-two and built like a male model. Broad shoulders, slim hips, and a chambray shirt which is no doubt covering a ripped torso. A pair of jeans has never looked better. He's obviously dressed down for the locals, but I know he could seriously do justice to a tuxedo. Thick sandy hair and deep-set pale blue eyes give him a bit of a beach boy look, while huge dimples come into play when he smiles.

Which he does as he gives the waitress a soulful look with those eyes. He gives his order with a deep voice smooth as silk. She turns while staring at him and walks right into a table. Her face flushes as she scurries back to the kitchen.

"You're a natural flirt, you know that?" I say.

He shrugs and furrows his brow. "What did I do?"

"Oh, nothing, you just make a patty melt sound like phone sex. If the waitress was named Patty, she'd melt."

"Well, Frank was certainly spot on about you."

Now it's my turn to shrug. "What did I do?"

"You're not shy about saying anything, even to people you just met."

"Part of my charm. That's why you guys hired me. I basically have no filter. Although, as you're aware, the lack of said filter got me fired from the network."

"Well, we'll make sure that doesn't happen here. Anyway, in regard to your phone sex comment, I used to do commercial voice-overs before I got into politics. I was blessed with a good voice, which will come in handy when I'm too old to do anything else."

"Hey, I know how you can lock up the election. Call up registered female voters and ask, *What are you wearing*?"

He leans back and laughs. "Twitter Girl, you are something else. I've run into some characters in politics, but you are definitely one of a kind."

"I'll take that as a compliment, Andrew. So, how does one become an advance man?"

"I was working in the Senator's office and a few times he was late for a few events so I had to basically keep the crowd warm."

I'm sure he could keep any girl warm…

"Anyway," he continues, "Becker thought I'd be good at getting the locals primed before his arrival because I'm from a small town and can relate to Joe and Mabel Sixpack. He calls me the *redneck whisperer*."

"Cute. Though you sure don't look like one."

"Well, for whatever reason, people open up to me. I grew up on a farm with a lot of blue collar folks. A lot of advance men show up in thousand dollar suits, and that screams New York carpetbagger. I try to blend in and get a sense of the mood so I can brief him before he gets here. I spend a lot of time in coffee shops and diners."

"Interesting. So you'll always be one day ahead of me?"

"Yep. Soon as we're through with lunch I'm off to Cedar Rapids. So I'll always have a little time to brief you when you arrive, but we'll always be sleeping in different towns."

So much for Plan B…

"Does that make you feel detached from the campaign?"

"In some ways, yes, but I do get back to the New York head-quarters quite often, since I live in Manhattan."

What the hell, take a shot. "So at some point when we're both in town we might actually have dinner instead of lunch."

"Or… breakfast."

Talk about not being shy about saying anything to someone you just met. His last words are followed by a smile that makes my heart flutter. Until he follows it up with…

"I love having meetings over a good power breakfast. I get a lot of ideas late at night and need to get them out of my head right away. And I know every great pancake and Belgian waffle place in the city. The way to my heart is covered with pure maple syrup."

Oh.

My phone chimes. "Excuse me," I say, as I pull it from my purse and see it's a text message from Ripley.

Not fair. You're getting a head start on Becker.

I quickly tap the keys and write back.

Don't worry, the runner-ups are spectacular.

I slide the phone back into my purse. "You getting all snarky already?" he asks.

"No. Quick note to my best friend. She, uh, wanted to make sure I'm keeping warm out here."

"Stick with me, I'll keep you warm." Another sly smile.

Aha.

"I grew up in Minnesota, so I know everything you need to know about dealing with seriously cold weather." He cocks his head at my coat. "You need something like a down coat from Eddie Bauer. It'll make you toasty even when it's twenty below. The one you've got isn't gonna make it."

Oh, again.

***

Frank and I are in a small room just off the auditorium stage, seated at a table in front of a monitor as the Iowa debate is about to begin. He has a yellow legal pad in front of him along with a laptop while I have fingers at the ready next to my own laptop, Twitter account already open and buzzing. My followers have been burning it up waiting for whatever darts I'm about to throw at the other candidates.

A digital clock shows there's one minute to go till the ninety minute debate begins. "You ready?" asks Frank.

I crack my knuckles. "Absolutely."

And then something happens that has never, ever happened to me on television.

My heart starts pounding.

Talking live in front of millions, I've never had a problem. Seated in a room with one guy ready to launch barbs at a bunch of sleazeballs with no souls, and for some reason I'm nervous as a virgin on prom night.

Probably because there's more at stake here. Let's face it, television news aint gonna cure cancer and if you screw up on the network no one is going to die. But what I'm doing could conceivably affect the future of the country. If you look back at previous presidential races, you'll often find one sentence that defines a campaign. The famous headline in the New York tabloid ("Ford to City: Drop Dead") during the race between Jimmy Carter and Gerald Ford is widely accepted as having had a huge influence on the outcome. "Read my lips" sank the first George Bush like a stone. A few words, history changed. Just like that. And if I end up providing what turns out to be the key words of the campaign, that's a potentially large gorilla on my back.

Luckily Frank is here to act as a filter in the unlikely event that I need one. (Oh, stop laughing.)

The monitor fills with a red, white and blue graphic and Frank says, "Here we go."

The music fades as the face of the moderator, public television anchor Jarvis Jones, greets the audience. Jones, who is probably in his mid sixties with a personality as dry as a rice cake, shows no emotion at all as he announces the names of the candidates.

"Hey, Frank, why do they always have these public TV bores as moderators?"

"Yeah, I hate it. Supposedly they're unbiased, but that's a bunch of bullshit. They're liberal as hell." He cocks his head at my laptop.

"Go ahead. Fire away."

"The debate hasn't started yet."

"I meant throw a zinger at the moderator."

"Really?"

"Sure. His eleven fans probably won't mind."

I lick my lips as my eyebrows do a quick jump and I begin to type.

#IowaDebates
@TwitterGirl
Jarvis Jones died in 2011, but hasn't gotten the memo yet.

I look at Frank for permission before I post it. "Do it," he says, laughing. "It's funny as hell. And probably true."

I post the tweet and watch the LOL and ROFL responses fly by at blinding speed.

"See, they love that kind of stuff," says Frank. "And regardless of who people are supporting, you've said something they all can appreciate."

The moderator pulls an index card from a stack and says, "So, let's begin the first debate on the road to the 2010 election." Snickers fill the room and Jones doesn't react, clueless that he hasn't changed refrigerator calendars in awhile.

"Good God, he doesn't even know what year it is," says Frank. He points at the laptop. "Hit him again."

#IowaDebates
@TwitterGirl
Re: Jarvis Jones death in 2011. I rest my case.

"Damn, you're quick," says Frank, wearing a big smile. Again, the responses fly by, and within seconds someone has created a new hashtag:

40

#RIPJarvisJones.

"Jump on it," says Frank. I start typing again.

#RIPJarvisJones
@TwitterGirl
In lieu of flowers, mourners are asked to donate a personality
to the Public Broadcasting System.

"You think he'll be upset?" I ask.
    "You really think he even knows what Twitter is?"
    "Good point."

* * *

The debate begins, with six other challengers flanking Becker, who, as the front-runner in the polls, is at the center podium. Nothing "tweet worthy" happens as the first four candidates answer a question about foreign aid. But then we come to Marvin Hensler, a sixty year old extreme whack job with an extreme following. The walking definition of "lunatic fringe."
    "Stand by," says Frank. "He's bound to say something stupid."
    Hensler, a wealthy private citizen who made his millions the old fashioned way (by inheriting it), has the classic look of a good ole boy politician; bloated, bulbous nose, grey hair styled in a helmet. He starts off rambling about cutting foreign aid completely. "If third world countries like England can't get by without help, well, that's not America's problem."
    "Go!" says Frank.

@TwitterGirl #IowaDebates
Please give to the United Kingdom indoor plumbing fund,
Hensler has designated the UK as a third world country.

"You're on a roll tonight," says Frank.

"Honey, I'm just gettin' started."

***

The phone rings just as I hit my hotel room at midnight. I'm tired but exhilarated, and when I see it's Ripley I take the call. "You've reached Twitter Girl. For sarcasm, press one—"

Beep. "Damn, Cassidy, you were hilarious tonight."

"I guess a few days off from being snarky will pay dividends."

"It must have built up while you were out of a job. God, that tweet about the moderator… I couldn't stop laughing."

"Well, the campaign people were very pleased."

"Okay, enough about your new job. You turned Becker's head yet?"

"It might already be spoken for."

"You're kidding me! Say it aint so! Who is it?"

"The drop dead gorgeous twenty year old flight attendant on our plane. She disappeared into his office for twenty minutes then came out needing lip gloss. Don't think she was inflating his life jacket for use as a flotation device."

"Well, shit, Cassidy. So I'm out before I even get there."

"I wouldn't say that. There's a huge age difference between her and the Senator. What could they have in common?"

"Duh-uh. You're seriously asking what might attract a middle-aged guy to a hot younger woman? Earth to Cassidy…"

"Sorry, it's late. But anyway—"

"You said something in your text about runner-ups?"

"No shortage of seriously attractive guys in this campaign. Between the adorable strategy guy in New York, the hunky advance man and the hotties on the plane, it's like a cute guy buffet."

"Okay, see you when you get back. At least now I know who the competition for Becker is. I'll have to go to DEFCON 1."

And where Ripley is concerned, that means seriously dressing up for her volunteer job. Her "A" game will turn mine into an "F".

***

I'm already buckled in for the flight home and watching through the window as the Senator gives a last minute interview on the tarmac to a TV crew with Frank standing at his side. Becker wraps it up and shakes hands with the reporter and photographer before heading toward the plane. Frank enters first and walks toward the seat next to me.

But I'm laser locked on the front of the cabin. Senator Becker steps into the center aisle and hands Jessica his coat. She hangs it up, turns around and gives him a big hug.

He hugs her back with a big smile on his face, then kisses her on the cheek as Frank plops down next to me.

"They're not terribly discreet, are they?" he says, shaking his head as he stares at them. "Someone should say something."

"No kidding." I'm still looking at the front of the plane where they've broken the embrace but Becker is now holding her hands. "Frank, I realize I'm new and this is probably not my place to say this, but don't you think you should be the one to do something about it?"

"Yeah, I know."

"I mean, it's only a matter of time before we have reporters on the plane and they see it. Aren't you worried about his image? How old is she?"

"Nineteen."

"Good God, Frank, people can't see the next President running around with a teenager."

"What can I say, he likes 'em young." Frank leans over and lowers his voice as the Senator heads toward the back of the plane. "No one's had the guts to talk to him about it. Including me."

Becker smiles at me as he passes. "Great job last night, Cassidy."

"Thank you, Senator," I say. He opens the door behind me and disappears into the meeting room. (Or should we call it the multi-purpose room?)

"You know," says Frank, "I think we'd all consider it a personal favor if *you'd* say something."

"Me? Are you out of your mind? I'm not going to tell the Senator he's looking like a cradle robber. I hardly know the guy."

"I meant say something to *her*. Maybe coming from a woman she doesn't really know it might sink in. Go on, you're not shy about saying anything. Go talk to her."

I'm not wild about the idea, but I know how reporters think. And if a member of the media sees that kind of behavior with a woman that young, Becker is done. Besides, we need to keep the dream alive for American women that he's available. I get up and walk toward Jessica, who is busy locking things away for takeoff.

She turns to face me and smiles. "If you want something to drink, I'll bring it to you as soon as we're airborne."

I shake my head. "It's not that." I gently take her arm and pull her away from the aisle into the doorway so no one can see us. "It's your... behavior."

She furrows her brow. "Excuse me?"

"Look, I know you're young and all but if the media sees you in a clench with the Senator, it won't be good."

Her face tightens a bit. "Really?"

"Sweetie, the media would eat it up, and not in a good way. It would be a huge scandal."

"So I'm not allowed to hug my own uncle?"

To say my face is turning beet red is putting it mildly. "Oh my God..."

Jessica studies my expression for a moment, then smiles and starts to laugh. She grabs my hand. "You thought... Uncle Will and I—"

"Please ask the pilot to make an emergency landing at the

nearest hospital so I can have my foot surgically removed from my mouth."

She slowly nods. "Yeah, I know what this is about. Frank told you to say something, didn't he?"

"How'd you know?"

"He basically initiates new people into the campaign with a practical joke. I've seen some good ones but this takes the cake." She looks around to make sure no one's listening. "You gotta get even."

"Oh, trust me, Jessica, I will. Payback will be a stone cold bitch."

"And just so you know, we're a really close family. Uncle Will is my mom's brother, and when my dad passed away he helped raise me. He's been like a father to me. I really don't want to be a flight attendant but he only wants people he can trust on the plane."

"That's nice to hear. Anyway, I'm sorry this happened."

"Nothing to apologize for. I'm used to it. Nothing is sacred on this campaign so it's good preparation for the real world."

"By the way, may I ask how old you are?"

"Twenty-five. Why?"

"You're mature beyond your years."

"Thank you. Oh, we're about to take off, so you need to buckle up."

"Sure thing."

"And please let me know if I can help you get some revenge."

I turn and head back to my seat staring daggers at Frank, while the rest of the passengers are biting their lips and doing their best not to laugh. "Okay, guys, you've had your fun." Everyone bursts into laughter as I pass them and take my seat, then look at Frank. "I *will* get even."

"I would expect nothing less." He extends his hand. "Welcome to the campaign, Twitter Girl."

Jessica's voice comes over the intercom as the plane's engines fire up. "Please fasten your seat belts as we're about to take off. Once we're at a cruising altitude I'll be bringing coffee through the cabin. And I cannot guarantee what will be in it... *Frank*."

Oh, I like this gal.

I sit back and melt into the soft leather seat and just as I'm about to flip my phone to airplane mode, it beeps with a text.

And as I read it, my blood runs cold.

CHAPTER FIVE

@TwitterGirl
President Turner in NYC today. Over/under on gaffes is four.
Bet the mortgage on the over.

"Cassidy. All is not as it seems. You're still a reporter. Start digging."

The text did not list a sender. In fact, when I hit reply button I saw something I'd never seen before.

Sender unknown.

This of course had made for a very stressful plane ride home.

After my blood pressure calmed down, I considered the possibilities. The text was from someone in another campaign. It was from a former employee of the Senator who had an ax to grind. Those were the most likely.

Or the worst possibility, it was someone who knew the truth. What that truth might be was anyone's guess.

But when journalism gets in your blood, it's as addictive as any drug. Tell a reporter there might be a story, and the reporter will always check it out, no matter how lame the tip might seem. The thought of another reporter getting a scoop because you didn't bother to do a little legwork drives everyone in the news business. It's not fear of failure, but fear of getting beaten.

My brother Sam, who is also a digital whiz, said the text was obviously from what is known as a "burner phone" which is disposable and therefore untraceable. He also thinks it's from someone in another campaign, but wants me to keep my eyes open. Gotta love my brother, he's always trying to protect me.

Between that text and the quick end to my dinner with Becker's deputy campaign manager, my reporter radar is up. I'm going to start quietly poking around.

Is Will Becker all that he seems?

Inquiring minds wanna know.

**

Meanwhile, after the "Will Becker is off the table rollercoaster" I went through last week thanks to a combination of my own suspicions and Frank's practical joke, Ripley and I are officially kicking off our own campaign to turn the Senator's head by ignoring him. My best friend had been disappointed after hearing that he was spoken for, but she perked up when I told her that he was not in a relationship with his niece. (Of course, had they been from Arkansas, an actual uncle–niece romance would not have raised an eyebrow.)

Anyway, Ripley is dressed to the nines (as far as office attire is concerned) as I lead her into the Manhattan campaign headquarters for her first day as a "volunteer." She removes her coat with a flourish and this brings every male in the room to a screeching halt. Jaws drop and eyes widen as they lock on her like a heat-seeking missile. The women who had simply glared at me give her the death stare. She follows me toward Becker's office, sashaying in a form-fitting red dress that shows off her bikini-perfect body even though it has a high neck, long sleeves and a knee-length hemline. Cut-out shoulders offer a little tease of perfectly toned skin while four-inch matching stilettos complete the package. Her outfit is sort of a combination between conservative and slutty, which only Ripley can pull off. I'm thinking I wasted my head start. She has taken ignoring a man to a new level, as no red-blooded male could possible feel indifferent looking at her in that outfit.

Becker's office door is open and he's on the phone as we arrive. "Yeah, I think we have more work to do in New Hamp…(long pause) shire…"

Said long pause was caused as he looked up and saw Ripley. She flashes a smile at him as his eyes bug out and jaw drops.

Yep, I've seen it before. He's been hit by the DeAngelo thunderbolt, which renders men momentarily speechless and unable to function, like some sexual Star Trek phaser set on stun.

I hear a voice on the other end of the phone. "Will? Will, are you still there?"

"Huh? Oh yeah," he says, as he turns his attention back to the phone call. "I'll get back to you this afternoon as soon as I run this by the staff. Talk to you then. Bye." He tries to hang up the phone but misses the cradle.

I turn to Ripley and roll my eyes. She bats her lashes and smiles. Round one to my best friend, no contest. A knockout by a knockout. The judges are unanimous.

Becker hangs up, moves around his desk toward us and extends his hand toward Ripley. "You must be Cassidy's advertising friend I've heard so much about."

She shakes his hand as I handle introductions. "Senator, this is Ripley DeAngelo. Ripley, Senator Becker."

"Great to meet you," she says. "I really admire what you're doing and hope I can contribute in a small way."

"Hey, it's great to have another person to brainstorm with our team," he says, eyes locked on her as he still hasn't let go of her hand. He places his other hand on top. "Should help to have someone who's not in politics. Sometimes we're too close the problem. I really appreciate you volunteering."

"Well, my agency can spare me from time to time. Of course, you can do that if you own it."

"I guess so." He turns to me. "Oh, Cassidy, Tyler is waiting for you in the conference room. Wants to run some stuff by you this morning."

"Sure."

He turns back to Ripley and gives her that famous smile. "And I'll give our newest volunteer a tour."

They head out the door as I watch for a moment before I'm off to see Tyler. I have to admit, they look like a couple on the top of a wedding cake right off the bat. There's some obvious sexual attraction there by the Senator.

Hey, she's my best friend. I'm happy for her.

Yeah, let's go with that.

***

"T.G., welcome home!" Tyler's face lights up as I enter the conference room. "You kicked ass in Iowa."

"Thank you, but it was the Senator who kicked ass in the debate."

"Yeah, but you started closing the lid on Marvin Hensler's coffin. A few more tweets like that and he'll be dead and buried."

"Hell, Tyler, he doesn't have a shot anyway."

"Yeah, but the best way to wake up his followers is to show that he's stupid."

"I think he does that on his own quite well."

"But you help take it to another level. You've heard the term *national joke*?"

"Yeah. What about it?"

"That's what you're doing to candidates like him. Some of the late night talk shows used your line. You should demand royalties."

"Hey, a job in the White House would be payment enough. So

50

what are you up to this morning?"

"Wanted to go over some homework for you."

"Homework?"

Tyler reaches over to the next chair and grabs a bunch of manila folders stuffed with papers. "The staff has compiled all the stupid things the other candidates and the President have said over the years." He plops them down in front of me.

"I would think it would fill an entire library."

"Good point. Perhaps if Top Dog gets in office we can get a pork barrel project for that. National Museum of Idiocy. Anyway, familiarize yourself with this because you can make these little sound bites rear their ugly heads and nip the candidates in the ass."

"Okay, it's a lot of reading but it will be fun."

He pulls a zip drive out of his pocket and hands it to me. "Here's your travel version. I printed it out so you can make notes in case you're old school."

"Actually, I am when it comes to journalism. I may be Twitter Girl but I'm like Robert Redford in *All the President's Men* when it comes to investigating a story."

"I love that movie! That scene where he works the phones and writes stuff on the legal pad—"

"That's me. And that's the most accurate film you'll ever see about how reporters actually work."

He nods and pulls his laptop in front of him. "Now to something fun. Do you have any plans Sunday afternoon?"

"Well, like most New Yorkers I was gonna sit down and watch the Giants playoff game. Why, do you guys need me to come in?"

"No, not at all. So you like football?"

"I love football."

"Great. I'll put you on the ticket list."

My eyes light up. "You guys actually have playoff tickets?"

"Top Dog is a season ticket holder and he likes to take the staff on outings. A team building sort of thing to get away from the campaign."

"But I just started here. Surely some people who have been here awhile are entitled to them."

"Most of our people aren't from this area. Not a whole lot of Giant fans on staff so the ticket is yours. By the way, this isn't a private box, so you'll be sitting out in the cold."

"Fine with me. After Iowa it will feel like the beach. You going?"

"Unfortunately I have to go to a wedding."

"Who the hell gets married on a Sunday during playoff season?"

"Jets fans. They knew their team would be awful, as always. Anyway, I'm taping the game so don't you dare call me and tell me how it went. Big Blue all the way."

***

Sam rolls toward the dining room table on this Saturday night carrying a bunch of dishes like a seasoned waiter along with a bottle of wine in his lap. I lick my lips as he slides a plate of cajun seafood Alfredo in front of me. Ripley already has her fork and spoon at the ready as she adores his cooking. Sam leans over and starts carpet bombing her fettuccine with freshly grated parmesan, as he knows she's a cheese fanatic. She digs in immediately, twirls a ball of pasta with a shrimp and pops it in her mouth. She closes her eyes as she savors it and licks her lips like a cat. "God, that's better than sex. Sam, you'll make someone a great wife."

"Cute," he says, as he moves to the head of the table. I'm older but he's the man of the house, so he sits at the head. I like tradition that way. By the way, Sam has had a major crush on Ripley since he hit puberty and says he would die if she ever knew. Of course it's so obvious the way he dotes on her that she figured it out long ago, but thankfully he doesn't know she knows. (Even my brother the genius is a typical man in that when it comes to women he misses the obvious.) I've always wondered if there weren't such an age difference if those two would make a good couple.

"So," says Sam, grabbing the bottle opener, "how's the political version of *The Bachelor* going? Has there been a rose ceremony yet?"

I cock my head at Ripley. "She's out of the gate like Secretariat," I say, just before I stuff my face with pasta.

Sam turns toward Ripley as he pops the cork on the wine and beings pouring her a glass. "Ah, do tell."

"Nothing to tell," says Ripley, too busy shoveling food in her mouth to bother looking up from her plate.

"Horseshit," I say. "Becker nearly tripped over his tongue when he saw her in that red dress."

"The one with the high neck and the cut-out shoulders?" asks Sam. I nod. "She looks great in that. Of course, she looks great in everything."

Ripley looks up and smiles at him. "You're sweet," she says, talking through the pasta, though it comes out, "Yur sreet."

I point my fork at her. "Becker gave her a personal tour of the office."

"And that's all it was," said Ripley, coming up for air and a sip of wine.

"Oh, come on, I could tell you two had a connection."

"Maybe so. But all he did was ask about you."

My fork is suddenly suspended in mid-air inches from my mouth.

"And the plot thickens," says Sam.

"Continue," I say. "What did he ask?"

She puts her utensils down and dabs her lips with a napkin. "Let's see... has Cassidy ever been married? Is she seeing anyone? What does she like to do for fun?"

"You serious?"

Ripley nods. "Yep. Anyway, I didn't react in a jealous high school manner because I am keeping the pact."

"You two have a pact?" asks Sam, putting down his utensils and resting his chin on his hands. "Oh, I can't wait to hear the details of this."

"We're both supposed to ignore him," says Ripley.

Sam furrows his brow. "I don't understand. I thought this guy was the ultimate catch for you guys. Why would you both ignore him?"

"Men always want what they can't have," I say, reaching for a piece of hot Italian bread. "Dating 101."

"Yeah, you have a point," says Sam. "But you two aren't exactly shrinking violets. What constitutes ignoring him? Grabbing his ass only once a day?"

"Hush, little brother."

"I'd agree to that," says Ripley, "if you wanna amend the pact." She goes back to attacking her food. "I almost forgot. After I basically gave him a dossier on the care and feeding of Twitter Girl he did invite me to the football game this weekend."

I drop my fork. "*You're* going to the Giants game? You hate football."

She shrugs. "Thought I'd give it a shot."

"Hell, Ripley," says Sam, "you think a tight end is one of your requirements for a boyfriend."

"That's why I got this," she says, as she leans down, reaches into her purse and pulls out a paperback titled *NFL Football for Dummies*. "I'll be cramming tomorrow morning."

I roll my eyes. "You can't become a football fan in a day. Name one of the Giants."

She searches the heavens for an answer, then looks at me and smiles. "Frank Gifford!"

"He retired in the sixties and he's eighty years old! You only know him 'cause he's married to Kathie Lee."

"You said name one Giant and I named one. So there."

"Name a current one."

"I'll know them all tomorrow."

"Really. How much is a touchdown worth?"

"Uh… ten thousand dollars?"

Sam shakes his head and laughs. "Man, I'd love to be a fly on

54

the wall when you talk football with Senator Becker."

"I'll record it on my cell," I say. "I can sell it to ESPN for a fortune."

***

The cold wind slaps us in the face as Ripley and I head down the concourse toward our seats. One look at her face tells me my best friend is not at all wild about dealing with the elements in pursuit of the ultimate catch. (Her idea of camping out is taking a nap on the sun porch in May.)

"Why couldn't we have gone to a Broadway show?" she asks. "At least there'd be heat."

"You can go home if you like, I'll tell him you weren't feeling well."

"Hell no, dear friend. I'll freeze my ass off for a shot at Becker's."

"Thought so. We'll get you some hot chocolate when we get to our seats."

"I think I'll need a stronger antifreeze," she says, pulling her suede coat tighter around her. "Couple of dirty martinis should warm me up."

I stop and turn to face her. "Oh, would you like some paté to go with it?"

"Great idea—"

"You're at a friggin' football game in New Jersey! You can have a hot dog and a beer!"

She face tightens. "Really? There's no place serving hot hors d'oeurves?"

I roll my eyes and continue toward our section, which is around the forty yard line. I pull the tickets out of my pocket and see we're both in odd numbered seats. "Hey, we're not sitting together. We've got seats nine and eleven."

She shoves her hands in her pockets and adjusts her hat. "Let's just get there."

We turn into the tunnel and I hand my tickets to an usher who points to our row. We head down the steps and I see the seat between nine and eleven is occupied.

By the Senator.

I stop, grab Ripley's arm and lean over to whisper in her ear. "Becker's sitting between us."

"Really? Hmmm, interesting. You think he planned it or that's just the tickets we got?"

"Guess we'll find out."

"Maybe he wants a three-way with the hottest members of his staff."

"Yeah, *that* will get him elected."

We head down the steps to our row. The Senator spots us as we arrive and stands up. "Hey, you made it. Hope it wasn't too much of a hassle getting here."

"Nah, no big deal," I say, as I slide past him and grab seat number nine as Ripley plops down in number eleven. I turn to face Becker and take in his outfit. Jeans, Giants ski jacket, stocking cap, wire-rimmed glasses. "You dress down really well."

"I can blend when I have to. If I sat in a private box people would bend my ear for three hours and I'd never get to watch the game."

"I never would have recognized you," says Ripley.

"By the way, we'll have a limo to get you guys home."

We're interrupted by two new arrivals, Andrew and another hot guy I haven't seen. Ripley hasn't met either one, and when she looks at me I gather by her "tell" (according to my brother) that she's not at all disappointed by the runner-ups.

The Senator introduces them. The new contestant in hot guy roulette is a political consultant named Vinnie Franco and looks as Italian as his name. Tall with black hair, deep-set dark brown eyes, a rugged face. One of those guys with a heavy beard who always looks like he has a five o'clock shadow. The jury's out on the rest of him until I see what's under the goose down parka. Vinnie grabs the seat next to Ripley while Andrew slides by and sits next to me.

This is one helluva hot guy sandwich for two gals from Staten Island.

Ripley no longer looks cold.

***

The Giants are up by ten as we get close to halftime. I don't think Ripley's watched one single play (not that I expected her to) as she's bounced her conversation between Becker and Vinnie. She's also managed to hide her lack of football knowledge by jumping up and cheering whenever everyone else does. I've been talking football with the Senator and Andrew as the game hits the two minute warning.

"Okay," says Becker, eyes riveted on the field, "if they can just avoid a mistake in the last two minutes." He's obviously a true fan as he hasn't mentioned politics once.

"Wow, the game is going fast," says Ripley.

"Not too much passing in this wind," says Vinnie. "Ground game eats up the clock."

"True," says Ripley. She looks at me and shrugs.

I give her an eye roll and she shoots back a Cheshire cat grin. She's actually pulling it off. As we say in television news, if you can fake sincerity you've got it made.

"Oh, we're going out to eat after the game," says Becker. "A friend of mine has a restaurant with a private back room. Hope you girls like Italian."

"Who doesn't?" I say.

"Cassidy, you want a snack during halftime?" asks Andrew.

"Hey, I'm a growing girl. I'll have whatever you're having. Long as it's something hot."

The Giants are stuck deep in their own territory as the game resumes and decide to run out the clock for the first half with three straight runs. The gun sounds and the crowd cheers as they head into the locker room with a ten point lead.

And then Ripley blows her cover as she jumps up and yells, "Yay, they won!"

The guys start laughing and I'm biting my lip. "Ripley, it's just halftime," says Vinnie.

She sits down. "Oh, right. I knew that."

But the men aren't buying it.

"Ripley," says Becker, turning to face her as he tries to hold back a grin. "Look at me."

She turns to face him and smiles.

"Who are the Giants playing? And don't look at the scoreboard." He puts up his hand to block her view.

Her smile slowly fades. "They're… obviously playing a team that isn't worth a damn."

"Who are they playing? Name the team."

"Thuuhhhhhh… Red Sox?"

We all double over in laughter as her face turns red. "Sweetie, the Red Sox play baseball," I say.

"Oh."

"You've never watched a football game?" asks Becker.

She thrusts out her lower lip in a pout and extends her arms like she's waiting to be handcuffed. "Guilty as charged." (Of course, when she uses this bad little girl look it turns men into quivering globs of flesh.)

"Not a problem," says Becker, now smiling at her, obviously charmed by this.

Another eye roll from me.

"Thought I'd try something new and get to know everyone a little better," she says, doing some damage control. (The girl is in advertising, after all.)

"I think this might be a good time for a trip to the ladies room,"

I say as I squeeze by Becker, grab Ripley's hand and lead her up the stairs. When we're out of earshot I stop and turn to face her. "I thought you were gonna read that book?"

"I did, but it was confusing. I mean, a fly pattern is in a Simplicity catalog, what's it doing in football?"

"What's even more bizarre is the guys think it's so cute."

"Part of my charm, as you like to say."

***

Ten minutes later we return to our seats and find two of the guys have played musical chairs. Andrew and Vinnie have switched seats.

"Excuse me, Sir, may I see your ticket stub," I say to Vinnie as I sit down.

"Hey, not fair for Andrew to hog you the whole game. Besides, he needed to get to know Ripley and I wanted to spend some time with you." He locks those dark eyes with me and my heart flutters.

Day-umm.

I glance over at Ripley and she's beaming. And after being her best friend for so long, I know what she's thinking.

Can this get any better?

And after the game, it does.

***

We're in good spirits after the Giants win, and need some real spirits because we're all frozen. A limo is waiting outside the stadium, exhaust coming out of the tailpipe and a chauffeur standing by the door. He smiles and holds the door as Ripley and I quickly get inside. We take seats on opposite sides as the guys slide in next to us. Thankfully the thing is toasty warm with the heat blowing full blast and we both whip off our gloves and hold our hands next to the vents while I eye the fully stocked bar. Becker and Andrew are on my side with the Senator next to me while Vinnie grabs a seat next to Ripley.

"Little cramped on this side," says Andrew, the only guy stuck not sitting next to a woman. He moves across the compartment and sits on the other side of Ripley, leaving her between two cute guys while I share my side with Becker, who starts taking drink orders. He leans over to play bartender as the limo pulls away. Ripley and I lock eyes for a moment, exchanging non-verbal best friend communication as we both do our best not to beam.

Three hot guys, two girls. Do the math.

CHAPTER SIX

@TwitterGirl
Air Becker off to frozen New Hampshire this week. Will try to convince Marvin Hensler to stick his tongue to a flagpole.

There's a definite spring in my step on this Monday morning. The Giants won, Ripley and I had a great dinner and drinks with three very eligible men last night. (Vinnie and Andrew helped pour us out of the limo when they dropped us off at my place. Becker couldn't exactly do it, as he didn't need to take a chance of ending up on the *Page Six* of *The Post* helping a couple of drunken staffers to the door.) Vinnie, whose body did not disappoint when he removed his parka at the restaurant, asked for my phone number while Andrew got Ripley's. So even though we're still in the Becker sweepstakes, our dance cards are not empty.

However, this semi-intoxicated conversation after we got inside had Sam howling:

Ripley: "So, you got a date with Vinnie?"

Me: "And you got a date with Andrew."

Ripley: "Who do you like the best?"

Me: "Of the three guys? All of 'em."

Ripley: "Yeah. I like them all too."

Me: "And I think they all like both of us."

At this point Sam interrupted by saying, "Ladies and gentlemen, welcome to America's newest dating show... Caligula's Palace!"

While this three guys and two girls romance polygon sounds like some sort of sixties commune, right now it makes for a very pleasant working environment.

Ah yes, back to the task of getting Becker elected president. This job, as you may have noticed, could seriously play havoc with my social life.

Frank wants me to check in first thing every Monday with Tyler, so I bounce into the conference room where I find him slumped in a chair yawning. "Late night?"

"Yeah, T.G. Didn't get done watching the game till one. Wedding went on forever."

"How was it?"

"The over and under is two years. Though I personally give it nine months."

"That bad of a couple, huh?"

"Well, not many people know it but she got herself knocked up to trap him into marrying her."

"I thought women were past that."

"Most are, the bride was not. If you knew her, you'd understand."

"Let me guess... bitchy and unattractive?"

"Correct on both points. One of her cousins was at my table and referred to her as Hannibal Lecter with boobs."

"Why do men put up with that?"

He smiles, flicks his wrist and makes a whip noise.

"Oh, that."

"And, as you would say, she has a good face for radio. You oughta see her complexion. Had to apply makeup with a paint roller. I think she was goalie on her high school dart team."

I crack up at that line as he offers a soft smile. His eyes are a little droopy, and I can tell he's not his usual upbeat self. "If you don't feel well I can come back after lunch—"

"Nah, I'm okay. I'll just pace myself today. I've been through

62

this before. But I always remind myself it's a blessing."

"What's a blessing?"

"My condition."

"Not sure I understand, Tyler."

He sits up straight and his eyes get a little misty. "My first job was in lower Manhattan, in the World Trade Center. On my usual Monday, Wednesday, Friday schedule. The 9/11 attacks were on a Tuesday. That's the only reason I'm still around. I had always wondered why God gave me this condition and that day I got my answer. Ever since, I've known He put me here to make a difference. If I'd been born with a normal metabolism I'd be dead like a lot of the friends I lost that day." He gives me a soulful look that makes my eyes well up a bit.

"Well, they say God works in mysterious ways. You have such a positive way of dealing with challenges, Tyler. You're a lot like my brother."

"Mine is no big deal compared to your brother, from what I read. Anyway, we all have certain gifts, even if we don't know they're good for us sometimes. Maybe God blessed you with sarcasm to change the direction of the country."

"Interesting way of looking at things."

"Speaking of which, that little town hall thing up in the *Live Free or Die* state offers all sorts of possibilities." He hands me a manila folder with two sheets of paper inside. "We've got a few plants in the audience and those are the questions they've been given."

"You planted *gotcha* questions?"

"Hell, everyone does *that*. I call 'em *button* questions."

"Huh?"

"Our questions are designed to push people's buttons."

I take a minute to review the papers and see each question is not a gotcha question but about a hot button issue that at least one candidate is passionate about. Or one which might send said candidate off the rails on a rant that could prove damaging. "These are all designed to get some wild, opinionated responses from different candidates."

"Right, we stay away from the usual economy, health care and foreign policy questions which bore the living shit out of the voters. If we're lucky we'll get one or two of those asked, so familiarize yourself with those and be ready with some clever tweets."

"Thanks for the heads up. I can work on those in advance. I gotta admit, Tyler, this is pretty devious."

He smiles and leans back, folding his hands behind his head. "Thank you, T.G., I take that as a compliment."

My phone dings, telling me I have a text. I take a quick look and see it's another from my unknown source.

Good Monday, Cassidy. The postman always knocks and knocks.

I furrow my brow as I try to figure this one out.

"Problem?" asks Tyler.

"Nah, just some friend playing a game of treasure hunt with me." I slide my phone back into my purse. The postman obviously means I need to check my mail. "By the way, do I have a mailbox here for letters and memos and stuff?"

"Sure, just outside the break room."

"Thanks. Anything else today?"

"Check back at four this afternoon. We'll do some FaceTime with Frank and Andrew."

"Frank's not here?"

"He went to New Hampshire to scope out the site for the Town Hall meeting." He reaches across the table, grabs an envelope, and hands it to me. "Oh, almost forgot. He told me to make sure to give you this."

I open the envelope and take out a memo:

Cassidy,
One of the higher-ups in the campaign wishes to meet you. Dinner is at Tre Bella at six. Ask for Mister Harris. Keep this confidential.

-Frank

I fold the note and put it in my purse.

"Anyway," says Tyler, "those button questions should keep you busy for awhile."

It will, but not all day. Which gives me a little time to start snooping.

***

I smile at the staffers who are buzzing around the office as I head toward the break room. I see an old fashioned wood set of cubbyholes with letters and manila envelopes crammed inside. I stop and scan the boxes to find my name.

It's on the bottom row, since I just arrived. And has one letter inside.

I pull it out and turn it over. No return address, the address printed with a computer. There's a letter opener on a shelf next to the mailboxes so I slide it through the top and open it.

Inside there is a single sheet of white paper, folded into thirds. And what's written on it pushes my curiosity to the front burner:

All is not as it seems. I know it but cannot prove it. You have resources I do not.
438903125267
What does it mean?

I stare at the message for a moment, put it back in the envelope, fold it in half and shove it into my purse.

I walk into the empty break room and fix myself a cup of coffee.

A twelve digit number.

And resources I have that our mystery guest does not.

What does it mean, indeed.

Tre Bella is an old restaurant in Little Italy. I've eaten there a few times; the food is excellent and the prices reasonable. Not the type of place I'd expect to meet a big wheel in a presidential campaign, but nothing about this campaign is normal. But hey, I don't mind Italian two days in a row. Make it three if you count Sam's better-than-sex pasta.

I hop out of a cab as a smiling older gentleman holds the door to the restaurant for me. The smell of garlic and fresh bread greet me along with the crooning of Dean Martin as I head for the hostess stand. A petite, middle-aged brunette smiles with the look of recognition I've grown accustomed to. "Ah, Miss Shea, you're with the Harris party. Right this way." I follow her through the mostly empty restaurant, which is not surprising since it is a Monday. She takes me to a door in the back of the restaurant and opens it. This campaign does like its private rooms.

I enter and what I see stops me in my tracks. Senator Becker seated at a round table.

He smiles and stands up to greet me. "Cassidy, right on time."

He moves around the table and pulls a chair out for me. "Thank you, Senator. I didn't expect to see you here."

"Please call me Will," he says, as I take my seat and he moves back to his own.

"So, Mister Harris hasn't arrived yet?"

He smiles. "He's already here. You're talking to him."

I furrow my brow, trying to quickly process what's happening. "I'm a little confused—"

"When you're running for president, it's hard to have a casual dinner off the grid. I've got a lot of aliases and restaurants with private rooms that I use to get away."

I slowly nod. "Make sense. So, anyone joining us?"

He shakes his head. "Nope. Just you and me. Hope that's okay."

"Sure, you're my boss."

"I'm not here as your boss, Cassidy. I hope that's okay too." Suddenly the man sitting across from me is not the next President of the United States, but a single guy about to have dinner with me.

Is he trying to tell me we're on a date?

"Of course it's okay. You just caught me off guard, that's all. I mean, you were the last person I expected to find here."

"I could have actually set you up with one of our billionaire donors who would have bored you to death."

"No, this is fine. It's a nice surprise."

Damn, is that an understatement.

"I've been following you a long time, Cassidy. I remember when you broke in with the local station here."

"Wow, you must really be a news junkie."

"You sort of have to be in my line of work. All it takes is for some reporter to ask you something you're not familiar with and you're toast."

"True enough."

"But I always looked forward to your stories. You had such a unique way of reporting... your life force really came through the screen."

"Thanks, that's a nice compliment."

"And then when you started doing the Twitter Girl thing it really gave me an insight into your true personality. It made you even more attractive."

"Sarcasm made me attractive?"

"Guys like a girl with a lot of spunk. And you took no prisoners as a reporter."

"I really loved what I did. But, as they say, all good things come to an end."

"Why would you say that? You could certainly go back to TV after the campaign."

I shake my head. "Along with being toxic right now my sell-by date is coming up. Once women hit forty in the business, they become producers behind the scenes. High def is not kind to those with wrinkles."

He waves his hand like shooing a fly. "Pffft. That's ridiculous. And you're stunning. Any news director would be an idiot to not put you on the air." He leans forward. "And I don't see a single wrinkle."

I can't help but blush. "Thank you, you're very kind. But if you want stunning, Ripley's your girl."

He nods and smiles. "Yeah, when the two of you are in the office at the same time, the guys all hit the pause button."

"Oh, stop it."

"I'm serious. Productivity hit an all time low that first day you were both there. May have to hide you guys in the supply closet."

So now I'm thinking after the "stunning" comment that he's interested. And then he hits me with… wait for it… this:

"I like to have a quiet dinner with all new members of the staff. Chance to get to know them better."

"Uh, yeah, this is nice."

"So to what does Twitter Girl aspire?"

I lean back in my chair, figuring I've returned to being an employee, albeit one he considers stunning. "Well, you know, what the average girl wants. A fun career and a guy who loves me. Men think we're complicated but when you boil it all down that's really about all that matters. Along with, you know, shoes."

He laughs a bit, then turns serious for a moment. "It's the same for guys, finding a soul mate." He gets a faraway look and I know he's thinking about his wife. "And the career thing as well, but nothing is as important as having someone to love. Anyway, I hope this job is going to be fun for you."

"Already is. Hey, getting paid to be sarcastic, I mean, talk about a dream gig."

"So now that you're working again you've probably got it all. I'm sure you have men beating a path to your door. Along with enough shoes."

Okay, now he's fishing.

I think.

"While I've got plenty of heels I'm pretty much a free agent in the dating department."

"Ah. Interesting."

What the hell does that mean?

***

I arrive home at eight-thirty to find Ripley playing gin rummy with Sam at the kitchen table. "So, how was your dinner with the high ranking official?" she asks.

"Confusing," I say, opening the fridge and pulling out an IBC root beer. (Can't beat ice cold soda out of a glass bottle.)

"So who was it?" asks Sam. "High roller?"

"Nope. Senator Becker."

Ripley sits up straight. "Senator Becker? And who else?"

I twist open the bottle and sit down between them. "Just Becker. He was the mystery guest."

"Interesting," she says, putting her cards down. "So, a private dinner with Mister Perfect. Was this a date?"

I take a long sip of my root beer. "To be quite honest, I'm not sure."

Now Sam puts his cards down and leans back. "Oh, this oughta be good."

"Soooo... what happened?" asks Ripley.

"Nothing *happened*. Half the time he talked to me like a guy on a date and the other half he was my boss. And the other half he talked about you."

"That's three halves," says Sam. "You're still bad at math."

"It would make sense if you were there."

"So when he talked about you," says Ripley, "what sort of things did he say? I mean, when he was the half who was a guy on a date."

"It was typical first date stuff. What do you like to do, tell me

69

about your family, where'd you grow up, favorite movies, lifelong goals, that kind of stuff. He seemed really interested in me as a person, though I don't think we have much in common."

"And when he talked about me?"

"He seemed to be asking if you were available. Of course he asked me the same thing."

"So let me get this straight," says Sam. "Will Becker, who is Mister Perfect for the two of you, asks you about her and her about you. That makes no sense if he's romantically interested in either of you."

I take another sip of root beer. "Nope, sure doesn't."

Sam gets a gleam in his eyes. "Unless...."

"Unless what?" we ask in stereo as we both lean forward.

"Ah, you actually need advice from the oracle."

"Spill, Sam," says Ripley.

"Unless he's interested in both of you and is so clueless about women he doesn't realize you shouldn't talk about another girl when you're out on a date."

"He can't be that clueless," says Ripley. "He's running for President."

"Put politics aside for a minute," says Sam. "Look, the guy got married at eighteen. If he hasn't dated since his wife's death, and I'll bet he hasn't since it was only three years ago and he's been campaigning for the last two, that means he hasn't asked a woman out in a quarter century. He's still operating on a high school level when it comes to women. And we all know how dumb guys can be in high school. As proven by the quarterback who was able to resist you two."

"You know," says Ripley, "that actually sounds plausible. He never did go through the dating thing in college or after."

My brother may be on to something. "And come to think of it, he almost seemed a little shy at dinner. Didn't have the confidence you'd expect."

"He might actually be scared of women on a romantic level,"

says Sam. "And he hasn't had any experience with them. I did read that his wife was his high school sweetheart for all four years. If he hasn't dated since she died, she might have been the only women he *ever* dated. And the only woman he's ever, you know…"

"But does that mean he's interested in both of us?" I ask.

"Alas, dear sister, I do not have a crystal ball to tell me if he's right for either one of you. But there is one sure-fire way to find out."

Ripley's eyed widen. "And that would be…"

"At some point, I need to meet this guy."

CHAPTER SEVEN

@TwitterGirl
In New Hampshire for tonight's Town Hall. Redcoats marching from Boston to attack Marvin Hensler.

In television news, a political event that attracts a horde of media people is known by the genteel term of "gang bang." (Hey, don't look at me, I didn't make it up.) I'm sure it's a reference to the fact that a lot of people (reporters) want to screw one person (the politician.)

Now as I look at things from the political side of the fence, I see the term can be taken literally.

Our Manchester hotel is filled with candidates and their staffs, and every single person has come armed with cutlery service for sixteen. A walk through the lobby and you can overhear any number of political flacks plotting against the competition accompanied by the quick *whoosh-whoosh-whoosh* sound made by knives flying through the air. And I thought media people had no souls. These guys are the devil's minions and already have their tickets punched for an eternity by a roaring fire.

Of course when I checked in I got several raised eyebrows along with some looks that said, "can you believe *she* is working in a campaign?" I'm definitely the wild card in the race. I've heard another candidate is looking for a snarky Twitter person, but according to Frank I'm a Jedi Master in sarcasm and any attempts to copy what I'm doing will pale in comparison. I guess it's a compliment that the guy known as "Viper" who is running a presidential campaign thinks I'm the snarkiest person on the planet. Personally, I was already thrilled that Senator Becker thinks I'm stunning even though I don't think I'm remotely close. He may in fact be clueless about single women, but at least he noticed me.

Frank and I are having lunch in the hotel restaurant when I see a familiar face heading our way. New Jersey Governor Rachel Schilling is perhaps our strongest challenger in the race, as she does for spunk what I do for snark. The petite late-forties brunette with the ice blue eyes is considered a maverick, as she doesn't believe in "going along to get along." She does believe in saying exactly what she's thinking and really doesn't have much of a filter. (I know, sound familiar?) Typical Jersey girl. She stops at our table and smiles at Frank. "Hey, Delavan, how's it goin'?" she asks in a sharp accent.

Franks puts his burger down, wipes his mouth with his napkin, stands up and shakes her hand. "Governor, nice to see you again."

She turns to face me. "And who do we have here but the famous Twitter Girl."

I stand up and shake hands. "Pleasure to meet you, Governor."

She looks back at Frank. "I must say, Frank, her hire was nothing short of inspired." She turns to me. "Honey, if your candidate drops out, you've got a job with me."

"Hands off the hired help, Rachel," says Frank.

"That offer goes to you too, Frank." She turns back to me. "Becker apparently beat me to him as well."

"I'll keep your offer in mind," says Frank. "In the unlikely event we lose the nomination."

She moves a little closer to me and drops her voice a bit. "Listen, Twitter Girl, do us all a favor and take Marvin Hensler out tonight. That idiot makes everyone in the party look like a bunch of whack jobs."

Frank nods. "On this we agree, and it's already on the agenda."

"Have no fear, you'll need a mop to wipe up the sarcasm," I say.

"Great," she says. "We need to drop that chump." Someone is yelling her name across the room and she turns her head. "Well, gotta go. Good luck tonight. But not too much."

"Same here," says Frank, as she leaves and we both sit back down.

"So," I say, "would you have gone to work for her?"

"She's an interesting flavor of the month. That in-your-face style of hers may play well in the Northeast, but it won't go over in Kansas. And she might be a little too honest for her own good."

"Honesty's a bad thing?"

"In politics it can be deadly. I know this is going to sound horrible, but there's a lot of stuff the general public doesn't need to know."

"What, like aliens in Area 51?"

"I can neither confirm nor deny the existence of extra-terrestrials."

I study his face and wonder what he actually knows about little green men. "Anyway, is Governor Schilling running-mate material?"

"Possibly. But we'd have to put a tight leash on her. You do know why she came over here, don't you?"

"Being polite?"

"Pffft. Polite doesn't exist in politics. She's hoping you like her enough so that she doesn't get one of your barbs tonight. So make sure you zing her at least once to let her know you can't be swayed."

***

Right now Frank and I are holed up in Becker's hotel suite as the Town Hall is about to get underway at the convention hall next door. All the questions will be asked by "regular citizens" though every campaign has its plants in the crowd. Frank has come up with an added twist to this strategy, as he actually found a Brit who had become an American citizen. If called upon he will hopefully provide the final nail to Marvin Hensler's coffin with a question about the whole UK third world thing. The event is moderated by network correspondent Hank Morell, who, though biased like everyone else in the national media against this party, will have no input into the questions. He's merely there to call on people in the crowd. Of course there's always the possibility that one or more campaigns has convinced him to call on their plants, but since he hates everyone that's not likely. If anything he'd favor the candidate least likely to win against President Turner in November.

And that would be Hensler.

So I'm determined to take the man down tonight. Death by snark.

We have seven "plants" in the crowd and Frank has taped eight-by-ten photos of each one around the flat screen monitor, along with the name of the politician whose button each will try to push. Of course our biggest hope is that our other Hensler plant, an attractive fortyish soccer mom, will be among those chosen.

With two minutes to go I've got my laptop in front of me, logged in to Twitter, ready to strike.

Frank points at the screen. "You should do a little welcome to your followers before we start."

"Good idea." I think for a moment as my muse goes online.

@TwitterGirl
Every time Hensler says something dumb, take a drink. Should put you over the legal limit in 30 minutes, so don't drive.

Frank shakes his head and smiles. "I don't know how you come up with stuff that fast."

"That's why you pay me the big bucks."

"You're worth every penny. Beats the hell out of negative ads."

A patriotic banner flashes across the screen as the event begins.

The moderator welcomes the crowd and the candidates, then briefly goes over the ground rules. He reaches into a large glass bowl filled with index cards, pulls one out and says, "Our first citizen is Danny Beaumont of Concord, who has a question about foreign policy."

Frank rolls his eyes. "Nothing bores the hell out of voters more than foreign affairs."

"Hell, it bores me."

The candidates, including Becker, basically "recite" memorized answers on the subject. No one impresses or says anything stupid, so I don't tweet.

Another question about health care doesn't inspire my muse.

And then the host picks one of our plants from the bowl. Frank sits up straight. "Get ready, it's a question for our Jersey girl."

A dark-haired slender young man in his mid-twenties is handed a microphone. "I'm a new parent and there's been a lot of talk about putting discipline back in public schools to give teachers more control. I'd like to know where each candidate stands on that, and how far you think that discipline should go."

I can tell Governor Schilling, a former private school teacher, is chomping at the bit as she bounces on her toes waiting her turn. Two other candidates give stock answers, and then she's up.

"Look, I taught school for ten years," she says. "And let's be honest… sometimes kids need a shot in the rear end to keep them in line."

Now I know about half the parents in this country think their precious little snowflakes can do no wrong and would sue a teacher who looked cross-eyed at their little angels, sooooo…

@TwitterGirl
Governor Schilling to replace "No Child Left Behind" with "No Child's Behind Left"

"Ow, that one left a mark," says Frank. "She'll get the message."

76

"Aw, c'mon Frank, I didn't hit her too hard."

Frank points at the screen. "Oooh, one of her plants is next."

"You know who the other candidates' plants are?" He dips his head and gives me a *seriously?* look and I nod. "Sorry, I forgot about your connections."

A middle-aged blonde woman who obviously dyed her roots brown takes the microphone. "While we have only one woman running for President in this group, I wonder how the rest of you would include women in some non-traditional posts should you be elected. For instance, since there are plenty of females serving in the military, do you think a woman is qualified to be Secretary of Defense?"

Governor Schilling smiles at this one, and of course says women are qualified to hold any position. The male candidates, knowing full well there is only one possible answer, follow suit.

Until Marvin Hensler.

"Well," he says, giving a sideways glance at the lone woman on the stage, "while women are certainly qualified to hold certain positions in public office, I don't think Secretary of Defense is one of them. I mean, if someone fires a nuke at us I can't be waiting around if she trips running to the Oval Office in her high heels."

The crowd groans as Schilling stares daggers at Hensler, then looks down and smiles. "At least I wear shoes that match, Marvin. Maybe your campaign staff needs to tag your wardrobe with Garanimals."

"Ha! She's almost as quick as you," says Frank.

"Damn good line."

The video cuts to a tight shot of Hensler's shoes, clearly showing one is black and the other dark brown. Hensler turns beet red, the crowd roars and Governor Schilling licks her lips while wearing a huge grin. Senator Becker turns away because he's laughing so hard.

@TwitterGirl
Marvin Hensler's global warming policy: dress in the dark to

save energy. Warning: he could show up in capri pants next time.

Frank cracks up, then I see our young Hispanic plant is next. This could be it.

"Good evening, candidates," he says in a strong accent. "I grew up in Latin America and go to college here. I want to become a US citizen because of the opportunity. I have learned to speak English and consider the United States to be my home. I want to know how each of you plans to deal with the immigration issue because I do not want to return to Latin America."

Most of the candidates give a variety of the usual responses. Build a wall on the border, grant citizenship to immigrants serving in the military, create a path to citizenship.

Hensler is shaking his head. "Well, it's nice that some of my fellow candidates want to put out the welcome mat for illegal aliens. But I cannot support such a program. However, young man, I will say it's very admirable that you came here speaking English tonight instead of Latin."

Frank nearly spits out his soda at Hensler's comment as the crowd explodes in laughter. "That's it! Finish him off!"

I'm laughing my ass off but I have to focus. Thankfully, the stuff I learned in Catholic school pays off.

@TwitterGirl
Carpe idiota (that's "seize the idiot" in Latin)

***

It is just past eleven when I get back to my hotel room in a great mood. The Town Hall had gone well for the Senator, I'd zinged each candidate at least once, and the word in the lobby was that Marvin Hensler would announce he was dropping out of the race tomorrow morning after his incredible gaffe. While Frank had wanted me to push him from the race with snark, let's face it, the guy did it to himself. But lawyers, doctors and priests, all of whom had been required to study Latin, joined my Twitter parade after Hensler's screw-up.

Veni, vidi, vici. I came, I saw, I kicked ass.

But right now I'm fried as I pour a single serving glass of wine from the mini-bar which probably cost the campaign ten bucks, toss off my clothes and crawl into bed.

And then the FaceTime ring tone on my iPad goes off.

I'm hoping it's not Frank needing me for something. I prop up two pillows, lean back, and when I flip open the cover I find it's Tyler calling. I accept the call and see his smiling face peeping out from under a blanket.

"Hey, T.G., I was hoping you were still up. Great job tonight!"

"Thanks, Tyler, though I don't think Hensler needed a push off the cliff."

"Hey, you still got in some serious barbs at the other candidates. One down, a bunch to go. Who does Frank want to target next?"

"Hey, you're the strategist, remember? Just pick someone and I'll be up his ass like a thong."

"Interesting visual, T.G."

"Trust me, the real thing is as uncomfortable as it sounds."

"Huh. You don't strike me as a thong girl."

"I'm not. Once was enough when it comes to butt floss."

"I can only imagine. Hey, did you get any of those great pancakes they serve up there?"

"Oh my God, those are incredible! I had no idea! And the fresh real maple syrup!"

"Can you get me a to-go box of those things before you leave? They actually re-heat very well."

"Done. Anything for you, Tyler."

The conversation moves from pancakes to the Giants to science fiction movies we both want to see to great books we'd read.

And then my tablet beeps again.

"You got another call?" he asks.

I check and see that I don't.

It's the device telling me my battery is about dead. I look at the clock. We've been talking for more than an hour.

"Battery's about to die, Tyler. I got two percent. Gotta go."

"Well, nice spending an hour in bed with Twitter Girl. Hope it was good for you."

"Tyler, you give good phone."

"And we were just getting into a good discussion on why Picard never fires his damn phasers. Kirk would seriously kick his bald ass."

Suddenly, I don't need sleep. "I could call you on the phone if you're not too tired."

"Operators are standing by, T.G."

My iPad goes dark. I plug it in to charge it up for tomorrow, grab my cell and call Tyler.

When it dies, I finally turn out the lights.

It's one-thirty.

And we weren't done talking.

CHAPTER EIGHT

@TwitterGirl
#ByeByeHensler
Hensler followers make Latin-English dictionaries number one on Amazon, send copies to Costa Rican missions

After an all-you-can-eat pancake feeding frenzy before leaving New Hampshire (and yes, I did bring a big stack back for Tyler, along with a quart jug of *real* maple syrup) it was a quick flight home and a late afternoon strategy session. Frank told me to keep hammering Hensler and his followers this weekend since that's one endorsement Becker doesn't want. Welcoming those whack jobs into our tent does more harm than good, and besides, they'll never vote for the President anyway.

Anyway, now the weekend is here and we can get back to the important stuff.

I'm on a date with Vinnie the consultant while Ripley is out across town with Andrew. (Now known as "Plan B")

If I thought Vinnie looked good after a football game, I'm blown away at how incredible he is in a suit. Seriously, the guy could model clothes for a catalog. And I don't need to see him out of the suit to know he's ripped, though the thought has already crossed my mind. Of course I cannot wait to hear my brother's first impression from when he picked me up, but I pretty much know what he's going to say.

Vinnie is, as my mother used to say in her wicked Noo Yawk accent, a smooth operatuh.

An hour and a half into dinner I can tell this is one of those first dates that's more about physical attraction than anything else. (And you're saying, "Uh… your point being?") The conversation is decent, but not easy. He wants to talk about nothing but politics, I want to talk about anything but. I think he's really more Ripley's type than mine, but hey, he aint chopped liver. And of course you already know I'm a horrible judge of character and bad at first impressions, so I shouldn't throw the guy back in the pond after ninety minutes. Besides, I have this huge slice of tiramisu to demolish and I'm a growing girl.

He glances at his watch, and smiles. "We're making good time," he says.

"Are we on a schedule?"

"We are if we want to catch a movie." He reaches into his pocket, pulls out a small sheet of paper and hands it to me. I see that it is the local movie listings. "You pick, if you're up for it."

Wow, a guy who plans. Interesting.

I scan the sheet and see the usual multiplex offerings of a few action movies, the latest teenage girl dystopian angst festival, two sparkly vampire flicks, and a romantic comedy I've been dying to see. I'm sure a macho looking guy like Vinnie isn't interested, so I throw the choice back at him. "I can go for the rom-com or the Liam Neeson shoot-em-up."

"Ladies choice. And I read some great reviews about the rom-com."

"You like romantic comedies? I didn't figure you for a chick flick guy."

"I'm Italian. Romance is in my blood."

And with that my interest in Vinnie picks up.

Three hours and a hilarious rom-com later, I'm seeing Vinnie in a different light.

Probably because it's the porch light from my house, and we've been making out in his car like a couple of teenagers.

***

Sunday brunch has been a tradition at my house for years. Ripley picks up fresh fruit, bagels and croissants; Sam whips up these incredible Belgian waffles; and I play bartender making mimosas with freshly squeezed orange juice. When it warms up we sit outside on the patio but it's way too cold for that in January. Besides, the Giants have another playoff game this afternoon and Ripley, amazingly, is going to stay and watch in the hopes of learning that a quarterback is not a twenty-five cent refund.

She and I haven't talked since Friday because she had a commercial shoot yesterday, so it's time for the Friday night dating postmortem as we sit down to this feast.

"So," says Ripley, slicing into her waffle, "how was your evening with Vinnie?"

"Not bad. Dinner, movie, and uh…" I see Sam smiling at me. "And small talk."

"Right," says Sam, turning to Ripley. "Ten degrees outside and they're *talking* in his car till one."

"Little brother, are you spying on me?"

"Just watching out for my sister."

"Did you meet him?" asks Ripley.

"Briefly, when he picked her up."

"And?"

"He's a player."

"If he were a player he would have taken me back to his place," I say.

"Did he ask you to go to his place?" asks Sam.

83

I feel a sheepish grin grow. "Uh…. yeah. But I told him to take me home."

"I rest my case," he says.

"Fine," I say. "Ripley, I think he's more your type. You both like to talk shop. The only common interest was physical."

"Your point being?" says Ripley.

"He scratched an itch, but that's about all."

"Well, if you're gonna toss him aside," she says.

I take a sip of my mimosa. "Meanwhile, how was your date with Andrew?"

"He's okay. Nothing special. I mean, he's cute as hell but we didn't seem to have much in common either. He's more your type."

"Well, if you're gonna toss him aside."

"Meanwhile, anything new on the Becker front after your private dinner?"

"I still can't tell if he's interested or not. Though he seemed disappointed that you weren't in the office when we got back from New Hampshire."

She leans forward and rests her head on her hands, eyes wide with excitement. "Really? What did he say about me?"

Sam rolls his eyes. "Aren't you two late for Algebra class?"

"Shut up, Sam," we say in stereo.

"By the way, dear brother, I seem to remember you had your third date with Stacy on Friday night as well. How'd it go?"

He shrugs. "Men never kiss and tell."

"Bull," says Ripley. "C'mon, we want details."

He suddenly gets a sad look. "If I'd gotten a kiss I'd be able to tell."

I stop eating and look at my brother, who I can see is a little down. "That bad, huh?"

"She's not interested in a romantic relationship." He gives me a look I know so well, his eyes deep pools of permanent hurt, the look that tells me the wheelchair was a factor and the girl wants to be just friends. Despite Sam's adaptability and independence,

84

the one thing over which he has no control is a single woman's view of a man who cannot walk. I'd like to bitch slap these girls and tell them they're missing a guy who is an absolute gem.

Ripley picks up on his body language, gets up, wraps one arm around his shoulder and kisses him on the top of the head. "Her loss, Sam. You're such a great guy. Any girl would be lucky to have you. You're the total package."

She hugs him hard as he locks eyes with me, his slightly misty, and our brother-sister non-verbal communication tells me exactly what he's thinking.

***

You have resources I do not. Use them.

The text hits my phone at halftime and I realize that with all this stuff involving our wheel-of-bachelors I've forgotten about this mysterious number I'm supposed to be looking for. Probably because subconsciously I don't really want to find anything.

Ripley notices the puzzled look on my face. "Everything okay?"

"I'm not sure."

"Why, what's up?" asks Sam, as he enters the room carrying three beers.

"You remember that mystery text? Whoever it is keeps contacting me."

Ripley furrows her brow. "What are you talking about?"

I tell her about the first text, then grab my purse and show them both the note I found in my mailbox, then the latest text. I turn to Sam. "Still think it's from someone at another campaign?"

"Not sure. I would think campaigns can get just about anything as far as information is concerned. Not sure what resources you would have that government people wouldn't."

"You're a reporter," says Ripley. "I'll bet your contacts are your resources."

I nod slowly as that makes sense. "Which means it's someone without great government or campaign connections. Meanwhile, where the hell do I start looking for this number? What could it be?"

"Swiss bank account?" asks Ripley.

"Possible," I say, "but even the feds can't get info on those."

"Guess we should start a list of things that have twelve numbers," says Sam.

"Is anyone at the campaign remotely suspicious?" asks Ripley.

I think a moment and recall my dinner with Frank's assistant. "Well, the deputy campaign manager, Roberta Willis. I had dinner with her and it ended abruptly when I asked about the Senator's personal life."

"Then that's where you should focus your attention," says Sam.

Ripley raises one finger. "But before you start going all Brenda Starr on this guy, consider this: what will you do if you find something?"

"How do you mean?" I ask.

"Well, suppose you stumble onto something sleazy that would kill the campaign. If you release it, you're out of a job and maybe President sleazeball wins re-election. Maybe you should let sleeping dogs lie."

"I have to know, Ripley. I can make a decision if I find anything substantial. Besides, wouldn't you want to know if the supposed perfect guy has skeletons in his closet before you sign on as First Lady?"

"I guess if you put it that way." Ripley loads up a chip with guacamole. "So where do you start with something like that?"

"That part's easy," I say. "Find someone with a personal ax to grind. With a politician, that shouldn't be too hard to dig up."

And when a reporter needs something like that, the best advice comes from none other than Richard Nixon.

***

"So, does Senator Becker have an enemies list?"

Tyler starts to laugh as he shakes his head. "Well, since you like *All the President's Men*, that question doesn't surprise me."

"Well? Isn't there a little bit of Nixon in every politician?"

He nods. "There is. Of course, you're not really paranoid if they really *are* out to get you. And in politics, there's always someone looking to stab you in the back."

"So, enemies list?"

"While we don't have a physical list *per se*, there are individuals who would do everything they can to see Top Dog fail. Why do you ask?"

"Figured there might be some people to discredit along the way with a tweet or two. You know, on the rare days when one of the competitors doesn't say something stupid. Call it pre-emptive snark."

"Hmmm. That's out-of-the-box thinking, but I like it."

"So who's public enemy number one?"

"That's easy. The Senator's former best friend, David Gold."

"His former *best friend*? Really?"

"You don't know the story?"

I shake my head. "Enlighten me, Tyler."

"Okay, so Becker and David Gold meet in college, both political science majors. Both get jobs as aides in Washington, then a few years later Gold decides he wants to run for some local office in New York and asks Becker to run his campaign. Anyway, the party has some sort of exploratory committee looking for candidates and Gold is supposed to meet with them. But that night Gold has the flu and rather than cancel he asks Becker to deliver his speech. The party falls in love with Becker and asks him to run. He tries to get them to run his friend instead but they want him since Gold really has no personality. Anyway, Gold has blamed him ever since for basically stealing his career."

"Did Gold ever go into politics? I mean, did he run for something else?"

Tyler nods. "He tried, ran a couple of times but his anger came through and eventually the party told him to get lost. Now he works for some watchdog organization and every chance he gets he puts out something negative on Becker. I met him once. He's a sad, bitter guy. But as far as his own political career goes, the point was moot, as he doesn't have one tenth the appeal Becker does and he's not exactly telegenic. Short, fat and losing his hair. He never would have gone anywhere in politics. The Senator even offered him a job but Gold thinks that would be demeaning."

"So he's our biggest enemy?"

"Enemy's the wrong term. He's simply a major thorn in our side, wants us to fail. You'll meet him eventually and he'll try to turn you against Becker."

"How will I meet him?"

"Oh, trust me, he'll show up as a heckler or do something disruptive at some point."

But I'm not waiting for "eventually." I need to know right now.

***

I walk over to the mailboxes to see if our mystery guest has sent any snail mail my way when I see Ripley heading toward me from the break room, beaming. I know something good has happened as our eyes connect. "Okay, spill."

She hands me an envelope. I open it and see something that looks very familiar.

Ripley,
One of the higher-ups in the campaign wishes to meet you. Dinner is at Carriage Trade at six. Ask for Mister Ferguson. Keep this confidential.
-Frank

I slowly nod as I hand it back to her. "So, Frank is apparently the campaign pimp and it's your turn with the mystery higher-up."

"Except we both know who that is. So he wants to play the field."

"At this point, who the hell knows? But good luck tonight."

"I'm betting he spends one of those three halves of the evening talking about you."

"And men say *we're* hard to figure out."

"Hey, Twitter Girl!"

Senator Becker's voice cuts through the chatter and I see him waving me into his office. "The master beckons," I say, as I head toward him. He smiles as I arrive at his office door. "What can I do for you, Senator?"

"Come on in," he says. I enter the office and he closes the door behind me, then moves behind the desk. "I just hadn't had a chance to tell you what a great job you did in New Hampshire and over the weekend. You not only put the nail in Hensler's coffin, you buried the guy and his followers at sea."

"Sir, it's easy when they do most of the work for me. I mean, talk about hanging curve balls over the middle of the plate."

"Yeah, really. And remember, when it's just you and me, please call me Will."

"Sorry, I keep forgetting. Twitter Girl's always good for me."

He leans forward, drops his voice a bit. "One more thing... I, uh, wanted to say how much I enjoyed having dinner with you the other night."

"Yeah, I had a good time."

"And I hope we can do it again. Just the two of us. If, you know, that's okay."

And his look tells me Sam may be right about his lack of experience with women. I haven't seen this body language since high school. Slump shouldered, hands in pockets, a shy boy asking a girl to dance.

"Sure, I'd like that, Sen— I mean, Will."

He exhales audibly like he's relieved at not getting shot down and smiles at me, not the famous smile America knows, but one that includes his eyes locking with mine and going deep into my soul.

Damn, I get an amazing shiver. The most eligible man in the country is interested in me.

I think.

And probably my best friend.

I think.

I'm totally confused.

Welcome back to high school, indeed.

***

The phone rings shortly after nine, and I see it's Ripley checking in with the latest breaking news on Becker. "You've reached Twitter Girl. For mixed romantic signals, press one."

Beep. "You called it," she says.

"Let me guess… the three halves again?"

"Yeah, it's the weird math formula for which there is no answer key. Half the time talking shop, half on a date, half talking about you."

"Kisses, hugs, pre-marital hand holding?"

"No, no and no. At this point two straws in a chocolate shake at a malt shop would pass for romance. Sweetie, I don't get it."

"I don't either. Maybe we're ignoring him too much?"

"Nah, that's not it. I'm beginning to think your brother's theory is on target."

"By the way, he called me in his office today and asked me out again. At least I think he did."

"What do you mean *you think* he asked you out?"

"He said he had a good time and asked if I was okay with having dinner with him again, just the two of us."

"Ah, that's something. So he's interested in you."

"Maybe, maybe not. Maybe he just wants a woman to talk to

and he's got a void in his personal life. The campaign is pretty much dominated by men, in case you hadn't noticed."

"I guess that's possible."

"Anyway, if the pattern follows, the next time he sees you he'll ask you out to dinner again."

"Maybe so." Heavy sigh. Long pause.

"What, Ripley?"

"I can't put my finger on it, but there's, I don't know, something not right about this guy."

"So, you dropping out of the Becker sweepstakes?"

"Hell no. Besides, if there really is something wrong with him, who better than me to fix him? However, I do think Sam needs to meet him."

CHAPTER NINE

@TwitterGirl
Marvin Hensler has head X-rayed during routine physical. The X-rays showed nothing.

Frank's pecan crusted chicken salad barely hits the table when his cell rings. He looks at it and shakes his head. "Dammit, gotta go."

"What?" I ask.

"Got a fire to put out back at the headquarters."

"You need my help?"

"Nah, I got this." He flags down a waitress and hands her his plate. "Can you box that up for me? I can't stay."

"Certainly," she says.

"See you back at the office. Save your receipt and the campaign will reimburse you," says Frank.

"No problem," I say, as he puts on his coat and takes off. Which leaves me alone in the busy Manhattan restaurant, so I pull out my tablet and start searching for something to read while I attack my pastrami sandwich. No sooner than I take a big bite than I'm interrupted.

"Excuse me, you're Cassidy Shea, right?"

I look up and see a handsome guy in a business suit about forty sitting alone at the table across from me. I put my finger up as I quickly chew, wipe the mustard from my chin, then take a sip of ice cold creme soda and swallow. "Last time I checked."

"I thought so. I really miss seeing you on TV. Loved your stories."

"That's very kind of you."

"That series you did on organ donation brought tears to my eyes. I think you're the only network reporter with a heart."

"Well, thank you, but now I'm a former network reporter. Still have the heart, though. The network let me keep it since they basically have no use for such things."

He laughs a bit. "Well, you'll get another gig. You're too talented."

"I already got a new job."

"Oh, really? What network? I'll be sure to watch."

I shake my head. "Not on TV. I'm working for Senator Becker's presidential campaign. Doing my Twitter Girl thing. I get paid to be sarcastic till November."

"Hey, that's terrific. Good for you."

The guy has a warm smile and pale blue eyes framed by thick dark brown hair. A lean, boyish face. Sort of a cross between handsome and cute. Probably because he's a cute guy wrapped in a thousand dollar suit. Oh, what the hell. "If you'd like to join me for lunch, my boss got called away. And I hate eating alone."

"Hey, can't pass up that invitation." He smiles, picks up his plate and slides into the seat opposite me, then extends his hand. "Jack Wheeler."

"Nice to meet you, Jack. So, did your lunch companion get called away as well?"

"Nope, flying solo today. Sometimes I like to get away from the office by myself to clear my head. Helps me think."

"Oh, I'm sorry. I'm taking you away from work."

"Much rather talk to you. And it's nothing that can't wait."

"So waddaya do, Jack Wheeler?"

"Public relations."

"That sounds like fun."

"Depends on the client, and right now I've got one that's taking

93

all my time. Gotta no-win situation that needs damage control."

"Well, as a former member of the media, I can only advise you that *no comment* is the worst thing you can say. When someone gives us that we only dig deeper."

"Yeah, I know from previous experience. Unfortunately my client didn't take that advice. Anyway, like I said, I'd rather talk to you."

And talk we do. And talk. And talk.

The conversation is easy, not forced, we have a lot in common. Lets put it this way; a half hour later I have only finished half of my sandwich, and it's killer pastrami on to-die-for rye bread with hot mustard. It's one of those conversations where you can't get what you want to say out of your mouth fast enough. And, news flash, the guy actually looks as if he's listening to me instead of giving me the usual guy-tuning-out-girl-yes-dear-bobblehead.

"So, are you liking politics?" he asks, as I give the waitress my credit card and ask her to wrap the rest of my sandwich. (I aint leavin' food this good. Like my mom said, kids are starving in some foreign country. And they probably wouldn't like pastrami anyway.)

"Only been doing it a few weeks. It's different than news. More cutthroat. But I think I've hitched my wagon to the right star."

"Yeah, Becker seems like a slam dunk. Love to see the idiot in the White House get his walking papers."

"Wouldn't we all."

"So, your job is to basically do the social networking thing?"

"Just Twitter. I'm supposed to simply launch sarcastic comments at the opposition when they say or do something stupid."

"Sounds like fish in a barrel with politicians."

"So far, it has been."

"And when you're not being sarcastic, what do you do for fun?"

He looks at me differently than Will Becker did. With the Senator it was simply a casual question. With this guy… I can tell he's definitely interested in me. "Being sarcastic *is* fun. For

94

me anyway."

"I meant when you're off the clock. Surely a household name like yourself has a full dance card."

Okay, now he's asking if I'm available. "Well, I like to travel, go to ballgames, binge watch shows on Netflix, play poker. But my dance card does have some openings."

"Might there be an opening for dinner and a show some night?"

I shoot him a slight smile. "Oh, I think I can fit you into my schedule—"

"Wheeler! Hey, Wheeler!"

A familiar voice interrupts me as I turn to see Tyler heading toward our table, not looking happy, eyes locked on Jack.

I turn back to Jack. "You two know each other?"

He slumps into his chair as he rolls his eyes and exhales a heavy sigh. "Uh, you could say that."

Tyler arrives, folds his arms and stares at Jack. "Well, well, well, isn't this an interesting lunch pairing."

"Hello, Tyler," says Jack, in a monotone.

I look up at Tyler. "So how do you two know each other?"

Tyler answers while still staring at Jack. "Uh, didn't he tell you? He's my counterpart for a certain governor from New Jersey."

I turn back to Jack with both eyebrows raised. "Oh, *really*? You sorta left out that little detail about your *client*." I look back at Tyler. "He said he worked in public relations."

"C'mon, Wheeler," says Tyler, "if you wanna spy on us why don't you just plant a volunteer in our headquarters? That's more your style anyway. Though it didn't work the last time."

Jack is turning beet red and looks at me like a child caught with his hand in the cookie jar. "Cassidy, I really was only interested—"

"Beat your feet, Wheeler," says Tyler.

I glare at Jack. "I'd take his advice if I were you."

"Fine. Listen, about that dance card of yours—"

"Get. Lost."

My almost dinner-and-a-show date gets up and leaves.

Tyler looks at me quizzically. "How the hell did you end up eating lunch with *him*?"

"Frank got called back to the office right after the food got here, Jack started chatting me up from the next table, we were both eating alone and I invited him to join me."

Tyler shakes his head as I grab the bag with the rest of my lunch and stand up. We start to walk out of the place. "I'm surprised Frank didn't notice him."

"He had his back to the guy."

"Can't believe he was stalking you. But that's typical of Wheeler."

"By the way, no nickname for him?"

"I have one, but not in front of a lady."

"I'm no lady, I'm Twitter Girl. C'mon, I can handle it."

"It's too crude and you have too much class. But he's known as Wheeler the Dealer in political circles."

He holds the door open and we walk out into the cold and bright sunshine.

"Well, I owe you one, Tyler."

He puts on a pair of Ray-Ban sunglasses as we head down the street, and for the first time since I've met him he's not the upbeat ball of positive energy who's the life of the campaign office. He looks serious, jaw clenched, as he power-walks down the street. "Just be careful, T.G. Nothing is as it seems in politics."

Nothing is as it seems.

I stop dead in my tracks, grab his forearm and turn to face him. "What did you say?"

"You gotta be careful in this business. Nothing is off the table and people will use every trick in the book—"

"No, no, when you said *nothing is as it seems*. What did you mean by that?" I study his face. Is Tyler my mystery contact?

"I mean the rules don't apply because there *are* no rules. Don't take anything at face value. Play your cards close to the vest."

"Oh." His expression offers nothing, no clue, though I cannot see his eyes. If he's my contact, which doesn't make much sense

96

anyway, he doesn't have a *tell*.

We start walking again. "Just be careful who you trust, that's all."

"I trust *you*, Tyler. Thanks again for protecting me from that guy. He had just asked me out to dinner and I was about to accept. I don't need my heart broken again."

"Yeah, and that's what would have happened. He would have been the perfect boyfriend till the convention, then dumped you."

Tyler's got his hands in his pockets so I curl one hand around his elbow and rest it on his forearm.

The guy reminds me a lot of my brother. Looking out for me, wanting the best for me, protecting me. Tyler Garrity makes me feel safe, like he would never let anyone hurt me.

And apparently there are a lot of people in politics who would like to do just that.

***

I head for Frank's office the minute we get back to the campaign headquarters and tap on his door. He's eating the lunch the waitress boxed up and gestures toward the chair in front of his desk. "C'mon in."

"Did you get your fire put out?"

"Thankfully, it didn't turn out to be anything serious."

"That's good."

"So what's up?"

"I had lunch with Jack Wheeler after you left."

His eyes widen and the eyebrows go up. "And you did this because…"

"Frank, I had no idea who he was. He was sitting right behind you all along. We started talking after you left and I invited him to join me at my table because I hate eating alone in a restaurant and he seemed like a decent guy. He told me he worked in public relations. Thankfully Tyler happened to come in and told me he

97

worked for Governor Schilling."

Frank's eyes narrow as he looks to the side. "That sonofabitch. The bastard was stalking us. How did I not notice him?"

"You had your back to him and Twitter Girl had your undivided attention. She has that effect on people."

"Thank goodness we didn't talk about anything confidential."

"Anyway, Frank, the guy hit on me after lying about who he was. I wanna get even."

"With him or his candidate?"

"I guess the road to him goes through his candidate."

"Fine, the primary is in two days. We need to knock her out anyway, may as well do it early. But be careful, we don't want any sexism charges. She *is* the only woman in the race. The term *bitch* is off the table."

"Don't worry, Frank. I know the rules of a good catfight. The only kick-ass bitch in Iowa this week will be me."

CHAPTER TEN

@TwitterGirl
#IowaPrimary
Governor Schilling driving through Iowa. So used to paying tolls she keeps tossing quarters out the car window.

Yeah, I started out with a cute, fun little tweet to lull the Schilling camp into a false sense of security. In a few hours I'll start carpet bombing the Internet with all sorts of snarky comments that will make them feel like they slept in itching powder. Might file them under **#Don'tLieToTheRedheadBitch.**

However, my "shock and awe" campaign to get even with Wheeler the Dealer is already underway after Tyler happened to mention the guy is an incurable chocoholic. My brother, who enjoys exacting revenge on those ne'er-do-wells who dare play with his sister's emotions, whipped up a batch of Ex-Lax brownies with enough laxative to give anyone a free colonoscopy prep. That's the shock part. I placed them in a decorative basket with red, white and blue ribbons and bribed a room service waiter to have them waiting in Wheeler's hotel room. So far our "public relations" guy is nowhere to be found, as I overheard another Schilling staffer say he was staying in today as he was a bit "under the weather." I did swing by his hotel room, tapped on the door, said, "housekeeping" and heard him yell, "come back later" followed by the sound of repeated toilet flushes.

And that's the… wait for it…

Awwwwww…

Then of course, I cover my tracks.

@TwitterGirl
#IowaPrimary
Love the hospitality here! Found a basket of delicious brownies in my hotel room! Sugar high!

But things are a little different this time in the wilds of Iowa. There's no debate, simply tomorrow's primary. (Known in Iowa as a "caucus" for some odd reason, and trying to explain it would take too long and not make much sense to you since it doesn't make any sense to me either.) So this time I'm not waiting around for a candidate to make a gaffe. I've got my tweets at the ready, scripted and with a specific schedule that will allow me to sit back, relax and watch the carnage. (Of course I'm always at the ready to throw more gasoline on the fire if necessary if there are any breaking gaffes.) Tyler, who also wants to get even with Wheeler, came up with the strategy and Frank already approved my tweets. While Senator Becker is making a last minute swing through the state along with the rest of the contenders, I'm going to make Governor Schilling waste all of her time doing something else.

Denying a rumor.

Of course I had to enlist some help to start said rumor so the origin cannot be traced back to me. One of my old co-workers and poker buddies, Kevin Frost, despises Governor Schilling almost as much as he hates the current President, as she has a tendency to treat photographers as the hired help.

So as I walk through the hotel coffee shop which is filled with nothing but media people, I see Kevin reading a newspaper while eating breakfast. He looks up, spots me, stands up and waves.

"Hey, Cassidy!"

All eyes in the coffee shop turn for a moment as I quickly move toward him and give him a quick hug. "Hi, Kevin, how's life on Air Force One?" I say in a louder than normal voice, at the level of those annoying people who discuss their sex lives on a cell phone while in a restaurant.

He replies in the same fashion. "Not bad, lotta frequent flyer miles. You enjoying your new gig?"

"Yeah, it's a lot of fun."

"So, what's Becker think about Schilling dropping out?"

Everything comes to a screeching halt in the place as all heads turn toward us. Now it's time for my best Academy Award performance as my eyes widen and I raise my voice. "Excuse me? Schilling's dropping out?"

"That's the rumor I overheard in the lobby. Figured you'd know for sure."

"Hadn't heard anything but let me check it out."

I pull out my cell phone as the place suddenly clears out. No one wants to be scooped on this.

@TwitterGirl
#IowaPrimary
Rumor has it Governor Schilling is dropping out. Trying to confirm. Stay tuned.

Of course now the New Jersey Governor will have to spend the rest of the day denying rumors and doing so without the help of her chief strategist, who is stuck in the shitter.

By the time she gets things straightened out, a lot of voters will actually think she's out of the race. And not bother voting for her.

***

101

@TwitterGirl
#IowaPrimary
Big win for Senator Becker! Thanks Iowa, will miss the brownies!

I'm feeling no pain as I lean back in the soft leather chair in Becker's suite. It's a party atmosphere after a huge victory, and the staff is watching the political commentary on television about the outcome. Of course, the big story isn't that Becker won, which he was expected to do, but that Governor Schilling came in fourth after running second in the polls here a few days ago. Most of the experts are attributing it to the rumor about her dropping out, which also resulted in a bonus as she got so tired of answering questions yesterday she bit one voter's head off and showed her true colors. Senator Becker played his role perfectly, sticking up for the Governor by saying the rumor was no doubt floated by the President's campaign in an effort to fracture our party. And Kevin the photographer stuck to his story about hearing it in the lobby "from a bunch of advertising people" he didn't recognize.

Meanwhile, Jack Wheeler never emerged from his hotel room. Sometimes, revenge is a dish served with chocolate.

So Twitter Girl is unscathed after getting even.

Meanwhile, back to the other campaign involving my romantic interest. Or, the man I think is my romantic interest. Becker has been making eye contact with me ever since he arrived in the suite after making his victory speech. He's sipping a beer, tie loosened, jacket off, sleeves rolled up, looking tired but happy. I, of course, have been smiling back at him after said eye contact. Though we haven't had our "second date" I'm thinking it's on his agenda.

And if he's "sweet on me" (love that old term) I'd like to know tonight instead of waiting for the next available date on Becker's dance card, which might be awhile.

The television commentators wrap up their analysis and the room starts to clear out. Becker doles out handshakes and back slaps as people leave the suite. Within a few minutes the only people left are me and Frank.

"Great job, guys," says Becker, as he closes the door. "I cannot believe the damage we did to Schilling."

I widen my eyes and put on my best playing dumb face. "Why Senator, whatever do you mean?"

He laughs as he turns to Frank. "You think she's toast, Frank?"

He shrugs as he tosses an empty beer bottle into the trash. "After that little outburst which has already gone viral, could be. No one wants someone with a hair trigger temper in the Oval Office. But I think she'll stick for a few more rounds. She's definitely off the short list for VP."

"Well, I've learned one thing," says Becker. "Don't get on Twitter Girl's bad side."

I drain what's left of my wine. "Hell hath no fury like a woman stalked."

Becker notices we're both out of booze. "Refill, guys? One for the road since no one's driving?" He looks at the bar. "Still got a half bottle of wine and a few beers."

"I'm fried," says Frank. "Gonna hit the hay."

"Well, I never let wine go to waste," I say as I hold out my glass. "Kids are thirsty in some foreign country. Hit me, Senator."

Frank says goodnight and leaves as Becker refills my glass, then sits down on the couch opposite me. "I must say, I'm amazed at what you and Tyler came up with."

"Well, I cannot take all the credit since it was Tyler's idea. But I think I did implement the plan with a certain flair and a little help from a friend in the media who will go unnamed."

"You really used Ex-Lax brownies on Wheeler?"

I shake one finger at him. "Senator, plausible deniability, remember?"

"Guess he'll be hiring a food taster." We both share a laugh as he leans back on the couch. "You're an amazing woman, Cassidy."

"Why thank you, Senator."

"Call me Will, please."

"Sorry, keep forgetting. But I'm really just an average girl."

"Yeah, right."

I tuck my legs underneath me and sip the wine, which is taking me past buzzed to a level Ripley calls *truth serum*. As in, I'd better shut the hell up unless I want to play all my cards in front of this man. "You're the amazing one, Will Becker."

He waves his hand. "Nah, I'm just an average guy."

"Yeah, right."

He sits there, staring at me with a longing look, and if he wasn't running for President I'd jump his bones. But this "relationship" (if it exists) will be a marathon, not a sprint, just like the campaign. I need to tread carefully, slowly, and not scare him away. "I heard you had dinner with Ripley the other night."

"Yeah, she's terrific. Smart gal."

Time for a little fishing. "You two look good together."

"Hell, I think she'd make any guy look good."

"She is a traffic stopper. Ripley's a real sweetheart, too."

"Why are we talking about her, Cassidy?"

Hmmm. An opening. Oh, what the hell, I'm tired of trying to figure this out. "I just figured, you know, you might be interested in her. Romantically. She'd be really good for you."

"I… uh… was sort of hoping *you* might be really good for me."

***

Between the booze and finding out the Senator thinks I might be good for him and wants to have dinner with me later this week, I'm practically floating down the hallway toward my room. It's a little after eleven.

Midnight back east.

Meanwhile, is he still up?

I open the door, pull my tablet out of my purse and check my email. I scan the dozens of congratulatory messages and find the one I'm looking for time stamped two minutes ago.

I hit the FaceTime button, tap his number and wait.

Tyler's smiling face fills the screen. "There she is! Congrats!"

"Tyler, you know the whole thing was your idea. You're the one who deserves the accolades."

"Fine, we'll share, but you fired the bullets. I just loaded the gun. Do we make a great team, or what?"

"We do. I saw that you had just emailed me so I knew you were still up."

"Yeah, I get kinda wired on election nights."

"It's the same when you anchor the late newscast. Can't go to sleep for a few hours."

I really wanna talk to him about my twenty minutes alone with the Senator, but realize it's probably not a good idea to do that over the Internet even though nothing happened.

So we talk about everything but.

An hour later, the battery on my tablet goes dead.

I want to continue our conversation, but it's wheels up tomorrow morning at seven.

Besides, I'll see him tomorrow.

CHAPTER ELEVEN

@TwitterGirl
Senator Becker has laryngitis today, so you biased media people better not put words in his mouth!

Yep, after countless speeches in below zero weather, Will Becker's vocal chords raised the white flag and surrendered. His doctor has put a medical gag order on him, telling him not to utter a single word for twenty-four hours. While he's in the office, he's not available for his campaign stops today and Frank has dispatched his Deputy Campaign Manager Roberta Willis as a stand-in. She suggested I tag along, since up till now I've been pretty much confined to hotels, back rooms and offices. Plus it's a gathering at a men-only exclusive golf club, and she didn't want to be the only woman. (However, when Becker gives talks at female-only organizations, it's fine to let him fly solo since the women won't be looking at anyone else anyway.)

It's a luncheon on what is known as the "rubber chicken" circuit, so named because group meals often consist of some nondescript poultry dish that was cooked hours ago and set up under a heat lamp during which time it has become vulcanized like a steel-belted radial. My mouth waters for that pastrami I had last week as I do my best to slice into my entree with a dull knife that probably wouldn't even cut butter. I'm sitting next to Roberta at the head table listening to her talk politics with the disappointed high rollers who though they'd be sitting next to Becker. Most of them are old, white haired guys who probably never heard of Twitter, much less Twitter Girl, so they probably think I'm some secretary. Of course that hasn't stopped them from leering at both of us.

My mind wanders as Roberta basically gives rehearsed stock answers to questions almost verbatim to the responses I've heard her give on the Sunday morning news shows. She's so rehearsed on everything and has a tendency to spin even the simplest question. I can only imagine a conversation with the man in her life:

```
Guy: So, you in the mood?
Roberta: It depends on your definition
of mood. From your perspective it might
be different from what I perceive it to
be. According to our latest focus group,
women who have to be asked if they're
in the mood usually aren't.
Guy: (grabbing TV remote): Guess I'll
watch the game.
```

I'm trying to process the conversation I had with Becker in his suite last night, and unfortunately Tyler called in sick so I haven't been able to get his opinion on things. Considering his condition, I was worried it was something serious so I called him but it turned out he just has a really bad cold and decided to work from home.

Anyway, Roberta wraps up her talk and everyone gets up for what will be about an hour of meet-and-greet around an open bar, which should take the leering up to groping stage. I take the opportunity to head toward the rest room, though unfortunately it probably doesn't have a shower which would enable me to wash off all the slime from the people I've met so far. The ladies room is dark since I assume it rarely gets used, so I have to turn on the lights, and because it's empty I can kill some time in here. An hour with that crowd and you'll have to dust me for prints.

Then the door opens and a middle-aged guy walks in.

I put up one hand to stop him. "Uh, hello, this is the ladies room. See any urinals in here?"

He doesn't say anything, turns and locks the door.

Oh shit. My pulse spikes. "What the hell?"

He puts up his hands. "Calm down, I only want to *talk* to you, Cassidy."

I don't recognize him. Short, fat, male pattern slug. "You can talk to me outside." I stretch to my full height, fold my arms and look down at him. "Unlock that door right now or I'll kick your ass. For good measure I'll use the taser in my purse on your balls and you can join the Vienna Boys Choir."

He doesn't back up. "I'm David Gold."

The name hits the pause button on my anger for a moment. "Oh."

"You've heard of me."

"I've been briefed. We could talk outside if you want."

"No. Roberta will see me."

I don't like his tactics but this is an opportunity I've been waiting for. "Fine. What's on your mind?"

"Becker's hiding something, Cassidy. Something big."

"And that something big would be?"

"I don't know."

"You're a lotta help."

"You're a journalist."

"Former journalist."

"It's in your blood, don't deny it. You people are all the same. You need to find it."

"Find what?"

"I don't know."

"Why don't *you* find it?"

"I've tried. But you have access now to a lot of stuff I do not."

"Are you the guy who's been texting me?"

He furrows his brow and if he's faking he sure doesn't look it. "What are you talking about?"

I can tell it's not him. I shake my head. "Nothing. So how the hell am I supposed to dig up this *something big* if you don't even tell me where I should start looking? If I'm going to find the needle you have to give me the location of the haystack."

"I don't know *where* to start looking. But I know *when*."

"Excuse me?"

"The year 2005. I've tracked his every move but things don't add up about that year."

"Like what?"

"Missing time, missing money, things like that."

"Missing time? What, he was abducted by aliens?"

"I'm being serious, Cassidy. The guy has always kept a strict itinerary but that year has a lot of blank spots. This country needs an honest man in the White House, and he's not it."

"I understand you were his best friend once."

"Once. Till he sandbagged me."

"Not what I heard."

"You as a reporter should know there are two sides to every story. And in this case there are three."

"Three?"

"Unfortunately the one person who could help you is dead. His wife."

***

The steam from the pizza box mixes with my breath as I shiver on the front step. I see a figure moving toward me through the beveled glass front door and know heat is a few seconds away.

Tyler Garrity opens the door wearing a robe, offers a smile to go along with bloodshot puffy eyes and invites me in. "You really didn't have to do this."

"Hey, you're sick, you live alone, you need to feed a cold. And you need to feed it with a shrimp scampi pizza from Rastelo's."

I crack open the pizza box, he looks inside and smiles. "Looks great, but I can't smell a thing."

"Smells as good as it looks," I say, as I take off my coat and hang it on an old fashioned wooden rack that's behind the door.

He leads me into the living room, beautifully decorated with antiques. The TV is on and the coffee table features a box of Kleenex while a nearby waste basket is filled with used tissues. "Excuse the mess," he says, as he plops down on a red leather sofa.

I look around and take in the decor, which is not what I would expect from a bachelor. "Damn, Tyler, this place is gorgeous. Did you hire a decorator?"

"Nah, did it all myself. Everything in the house is from an auction or garage sale. Old furniture was built a helluva lot better than the new stuff, and most of the new stuff is flimsy particle board from China."

"Good point." I slide the pizza box on the coffee table, pull a giant slice from the box, slide it onto one of the paper plates I brought, and hand it to him. "You're in for a treat."

He takes the plate and eagerly bites into the pizza. "Oh, my. That is wonderful. I had no idea there was such a thing as shrimp scampi pizza."

"Not many places make it."

"Well, it beats the hell out of Nyquil. I'd like to retract my comment about you not having to do this." He takes another huge bite. "I may have to get sick more often."

"Anyway, I remember what it was like to be single and live alone. Opening a can of soup is a chore." I take a bite of the pizza and savor the garlic shrimp. "Besides, I missed your smiling face at the office today. It's not the same without you."

"You bring a lot to the party yourself, T.G. So how did things go today? I heard Top Dog coulda worked as a Central Park mime."

"Yeah, blew out his voice in the Iowa cold. I shadowed Roberta most of the day."

"Ah, a day with Number Six."

"Huh?"

"Cylon on *Battlestar Galactica*. Roberta's an android, though not nearly as hot as the actress who played Number Six."

"Yeah, she is kinda robotic." I pull a six-pack out of a bag and hold it up. "Beer? I wasn't sure if you could handle alcohol."

"Bring it on. Just so you know, I can do anything a normal person does. Just not two days in a row. Think of me as a cell phone that has to get charged up."

"You got it." I hand him a beer, open one for myself and take a sip. "I, uh, met David Gold today."

He leans forward. "Really. Tell me more."

"He cornered me at the golf club luncheon. In the ladies room of all places."

"He probably needed a tampon."

I can't help but laugh. "Anyway, he told me I needed to investigate something that happened in the year 2005."

His eyes widen. "Investigate what?"

"He didn't know. He just said some strange things happened during that year."

Tyler takes another bite and shakes his head. "That guy really needs to move on and get a life."

"So how long have you known the Senator?"

"About nine years. Started working for him during his first Senate campaign."

"Have you ever seen anything at all that made you question his honesty?"

He shakes his head. "Nope. Decent guy. What you see is what you get. However…"

"Yeah?"

He grabs another slice of pizza and leans back on the couch. "There was one thing that struck me as odd."

111

"Really? What's that?"

"His wife. She always had this underlying sadness about her. I always suspected she hated politics, but was too supportive to ever say anything about it. She was the classic stay-at-home mom, really committed to raising her kids right, and when you meet them you'll see she did a wonderful job. And the woman was beyond shy, practically a recluse. I know he really loved her, and was told she was head over heels for him, but they seemed like an odd match to me. Opposites attract, I guess."

"Why would you marry a politician if you hated politics?"

Tyler takes another bite. "Heart wants what the heart wants, right?"

"Guess so."

He turns serious for a moment. "Speaking of hearts wanting, you really like him, don't you?"

I try to stop myself from smiling but am unsuccessful. "Yeah, I mean I wouldn't be working for the guy if I didn't."

"I didn't mean that. I meant you *like him*. Like millions of other women."

"Fine. I'm interested. And apparently he's interested in me."

"Well, that's understandable as smart and beautiful as you are."

"You're sweet, Tyler. But the guy could have any woman he wanted."

"Yeah, I guess when you add the fairytale First Lady thing into the mix, he could. But what a lot of women don't realize is that being a political wife is a different kind of life. If you like spending your life in the shadows, fine. If you want to cast your own shadow, you need direct sunlight."

We talk for a couple of hours, then I notice he's yawning. "Hey, that's my cue. You need rest," I say, standing up.

"Nah, I'm good."

"God, men are stubborn when they're sick."

"I won't argue with that. Guess you're right. But I am feeling better after the pizza."

"See, a little butter, garlic and spices and you'll be good to go tomorrow. But only after a good night's sleep, young man. Off to bed you go." I point and wave my hand around. "Wherever your bedroom is."

"Yes, doctor. And it's upstairs." He gets up and we head toward the door. "Can't thank you enough, T.G. That was really nice of you to bring dinner and I enjoyed the company." I grab my coat from the rack and put it on. "We should do this when I'm not sick."

"Love to, Tyler."

"I'd give you a hug but I don't want to infect you."

"I'll take a rain check on that, too. See you tomorrow."

"Tomorrow's Thursday, remember?"

"Right. FaceTime?"

"Look forward to it."

"Great. See you Friday then."

"Okay. G'night."

He opens the door for me and the cold air smacks me in the face as I head for my car. I carefully maneuver past the patches of ice on the brick walk, hit the street and open the door to my car. I look up and see Tyler standing there, door open, watching me. "What, you wanna heat the whole neighborhood?"

"Just wanted to make sure you got to your car safe."

"I'm good, now go back inside before you get pneumonia!"

He smiles, waves, and closes the door.

Damn, he reminds me of Sam. It's like having an extra brother looking out for me.

CHAPTER TWELVE

@TwitterGirl
**The PC Police want me to change my handle to Twitter Woman.
Seriously, get a life.**

In the newsroom it is known as getting "two fingers."

Nope, not having someone flip the bird at you using both hands. It's when a manager uses his index and middle finger, glares at you, waits a beat, then gives you the "come here" signal with the two fingers. Sorta like a spider does to a fly.

And it never, ever means anything good.

So when I see Frank give me the two fingers, my heart gets hung up on my tonsils.

What the hell have I done? I thought they were happy with me.

I get up from my desk and walk on eggshells into his office, head down. He closes the door and gestures toward the chair opposite his desk. "Cassidy, have a seat."

"Uh-oh," I say, as I sit down. "This doesn't sound good."

"Relax, Cassidy, you haven't done anything wrong. In fact, we're all thrilled with your work."

"Then why do you look like you just had a prostate exam with a paid of salad tongs?"

He chuckles a bit and shakes his head. "Honestly, you are the quickest wit I've ever met."

"Why, thank you. Meanwhile, got a joke for ya. Frank walks into a bar. Bartender says, *why the long face?*"

"We've run into a serious situation, Cassidy. And it involves you."

Oh, shit. They found out I talked to David Gold. Or did they? "You said I didn't do anything wrong."

"You haven't." He shakes his head, reaches into his desk for a huge bottle of Tums, shakes out a few and pops them in his mouth. "I knew this would happen eventually, I just hoped it would be after the campaign."

"For goodness sake, Frank, you're like a newscast producer teasing the same story for an hour. What the hell is it?"

"Senator Becker wants to... date you."

"Yeah, I kinda picked that up," I say, trying to sound casual, but knowing my widening eyes are betraying me.

"First, I want to know if this is okay with you. I mean, you are an employee and he is the boss. I don't want you to feel like you're obligated because we don't need to get into some sort of harassment thing here."

"It's fine, Frank, really. He's a nice guy who just happens to be running for President. If he wasn't my boss and asked me out, I'd accept."

"I figured as much since you once said he was smoking hot."

"My, we were taking notes."

"You don't forget a comment like that in politics." Frank leans forward and folds his hands. "I guess I don't have to tell you that whatever happens between you two has to be very discreet."

"I'm not expecting him to take me dancing."

"Good. I didn't really think I needed to tell you to be quiet. But keep it under your hat."

"Sure thing." I do the zipper thing across my lips and toss away the imaginary key. "I'm a vault. Well, except that Ripley and my brother know, but they'd never say anything."

"Good. If something like this got out... Cassidy, I hate to sound

115

so crass, but… we need to keep the dream alive."

I furrow my brow for a moment, then I get it. "You mean the shot every American woman has at being First Lady?"

"Twitter Girl, you're too damn smart."

"I'll play ball, Frank. I know the fantasy needs to stay out there. Really, you don't have to worry about us ending up on *Page Six*."

***

Ripley smiles as she clinks my glass two nights later. "Congratulations. Can you get me a night in the Lincoln bedroom next year?"

"Oh, stop it."

"Hey, he chose you. You got the brass ring."

"I've had two dinners with the guy under a veil of secrecy and didn't even get a goodnight kiss, so that doesn't exactly constitute a brass ring. Right now the only ring I've got is the one around the bathtub."

"This has got to be the weirdest romance ever," says Sam. "You get the guy you wanted and you're out on a Friday night with your brother and best friend eating fried cheese and nachos."

"Yeah, something's not quite right," I say. "But it's a unique situation. And you guys are the best company a girl could want."

Sam turns toward Ripley. "So, which of the so-called *runner-ups* will you be setting your sights on?"

"Vinnie," she says, then smiles at me. "Actually, we went out last night and I *did* get a goodnight kiss."

I raise my eyebrows.

"Okay," she says. "I got several."

"Careful," says Sam. "He's a—"

"I know, I know," says Ripley, putting up her hand. "He's a *player*. But he can play with me for awhile. One can always assume the savage beast can be tamed."

Sam pops a chip dripping with cheese in his mouth. "You

know, I don't get that about women. What exactly is the appeal of changing a guy? I mean, why don't you simply find a guy you can, you know, for lack of a better term, drive off the lot."

We both crack up at his metaphor. "Because, dear brother, if we mold a guy the way we want, we're in control."

"Shoulda figured it was something like that."

Ripley pats his hand. "You just haven't been around the block as much as we have."

"However," I say, "our odometers are in danger of turning over to all zeroes, so we may soon be heading to the cat lady junkyard."

"So, hypothetically," says Sam, leaning back, "if you guys were to mold me, what exactly would you want to change?"

Ripley shakes her head. "Honestly, Sam, I could drive you off the lot right now. You're the best thing on the showroom floor."

"C'mon, I'm serious," he says. "I haven't had the greatest luck with women lately. What do I need to change? What's wrong with me?"

Ripley looks at me and puts her palms up. "I got nothin'."

"Me neither," I say, leaning over and giving my brother a kiss on the side of the head.

"You're biased, you're my sister," he says to me, then turns to Ripley. "And you're too sweet to say anything negative."

"My dear brother, the stars simply have to align."

"Yeah," says Ripley, "it's smart to take advice from two thirty-five year old women who have never been down the aisle."

I look up and see lots of couples in the bar, enjoying the evening out. It occurs to me that even if I do catch that brass ring, it won't be until after the November election that I can be seen alone in public with Will Becker.

A waitress drops by and slides a drink with an umbrella in it in front of Ripley, which is a very common occurrence when we're out. (I've always been her wing girl.) She points at a fortyish guy in a white shirt and tie who is locked onto her. "From the gentleman at the bar," she says.

Ripley looks up at the man, who would qualify as classically tall, dark and handsome, and places the drink back on the serving tray. "Tell him thank you, but I'm not interested."

"Sure thing," says the waitress, who heads back to the guy.

"Didn't wanna mold him?" asks Sam.

She shakes her head. "Phony smile. Looked like a car salesman. And you know I never go out with people I meet in a bar."

"Now there's a good piece of advice from your focus group of unmarried thirty-five year olds who have been around the block," I say.

We share a laugh and all of a sudden the guy is standing next to our table between Sam and Ripley. "Looks like you're short one guy at this table," he says.

Ripley looks up at him. "Look, I'm not interested, okay? Thank you for the offer, but you can send your drink to someone else. There are plenty of unattached girls in the bar."

"I was just wondering if you got hurt when you fell. From heaven."

I roll my eyes at the lame pickup line as Ripley shakes her head. "I'm out with my friends here tonight. Not looking for anyone right now and I don't go out with strange men I meet in bars."

He stares right down her cleavage. "Aw c'mon, you didn't dress like that 'cause you wanted to be with your friends."

Ripley narrows her eyes. "Well I sure didn't dress this way for you. Now please leave me alone."

The guy shakes his head and starts to turn away. "Damn cock tease."

In a flash Sam reaches up, grabs the guy's necktie and yanks it, slamming his head into our table. The sound makes everyone in the bar look in our direction and everything goes quiet. Sam quickly uses his other hand to bend the guy's arm behind his back in a hammerlock. The man winces in pain. "Apologize to the young lady."

"Ow, you're hurting me."

"Apologize or I'm gonna hurt you a lot more."

He's barely able to turn his head toward Ripley but does so. "Sorry."

"That didn't sound very sincere."

"I'm sorry… for what I called you. It was… very rude."

"That's better," says Sam. "And for future reference, when a lady says she's not interested, you leave her the hell alone. Got it?"

"Uh-huh."

"Got it???"

"Yeah, I got it, I got it."

"Good. Now you're gonna pay your bill, leave the waitress a huge tip, and never come to this bar again because this is our hangout and your kind aren't welcome here. Agreed?"

"Yeah."

Sam releases the guy who stands up and rubs his arm, then walks to the bar red-faced through a horde of women laughing at him. He tosses a bill on it, grabs his coat and heads out the door. The minute he's gone the crowd starts applauding, and a few women come over to give Sam a pat on the back. A few others drop by and give him phone numbers.

Ripley and I are sitting there with our mouths hanging open, saying nothing. Sam looks at both of us. "What?"

"Damn, where the hell did that come from?" I ask.

He cocks his head at Ripley. "He insulted her. It pissed me off. No one talks to Ripley that way."

She leans over, wraps one arm around his shoulders and kisses him on the cheek. "Guess we'll have to add *white knight* to your résumé. And judging from the looks you're now getting from the women in this bar, you're definitely ready to drive off the lot."

CHAPTER THIRTEEN

@TwitterGirl
Ah, so we have a challenger on the political Twitterverse. Okay, let's rock. (My candidate can beat up your candidate.)

Monday morning is starting out well. Sam is in a good mood after having a great date on Saturday (a seriously cute waitress who gave him her number at the bar), the sun is out and it is unseasonably warm. I'll be leaving for the New Hampshire debate tomorrow, the country's most eligible bachelor wants to date me, Ripley seems happy with her runner-up and other than the fact that I am craving fried cheese and nachos for breakfast, all seems right with the universe.

And then my favorite New York tabloid swats my front door and greets me with this:

PRESIDENTIAL CAMPAIGN ALL ATWITTER

By Jim Harlin

Using social media in a political campaign is nothing new. Adding a snarky Twitter person to your staff is.

Eyebrows were raised a few weeks ago when former network reporter Cassidy Shea, a/k/a @TwitterGirl, was hired by Senator Will Becker's campaign a few days after she was given the boot by her employer because of a controversial tweet. The snarky queen of 140 characters has been sending out often hilarious remarks, shooting pointed barbs at the President, other candidates and even the moderators at the debates. All designed to take the competition down a notch, lighten things up and attract young voters in the process. Her huge following must be considered an asset by the Becker campaign, as her sharp witty comments can go viral in a heartbeat. And have done so during her tenure.

Well, another candidate has obviously taken notice as Congressman Dwayne Rodgers has hired comedian Dan Carrington to man the Twitter desk in his campaign. Carrington, known for his satirical political show on cable, will work from his Hollywood home whereas Ms. Shea has been seen traveling with the Becker campaign.

Becker's Campaign Manager Frank Delavan wasn't surprised by the move. "It was only a matter of time before someone copied our strategy. Carrington's a funny guy and I enjoy his show. But there's only one Twitter Girl, and she's on our team. Personally, I wouldn't want to be on Cassidy Shea's bad side so Mister Carrington needs to tread lightly if he has any intention of personally taking her on."

Rodgers is currently running fifth in the polls and seen as a long-shot for the nomination, so obviously has nothing to lose with this tactic and should at least see his name recognition increase.

In any event, seeing two of America's wittiest people go toe-to-toe on Twitter should be more entertaining than the debates.

"Glad to read that you think I'm unique," I say, as I enter Frank's office.

"You are definitely one of a kind, and that wasn't just a sound bite I handed out."

"Well, I appreciate the compliment. So what do you make of this? Is everyone going to hire a snarky Twitter person now?"

"It's possible, but I don't think it's likely. Though I was surprised Governor Schilling wasn't the one to do it."

"You think it will do Rodgers any good?"

"Look, Carrington is hilarious. He's a professional comedian and he's got a very quick wit, like you. Terrific ad-libber. But don't let him suck you into a Twitter war. His guy is fifth, ours is first. Keep your interaction with him at a reasonable level. No name calling or anything like that. Remember, go after the candidate, not the staff."

"That wasn't the strategy with the Ex-Lax brownies."

Frank laughs a bit. "That was a unique circumstance. Besides, they have no idea you were behind it. Wheeler the Dealer probably thinks he simply got food poisoning." He gets up from behind his desk and closes the door. "I didn't see you on Friday so I didn't have the chance to ask how dinner went Thursday night."

"Why Frank, you're acting like a high school girl."

"Just protecting the Senator."

"Eh, I'm just yankin' your chain. We had a nice dinner. That was it. I was home by nine, I'm sure I wasn't followed and I'm not eating for two."

"Well, I appreciate your discretion. I know this whole thing is pretty strange."

Driving myself to a date, meeting a man under an assumed name in the back room of a restaurant, getting myself home, not telling anyone except Ripley and my brother about it. Hey, what could be strange about that?

"Unfortunately the one person who could help you is dead. His wife."

Despite the enjoyable weekend, that line from David Gold is bugging me, and it is time to seriously start checking things out. If I am about to enter into a relationship with Will Becker, I need to know if there really *is* something underneath the political persona. I know most people might think it would be odd to actually vet someone before dating, but reporters are like that. If there are skeletons or red flags, may as well find out what they are so you know what to expect going in.

The campaign headquarters has a media library, with video, newspaper clips, political ads, brochures and just about everything you could imagine on the other candidates.

It also has everything you could possibly want to know about Will Becker.

And his wife.

I had a few hours to kill so I told Frank I was going to spend them in the media library, getting to know the players a little better. It's a small room with a desk, large computer monitor, some DVD dubbing machines and a couple of file cabinets. And since Becker and his senior staff are going to be out all morning, I am reasonably sure I won't be bothered.

I spend thirty minutes actually looking at stuff pertaining to the other candidates, just to cover my tracks if anyone asks. I don't know if anyone will check the history on the computer, but want to be safe.

After a half hour of campaign commercials, various talk show clips and gaffes, I'm ready to put on my reporter's hat.

There's a folder off to the side on the computer's desktop simply marked "Jennifer."

His wife.

I click on it and see a relatively small amount of files. I start with the photos first, wanting to put a face to the name as I'd never seen her. Or if I had, I hadn't paid attention. (Who would, when you're looking at Will Becker?)

She was a petite blonde, surprisingly plain. Not what I expected. Straight hair, slender, little makeup to be seen in any of the photos. Typical Connecticut girl. The only bright smiles are found on the wedding pictures, the ones with their two daughters or on campaign brochures. The rest are a collection of pictures from various campaign victories or standing by Becker's side as he took the oath of office. They all show a forced expression. Tyler was right. You didn't have to meet her to know this woman didn't like politics.

A bunch of video clips reveal the same thing. Jennifer Becker standing behind her husband as he campaigned or thanked a crowd. Holding hands with her two daughters instead of her husband.

Standing behind him.

In the shadows.

The standard political commercials show what seems to be a typical perfect American family. Jennifer smiling on cue, playing the supportive wife and mother.

The key is in the woman's eyes, and you wouldn't notice unless you were looking for it. Full of life when with her children, dead otherwise.

And then there is the picture from high school. He the star football player, she the bright cheerleader staring up at him with a look that was obviously love.

What had happened to the happy cheerleader and smiling bride?

Politics happened.

But the journalist sitting on my shoulder tells me there was something else.

***

124

The latest national poll shows Senator Will Becker defeating the President by four percentage points if the election were held today. All the other candidates in our party don't fare very well against the Sleazeball-in-Chief.

Which means the President wants to see anyone but our guy on the top of the ticket.

Which means network anchor Jon Hanley, who is so far up the President's ass he can't get a cell phone signal, will do everything in his power tonight to make Becker look bad.

So Frank has me defending our turf on three fronts. I've got the other candidates to worry about, the comedian in Hollywood who will do doubt try to lure me into an Internet debate, and a news anchor who makes no attempt whatsoever to conceal his negative feelings about our party.

I ran into Hanley a few times when he was a reporter. He's the classic square-jawed television news personality born with a silver spoon in his mouth who thinks his Ivy League education makes him better than anyone else, when in reality he needs Cliff Notes to do a story on foreign policy. And he paid no dues either, which really pisses me off, as he's the son of a former network anchor. He actually got on my shit list several years ago when he walked through my live shot on purpose, and when it comes to revenge, I never forget. Tonight (with a lotta help from Tyler) I've got something in my bag of tricks to take him down a notch by shooting his credibility to hell, and I'll be saving it for the perfect moment.

Once again Frank is at my side in a room off the stage as the debate is about to begin. I've got two laptops open as I'm using one to monitor whatever Dan Harrington does. Frank also has two, as he is monitoring Twitter and has another tied into a focus group back home.

And, right on cue, Carrington lobs the first shell in our direction.

@TheRealCarrington
#NewHampshireDebate
Polls show President trailing the Ken doll by four percentage points in a hypothetical election.

My eyes narrow as my hands head toward the keyboard, but Frank grabs my wrist. "Nope. Leave it alone."

"He called our guy a plastic toy."

"Let him do the name calling. That's juvenile. You stick to the snark. Don't stoop to his level, because that's what he wants you to do." Frank looks at the monitor as Jon Hanley welcomes the candidates. "Why don't you fire a shot across the bow of the moderator to get the ball rolling?"

I crack my knuckles and start to type.

@TwitterGirl
#NewHampshireDebate
If President Turner came to an abrupt halt, Jon Hanley would break his nose.

Frank throws back his head and laughs. "Good one, Twitter Girl."

"I'm just gettin' started here," I say, in a really bad Al Pacino impression.

The debate begins and we go through the first two questions with nothing earthshaking and no opportunities for me. Then all of a sudden Frank sits up straight and points at the monitor during a crowd shot of about a dozen people. "Look, half of 'em got their cell phones out. Have something ready the next time they show a reaction shot of the crowd. I wanna see if they're logged in to you."

"Anything in particular?"

"Give Hanley another shot."

I quickly ready a digital blow dart, then await the next cutaway as my finger hovers over the "enter" key.

And about ninety seconds later, the network provides us with what we need. "Now!" yells Frank.

@TwitterGirl
#NewHampshireDebate
Please warn Jon Hanley the teleprompter is out in the men's room, so he'll have to hold it.

About half the people looking at their cell phones start chuckling.

"They're paying more attention to you than the debate," says Frank.

I shrug. "Once again, I'm more interesting." I look at my other laptop. "Meanwhile, still nothing from my counterpart in California. They're not getting their money's worth."

"You should add up all your tweets at the end of the campaign, and see how much we paid you per word."

The topic turns to education, which, of course, affords our moderator the chance to beat his own drum.

"Let's talk about astronomical tuition costs," says Hanley. "I was fortunate to get an Ivy League degree, but these days few can afford even the substandard education offered by a community college."

I quickly cut and paste the tweet I've had ready and send it on its way.

@TwitterGirl
#NewHampshireDebate
Jon Hanley's "nolo cum laude" college transcript! (That means he wasn't on the dean's list). Link.

Said link was provided by Tyler who set up some untraceable website with all sorts of unflattering material about Jon Hanley,

127

including his less than impressive grades in college, one of which was an "F" in political science. And the fact that Hanley's wealthy dad made a million dollar contribution to the school right before he was accepted. Said link was also sent to each candidate's campaign team an hour before the debate.

@TheRealCarrington
Hanley's "F" in poly sci was due to the fact he thought Soviet Georgia was a suburb of Atlanta with Russian immigrants.

"Meh," says Frank. "If that's the best he can do, you've got nothing to worry about."

***

Another campaign stop, another party atmosphere in Becker's hotel suite.

But what's different this time is I'm in the room next to it. And there's a connecting door.

As before the staff has a few drinks and filters out. I don't want anyone to see a pattern here, so I'm one of the first to leave.

The minute I get back in my room I whip out my iPad and FaceTime Tyler.

The screen fills with his smiling face and I recognize the setting as his living room. "Hey, T.G, another great job!"

"You too, Tyler. That untraceable website was a stroke of genius."

"Well, Jon Hanley's transcript in the number one thing trending on the Internet. The debate isn't even in the picture."

"That ought to shoot his credibility to hell."

"No kidding. Hey, off the topic, wanted to ask you if you wanted to go to the Giants game this weekend. I've only got one ticket this time. Frank is taking the commercial production team."

"You going?"

"This time I don't have a wedding, so yeah."

"Then count me in."

"Great." I hear a female voice and see him turn around. "What? Talking to a friend with the campaign. I'll be right there." He turns back to me. "Hey, got company so I gotta run. But see you when you get back into town tomorrow."

"Okay, Tyler. Bye."

"Bye, T.G. Pleasant dreams."

The screen goes dark and I wonder about the identity of the female voice I heard. Nice that Tyler has a woman in his life. He's a great person and deserves someone good.

After all, he's a guy you can drive off the lot.

***

An hour later there's a gentle tap on the connecting door.

I haven't changed clothes because I was hoping for this. I hop up, run to the door, open it, and find Will Becker standing there with a bottle of champagne and two glasses. "I figured you were up," he says. "Saw the light on under the door."

"Yeah, I was checking out the reaction to the debate on the Internet."

"How'd we do?"

"Very well, nothing negative. Lotta cheap shots at Jon Hanley from the other networks, which he deserved."

"Good. Maybe he'll back off a bit now that you've taken him down several notches." He sticks his head inside the room and looks toward the window. "Uh, you need to close the drapes."

"Huh?"

"Never know who's out there with a telephoto lens."

Well, this is new as far as dating is concerned. "Oh, sure thing." He stands in the doorway until I close the drapes, then moves into the room and hands me a glass. "Celebrate with me?"

"Absolutely. Hit me, barkeep."

He pops the champagne and pours me a glass, then fills his own and raises it. "To the best addition to my campaign."

I clink his glass. "Why thank you, Senator."

"Are you ever gonna remember to call me Will when we're alone?"

"Probably not. And next year I'll be calling you Mister President. Besides, if this is going to be discreet, I don't need to slip up in public and call you by your first name."

"Very well, Ms. Shea."

"I prefer Twitter Girl if you're not gonna call me Cassidy."

He smiles at me, drains his glass, puts the empty on an end table and moves closer. "You're like no one I've ever met," he says, as his hands slide up my arms and rest on my shoulders. Our eyes lock, our lips part to meet—

And his cell phone rings.

"Sorry," he says, as he pulls it out of his pocket and looks at it. "Dammit, got a big opportunity. And this might take awhile. Rain check?"

"Not going anywhere," I say.

"Thanks." He turns and leaves my room, pulling the connecting door closed.

I'm left with a half empty bottle of champagne, wondering if "awhile" means I should get undressed and go to bed.

I'd call Tyler to kill some time, but he's got some babe with him.

An hour later the champagne is gone, and Becker is a guest on a late night talk show at a TV station way across town.

I fall asleep in my clothes. Just in case.

Just in case never arrives.

CHAPTER FOURTEEN

@TwitterGirl
Becker campaign finds proof of life after death! (Investigation shows thousands of dead people voted in last election.)

Oh, I'm gonna have so much fun with this little bit of breaking news. Apparently a whole lot of people who had reached room temperature in a swing state carried by the President in the last election cast ballots long after lying down for a dirt nap.

@TwitterGirl
President Turner announces endorsements from Abe Lincoln, George Washington and Thomas Jefferson. Considers Lincoln as running mate.

Of course the other party denies that any chicanery happened, and this is all due to a "clerical error." Okay, maybe a few thousand clerical errors.

@TwitterGirl
President Turner hires medium to arrange focus group with deceased voters. New campaign slogan: "I see dead people."

Anyway, Ripley's working in the campaign headquarters today and we haven't had a chance to chat about what almost happened in New Hampshire. Rather than take the chance of having someone overhear our conversation, I decide this is best discussed in a restaurant over lunch. She waits a moment after giving her order to the waiter, then turns toward me with a very eager look. "Sooooo?"

I shake my head. "Saved by the cell."

"Huh?"

"The guy was about to kiss me and his phone went off. Then he ran off. Then I went off to bed fully clothed. Then—"

"Whoa." She waves her hand to stop me. "Hang on a minute. Why did you sleep in your clothes?"

"In case he came back."

"Sweetie, it's generally accepted that taking one's clothes *off* is the way to attract a man."

"It wasn't my intention to seduce him."

"Obviously not if you're sleeping in your dress. How long have been going to bed in the Amish overnight collection?"

"You don't understand." I explain the whole adjoining room thing, how I had to pull the curtains shut in case the paparazzi was in a tree with a night vision camera, how he ended up ditching an opportunity to play tonsil hockey with me for a male late night talk show host, how I thought he might come back shortly so I kept my clothes on because I want to take this slow.

"Did he call you when he was done with the talk show?"

"No. He told me on the plane that he figured I was asleep."

"Oh. So where do you guys go from here?"

"I don't know."

"How far do you think he wanted to go before his phone rang?"

"Don't know that either."

"You are definitely in one weird relationship."

"It's not even a relationship yet. I don't know what it is."

She reaches across the table and pats my hand. "Patience, dear friend. "I'm sure he's worth waiting for."

***

When we get back I notice two very attractive young brunettes in the Senator's office, sitting opposite his desk. They're maybe late teens, early twenties. The door is open, Becker spots me and waves me in. I walk into his office, turn and smile at the two girls.

"Cassidy, meet my daughters Kristin and Laurie."

"Hi guys," I say, as I lean over and shake hands with both. Anyone could tell they're sisters, and both look like their dad. Caps of straight chestnut hair, big green eyes, medium height, slender like their mom.

"Can't believe you hired Twitter Girl, Dad," says Kristin, turning to her father. "Very cool."

"So I'm cool, huh?" I ask.

"In our college you are," says Laurie. "You rule."

"You guys home for spring break?"

"They're back for the day to shoot a commercial with me," says Becker, who suddenly looks out into the headquarters. "Hey, Frank needs me. You two wait here, we'll be ready to go in a few minutes."

Becker leaves so I figure this will be a good opportunity for me to get to know the family. "So, where do you two go to school?"

"Francis College in Pennsylvania," says Laurie. "Outside of Philly."

"Don't feel bad if you've never heard of it," says Kristin. "No one has. It's a really small school and a good place to hide if your father is running for president."

"I would imagine," I say. "What are you studying?"

"I want to go into advertising," says Laurie. "Commercial production. So this is a good learning experience for me."

"Well, you need to get to know my friend Ripley." I point at her through the window. "She's the supermodel talking to Tyler. Owns her own agency." I turn to Kristin. "And what do you wanna be when you grow up?"

"I don't wanna grow up," she says. "But when I graduate I'd

133

like to do what you do."

"Be sarcastic on Twitter? Not sure you'll find a whole lotta openings."

"No, be a reporter."

"I'm not a reporter anymore."

"Sorry, I didn't mean to bring that up."

I wave my hand. "No big deal. Life goes on and this campaign is a blast. You do realize it's going to be twice as hard for you, right?"

"I would think my last name would open a lot of doors."

"It will also bring a lot of jealousy if you don't pay your dues. That's one of the reasons all the reporters at Jon Hanley's network hate him. He started at the top because of his father."

"So I should start small and work my way up?"

I nod. "Exactly. So why do you want to go into journalism? And please don't say *I've always wanted to be on television*."

"I always liked solving puzzles, treasure hunts. I guess the search for the truth is like that. I'm already writing for the school newspaper and I really enjoy it. And I'd like to make the world a better place."

"You could do that working for your dad."

Her smile fades and she shakes her head. "Ugh. No way. I hate politics."

"We both do," says her sister. "Of course, you can't tell anyone or Frank will wish you into the cornfield."

"Listen," says Kristin, "could we maybe go to lunch when I'm home for spring break? I'd love to pick your brain."

"Absolutely. And Laurie, I'll set something up with Ripley for you."

Becker sticks his head in the door. "Okay girls, off we go."

They both stand up and grab their coats. "It was nice meeting you, Ms. Shea," says Kristin.

"Really," says Laurie.

"My pleasure, and call me Cassidy."

They nod and head out into the headquarters, heads down,

wearing looks like they're headed to the dentist.

They may look like their father, but they obviously take after their mother.

***

I slide into Tyler's car on Sunday afternoon and thankfully it's already toasty warm. "We are gonna freeze our asses off at this game."

"No we're not. Didn't I tell you we're in a luxury box this time?"

"No, how did you swing that?"

"Friends in high places."

"Well, while I really enjoy sitting out with the real fans, I'm certainly not going to complain in this cold."

"You'll enjoy it. Beats sneaking a snack in your parka."

An hour later Tyler flashes his passes at a security guard and leads me into the luxury suite. My jaw drops as I take in the accommodations, which look like something for a high roller in Vegas. We're on the fifty yard line, and the huge floor-to-ceiling window offers a terrific view of the field as the Giants warm up. Three large flat screens hang from the ceiling, a bartender in a tuxedo shirt and red bow tie is behind the bar, and steam is rising from what looks like an incredible hot buffet. A sharply dressed young lady takes our coats and Tyler leads us down to a couple of plush blue reclining chairs in front of the window.

"So this is how the other half lives," I say, as I melt into the chair which features the Giants famous lowercase *ny* logo on the headrest.

"Yeah, pretty nice huh?"

"Nice doesn't even begin to describe it. Are we the only ones here?"

"Nah, we're early. There will be about twenty people here by kickoff. May I take your drink order, young lady?"

"Why thank you, sir. I'll start by warming up with some Irish coffee. Light on the coffee."

"Coming right up. And I'll bring you a sampler from the buffet, unless you wanna check it out yourself."

"A variety sounds good. Bring it on."

Tyler heads up the steps as I look around the suite. I see a tall, hot blonde enter the room, smile at Tyler and give him a hug. He gestures toward me and she heads in my direction.

If this is the woman who was at his home when I called the other night, Tyler's doing okay for himself. The woman is a classic beauty built like Ripley; slender but stacked, high cheekbones, ice blue eyes, honey hair to her shoulders. She hits the bottom step and turns to face me, eyes narrowed a bit, arms folded. "So, this is the girl who's on the phone with Tyler all the time."

My shoulders tense up. Uh-oh. "Yeah, but we're just friends—"

She suddenly offers a warm smile and a handshake. "I'm Rachel, his sister-in-law. I was at his house the other night when you called."

I relax. "Oh, I thought you were his girlfriend."

"No, unfortunately we haven't found that someone special for him yet. But I'm always on the hunt."

"I'm Cassidy, by the way."

"I know. You're all I heard about the other night. Cassidy this, Cassidy that. Cassidy's so smart and witty. Cassidy's so tall and pretty."

"He called me Cassidy?"

She shrugs. "Sure, that's your name, right?"

"Yeah, but at the campaign he calls me T.G. for Twitter Girl."

"Oh yeah, his nickname thing. Now that you mention it, I don't think I've ever heard him call anyone by a real name. He calls me *Sil*."

"*Sil*? How do you get Sil from Rachel?"

"Sister-in-law. S-I-L. Anyway, he's just thrilled he found someone who likes to talk as much as he does."

"Yeah, I guess we both never shut up." I look around and don't see anyone else in the room. "Your husband with you?"

She shakes her head. "He's in Florida. I'm jealous cause he's warm and he's jealous cause I'm at the game."

Tyler returns carrying a huge tray of hot goodies and a cup of Irish coffee. "You two getting acquainted?"

"Yeah, I like her," says Rachel. "Gets me off the phone with *you* for at least a few hours a week." She wraps an arm around his shoulder and kisses him on the cheek. "He knows I love him, Cassidy." I hear some voices and turn to see more people entering. "Well, gotta go say hello. Nice meeting you, Twitter Girl."

"You too, Rachel."

Tyler places the tray on a small table in front of us. The dish is filled with bacon wrapped shrimp, little quiches, escargot in garlic butter, assorted cheeses and two small cups of steaming lobster bisque. "Wow, this looks terrific, Tyler. Thanks." I grab a toothpick with a huge shrimp and take a bite. "Oh my, that's wonderful."

"Beats the hell out of a hot dog and beer, huh?"

"No kidding." (Ripley would kill me if she saw this. Wonder if there's any pate'?)

"So, that was your sister-in-law keeping you company the other night."

"Yeah, she comes over for dinner a lot when her husband's out of town. Or just to watch TV. We get along great. My brother sure picked a good one."

"She seems really nice." I grab the Irish coffee, take a sip and lean back. "So, she mentioned she was looking for someone special for you. Is there a nice girl who's *not* your sister-in-law that comes by for dinner?"

"Well, this smoking hot redhead dropped by with a pizza the other night."

I playfully slap his arm. "I mean are you seeing anyone? Isn't there a nice girl in your life?"

"Not right now. I'm kinda particular and there has to be a

woman who understands my situation."

I reach over and gently take his forearm. "There's no *situation* with you Tyler. You're terrific."

He turns and stares straight ahead, the smile disappears. "Yeah. I keep hearing that."

***

Four hours later we're cruising home fat and happy after the Giants overtime win which puts them in the Super Bowl. I lean back and pat my stomach. "Damn, Tyler, I ate too much. I'm warning you, if the button on my jeans goes it could take out your windshield."

"Yeah, I'm stuffed too." He shoots me a look as we crawl through traffic toward the toll booth. "Honestly, I don't know where you put it."

"I've always had a huge appetite and never gain weight. When I was a kid I used to say *I'm a growing girl* but that excuse didn't work when I hit six feet. But I still use the line out of habit."

"Wow, you're six feet tall? I thought you were five-eight and wore platforms all the time."

"Smart ass."

"Seriously, you wear your height very well. A lot of really tall girls look, I don't know, gawky. And they hunch over or wear flats to minimize their height. But you look great. You could model."

"Yeah, right. But thank you for the compliment, Tyler. You're always so sweet to me."

He gives me a devilish sideways glance. "Of course it's good that you're so tall since you eat like a horse."

Now I slap him on the arm. "Hey! That snark burns a lot of calories."

"I'm just yankin' your chain, T.G. Seriously, nothing is worse than buying a girl an expensive dinner and having her only eat half of it. Anyway, I'm glad you enjoyed the food. By the way, we'll be having a Super Bowl party at the headquarters now that the Giants are in, so hope you'll come by."

"Sounds like fun. Will there be food?"

"Not as good as what you just had, but of course."

"So Becker won't be going to California for the game?"

"I'm sure he would if it weren't an election year." We get through the toll and the traffic starts to lighten up.

"Speaking of Becker, I met his daughters the other day."

"Yeah, nice girls. Always enjoy when they come by."

"They told me they both hate politics."

"Uh-huh. That's a tightly guarded secret. They're really shy, like their mom. It hit them real hard when she died. She home-schooled them, you know, so they were with her constantly. They went from the ultimate stay-at-home mom to one parent who's on the New York to DC shuttle a lot. It's been a tough adjustment. I think going off to college is helping, though."

"So will they be on the campaign when school's out?"

"That's a sore spot with them. Frank wants them but they're resisting."

"Do they even *want* their father to be President?"

"Honestly, T.G. I don't know. But I do know one thing. If he does get to the White House, they'll see even less of him than they do now."

CHAPTER FIFTEEN

@TwitterGirl
**In warm, sunny Florida for the latest debate… hot air provided
by President Turner.**

About six staff members fill the living room of the secluded beach
front condo as a warm evening breeze blows through the patio
door from the Atlantic. I let the salt air fill my lungs as I listen to
the strategy session for tomorrow's debate. Becker decided we all
needed to come down a day early to do some campaigning and
give his senior staff a break from the frigid polar vortex that has
a hammerlock on the Northeast. (Global warming, my ass. If you
see Al Gore, hit him with a snowball.)

Becker gives me a look and a quick smile from across the room
which distracts me from whomever is talking, as voices become
audio wallpaper.

A half hour later the meeting starts to break up, with staffers
heading back to their respective condos. (No connecting room
this time.) Becker will be off to make an appearance at a classical
concert in an hour and needs to put on a tux. I grab my purse
to leave but Becker places his hand lightly on my forearm and
says, loud enough for everyone to hear, "Cassidy, stick around
for a minute. Wanted to go over some stuff with you before I go."

Frank shoots me a wink as he heads out, leaving me alone with Becker.

"Don't you need to get ready?" I ask.

"I'm a quick dresser," he says. "I left you in a hurry back in New Hampshire and I wanted a little alone time with you. I've got a few minutes."

"Well, okay, if you twist my arm."

"A shame to waste the view in this place, don't you think?" He moves toward the patio door and looks out at the water. "Don't you just love the ocean?"

I follow and stand next to him. "Yeah. Little different than Staten Island. It's so quiet here, only the sound of the waves. And the water's not frozen."

He turns to look at me. "By the way, my daughters both like you. They think it's cool that Twitter Girl is on the campaign."

"Well, that's nice to hear. They seem like nice normal girls. Did you tell them that we—"

"No," he says quickly, shaking his head. "They still miss their mother too much. And seeing me with someone else... not sure they're ready for that. Another reason for keeping this discreet. Actually, as far as I'm concerned that's the *main* reason, despite what Frank says."

"Sure. I understand completely."

He reaches one arm out and snakes it gently around my waist, sending my pulse up like a rocket. "Now, where were we when I was so rudely interrupted?"

***

My cell jolts me out of a wonderful deep sleep. I crack one eye open and see it's a few minutes after six, and a quick look at the phone tells me Ripley's calling. I answer it. "For a cranky morning greeting, press one."

141

Beep. "Sorry, did I wake you?"

"No, I had to get up anyway to answer the phone. Do you know what time it is?"

"Sorry, this was important. Fire up your laptop and look at the front page of *The Post*."

"Can't this wait? I don't have to be out till ten and I'm only in my second dream."

"No. Now."

"Fine. Hold on."

I grab my computer and click on the bookmark which will take me to my favorite New York tabloid.

My jaw drops as the front page features a photo of me.

Kissing Senator Will Becker.

***

Wondering what your parents think of your choice of men is one thing. Wondering what the country thinks, something else.

Who knew dating a guy would require damage control?

Within an hour the photo has gone viral. I'm in a robe curled up in a chair, sipping coffee while Frank, Vinnie and Andrew discuss how to "handle" the next President of the United States having a love interest. Tyler is chiming in on a computer monitor via Skype.

"It's my fault," says Becker, sitting on a couch. "I thought we were safe here and didn't close the curtains. Figured no one could look in from the ocean."

"Obviously the paparazzi used a boat," says Frank, who doesn't look happy. "But the horse is out of the barn, so we have to deal with it."

"Am I the horse?" I ask. "I'd rather be the ship that sailed."

No one laughs at my attempt to lighten the mood.

Becker rubs his hands over his face. "Dear God, what are my daughters going to say? I should have told them I was interested

142

in dating again."

Frank gets up and pats Becker on the shoulder. "They'll understand, Will, and you said they liked Cassidy. They couldn't expect you to be alone forever."

"What about the voters?"

"Honestly, Will, we're in uncharted territory. It's not like you cheated on anyone, and you *were* named America's most eligible bachelor. People are rooting for you to find Miss Right. Why not now?"

"But will it look like I'm not focused on the campaign?"

"Don't know."

"What do you think the reaction will be from the other candidates?"

"We'll find out tonight, I guess."

I take a sip of my coffee but it's gotten cold, so I start heading down the hallway to the kitchen for a fresh cup. "Anyone want anything?"

"I'm fine," says Frank. Vinnie and Andrew both ask for a donut.

Becker shakes his head, looking like someone ran over his dog. Just what a girl wants to see after a first kiss.

I walk into the kitchen when I hear Vinnie. "You know, we can use this if we play it right."

"Excuse me?" says Becker.

Vinnie continues, lowering his voice, probably thinking I can't hear him as I quietly pour a fresh cup of coffee. "Think about it, we've been keeping this fairy tale thing alive for women who hope to be the next First Lady. Now they can watch the equivalent of a royal romance. Look, the Brits were beyond excited when Prince Andrew started dating Kate Middleton. I'm telling you, we can use this to our advantage. Like Frank said, they're going to root for you guys. She's pretty and likable and has a terrific sense of humor. So don't hide anything. Date like a normal couple."

This sounds fine with me. I stir some cream and sugar into the coffee.

Vinnie continues. "This should be worth more than a few percentage points so you'll at least need to keep the relationship going till November."

Suddenly I go cold.

"Dammit, she's not a campaign prop," says Becker in an angry whisper. "I'm not gonna *use* her or fake a relationship for votes." Long pause. "And now I'm not gonna use you. Get out, Vinnie. You're fired."

My blood starts pumping again.

He stuck up for me.

I hear footsteps and a door slam as I head back into the living room carrying a coffee cup and a plate of donuts, acting like nothing happened. Everyone turns to face me wearing a pained look and I can't let them know I heard everything. "I know, I know, I look like shit. Sorry I didn't warn you I resemble the cryptkeeper when I first get up. I'll go put my face on so as not to scare away the seagulls. So, Senator, now that you've seen me in the morning, you still wanna take me out?"

He offers a soft smile. "Yeah, Cassidy. I'll be proud to be seen with you."

An hour later the plan is in place. We hide nothing, which thrills me even though it was Vinnie's idea. (As soon as I tell Ripley, she'll cut him loose. And once again, my brother is right.) So no more restaurant back rooms, no more closing curtains, no more fake names, no more driving myself to dates. Everyone clears out to get ready for a luncheon, which will no doubt attract a media horde, leaving me alone with Will Becker. I move toward him, wrap my arms around his waist and lay my head on his shoulder. "Thank you for sticking up for me and getting rid of Vinnie."

He grabs my head and pushes it back so he can look at me. "Oh my God, you heard that?"

"Yeah."

"Cassidy, I'm so sorry."

"What the hell are you sorry for? You defended my honor like a white knight." I lay my head back on his shoulder and hug him tighter. "That's why people want you for their President."

"Glad you're taking it so well."

I lean back to look at him. "But you should know, Mister, that had you agreed with him, I woulda been outta here."

***

Media gangbang. And the shoe is on the other foot.

I see exactly what I expected as we pull up to the restaurant for our luncheon. Satellite trucks lined up, dishes pointed toward the sky like electronic petunias. A horde of reporters and photographers between us and the front door.

Frank turns to me with a worried look I've never seen. "Maybe this isn't a good idea. You can stay in the car if you don't feel like running the gauntlet."

"Frank, I got this and I'm not running from anything. I know exactly how they think, what they need and what they'll ask. We have to deal with it eventually so better to do it now before the opposition has time to come up with gotcha questions. And the longer we wait, the longer the focus is on me instead of Senator Becker. Every reporter knows that the more you avoid something the better chance you have something to hide. We're not hiding anything."

"Yeah, you're right. It's just that you've never been on the other side of the microphone."

"Twitter Girl is ready to rock. Let's do this."

Frank opens the door for me and I step out into the bright sunlight, which suddenly turns into a blinding glare thanks to all the television lights as I'm surrounded and peppered with questions.

"Cassidy, are you and Senator Becker in love?"

"Did you sleep with him last night?"

"How long have you two been dating?"

I pause a moment, scanning the faces, most of which I recognize. "Tell you what, guys. The Senator has an important campaign announcement and you're gonna miss it unless you get inside. After that I'll answer all the questions you want for as long as you want."

Becker is standing at the center of a long table at the front of the restaurant. There are so many media people in the room the restaurant has run out of chairs and it's standing room only along the back wall. The Senator is wrapping up a speech in which he's outlined some new ideas to balance the budget.

No one cares. They're all staring at the redhead sitting at the far end of the table. Every camera is pointed in my direction.

"Hello, Buckingham Palace? Can I speak to Kate Middleton? Hi, Kate, you don't know me but I wanted some advice..."

The Senator wraps up his prepared remarks. "And now I'll take a few questions. Though for some reason I have a feeling you don't want to talk about tax reform."

The horde yells questions all at once. "How serious is your relationship with Ms. Shea?"

"She and I have had dinner a few times. That's about it. And the photo that has been whipping around the Internet is one of our first kiss. If you're looking for something out of a romance novel, I'm sorry to disappoint you because nothing else happened. I will say that we are both single and interested in dating, though it's not the easiest thing to do in the public eye in the middle of a campaign."

"Have you talked to your daughters about this, and how do they feel about it?"

"My daughters have both met Cassidy and they like her. They also feel she's a lot cooler than their father. I think they understand

146

their dad is human."

"Do you think your relationship will hurt the campaign?"

"You know what? I don't really care. I'm interested in getting to know her, and my personal life is separate from politics. If voters have a problem with two single people dating, I don't know what to say. Who I have dinner with has no bearing on how I'd act as President."

Becker takes about ten minutes of questions and then a reporter calls me on my promise. "Twitter Girl said she'd answer questions. Unless you don't want her to."

"I don't tell her what to do," says Becker, who cracks a smile. "Frankly, I don't think anyone does."

The crowd laughs as he steps aside and I move in front of the microphone, followed by the sound of auto-winders and lit up by flashes from still cameras. "You guys are looking at me like my parents did in high school, so I'll just say he doesn't have a motorcycle or any tattoos, I was home by ten and finished my Algebra homework."

That gets a laugh and then the questions begin from people I've worked side-by-side with for years. "So what's it feel like to be the girl who caught the most eligible bachelor in America?"

"I haven't caught anything yet. Like the Senator said, we've had a few dinners and plan on having a few more to see where this goes." I turn and give Becker a sly smile. "Then again, maybe I'm the one who has to be caught." He smiles and nods.

"But you're dating the man running for President. Surely the fact that you could be the First Lady has got to be in the back of your mind."

"Look, there's Senator William Becker, the man who might be the next Commander-in-Chief and leader of the free world. And then there's Will, the nice guy I recently met who asked me to dinner. You have to separate the two. And my life's ambition has never been to redecorate the White House like Jackie Kennedy. I would start weekly poker games, though."

"Senator Becker is also your boss. Did you feel any pressure to go out with him in order to keep your job?"

"Of course not. Senator Becker is a complete gentleman. He has a get-to-know-you dinner with all the new members of his staff, and after ours he asked if I'd like to have dinner again. If we'd met under different circumstances and he'd asked me out I would have accepted."

I get a question from a famous male reporter who's probably pushing seventy and wrinkled as a prune. "How would you feel about having sex before marriage?"

"I'm way too young for you, Hal, but thanks for the offer."

That one gets a huge laugh.

"So will Twitter Girl be tweeting about the relationship?"

"Sorry, if you want *fifty shades of politics*, I'm not your gal."

"So, how was the kiss?"

The question from a young female reporter stops the crowd cold. Everything goes silent as they await my answer.

***

The unbelievably long day finally ends. It seems like eons ago that Ripley woke me up with a phone call. The strategy session, the luncheon, being hounded all friggin' day about my love life, which, up till now includes one kiss. Long phone conversations with Ripley and my brother, the latter of whom told me to "be careful" at least a dozen times. At least the debate gave me a break and I got back to my sarcastic self on Twitter. Dan Carrington tried to draw me out about the relationship, but I stuck to political snark.

And though Will Becker is in the next condo, the only alone time I want is with my bed.

I toss my purse on the dresser and begin to get undressed when my phone chirps. I check it out and find a text from Tyler.

I'm up if you need to talk.

148

And though I'm exhausted, I do.

I prop up a few pillows on the bed, lay back, connect and find Tyler already turned in, covers up to his neck. "Hi Tyler, glad you called."

"Rough day, huh?"

"I never expected anything like this. To be honest, it's a little scary. I've been in the public eye for a long time, but my personal life has never been under a magnifying glass."

"Well, you handled it beautifully. You were really charming at the luncheon. All the commentators thought you were a breath of fresh air."

"Charming?" I point at my face "*Moi*?"

"You were funny and cute at the same time. It's all anyone's talking about. Nobody gives a damn about the debate. They wanna know about the next President's girlfriend."

"Well, I'm not his girlfriend yet."

"You will be thanks to Photoshop. Can't wait to see the morning papers."

"*Page Six* here I come. But right now I'm trying to figure out how I'll deal with all this scrutiny."

"Just be yourself, T.G. It's what makes you so uniquely attractive. There are lots of beautiful women out there, but none has a personality like yours."

"Thank you, Tyler, it's very nice of you to say that." I stifle a yawn. "Oh, excuse me."

"You need sleep, go to bed."

"I can talk awhile."

"Hey, you made me go to bed when I was sick, now it's your turn to listen. Lights out, young lady. You're past your curfew."

"Yes, sir. I'll see you when I get back."

"Look forward to it, T.G. Pleasant dreams."

"You too, Tyler."

We sign off and I slide the iPad on the nightstand, throw my clothes on the floor, get under the covers and turn out the lights.

But while my body is exhausted, my mind is wired, going over the events of the day, wondering if tomorrow and the next few months will be the same. Now I know what it's like to be on the other end of the media. I roll over on my side and hug my pillow.

***

It's wheels up at seven but I've been on the plane since six. I didn't feel like running another media gauntlet at the front gate of the condo complex so I bribed a maintenance guy to drive me out in the back of his pickup. Nothing like hiding under a tarp when dating someone new. It's the political equivalent of sneaking out the bedroom window when your parents think you've gone to bed.

Right now Becker's niece Jessica and I are the only ones on the plane. I'm ravenous from the stress and have already downed a bagel, some eggs, a jelly donut and about a quart of orange juice. I look out the window and see a caravan of cars pull up to the plane. The cars are unloaded and baggage is transferred to the plane as staffers make their way up the stairs. Another media horde is on the end of the tarmac, hoping for a look at what they consider to be America's First Couple. Ha! You've got to get up pretty early in the morning to outsmart Twitter Girl. (Like, around five-thirty.)

Frank enters the plane and makes his way down the center aisle carrying a stack of newspapers. He plops them down in my lap and sits down next to me. "Some light reading material for the flight."

"How did they say we did in the debate?"

"That's not exactly the lead story."

I turn over the paper on top of the pile to look at the front page and see a picture of myself with Becker at the luncheon under the blaring headline: **BECKER'S RUNNING MATE?**

I roll my eyes. "Oh, this can't be good."

"Actually, it's all *very* good," says Frank. "Turn the page."

I flip open the paper and start reading.

MEET WILL BECKER'S TWEET-HEART

By Jolene Parker

Sorry, girls, Senator Will Becker may be off the market. His eye has been caught by a snarky redhead who would probably make the most entertaining First Lady in history.

After a paparazzi photo of Becker and campaign staffer Cassidy Shea stealing a kiss went viral, the two came clean about their relationship at a political luncheon yesterday. And clean it apparently is, as that kiss in the photo is as far as they've gone.

Geez, I woulda guessed a guy who looked like Becker would have no problem getting to second base with a woman.

Shea, the former network reporter known as Twitter Girl who was canned in December over a controversial remark she made on social media, joined the campaign in January to bring her digital sarcasm to a presidential race that badly needed some levity. Dressed in a stylish emerald green dress that showed off killer legs atop four inch heels, the towering copper-top fielded questions with ease from the media about the relationship, which so far consists of a few dinners. And when asked to rate that now famous first kiss, she tap danced like a seasoned politician and said, "Next question."

Ms. Shea, who is thirty-five and has never been married, was a fixture on the CBJ network for several years and had a Twitter following of more than one million when network executives deemed her snark had gone too far in a comment about a tornado. She was quickly snapped up by the Becker campaign, and has been launching hilarious barbs at just about everyone involved in the Presidential race, including the debate moderators.

Both Becker and Shea stressed that their private lives were just that, but good luck trying to keep something like this under wraps.

And while this bit of breaking news may have broken the hearts of millions, this reporter has to admit they look good together.

I snap the newspaper shut. "Well, she was certainly nice."

"All the articles are positive," says Frank. "Everyone loves you. Women want to be you and men want to... well..."

I put up my hand. "I get it. I was worried I was going to have a negative affect on the campaign."

"Cassidy, I think it's just the opposite."

CHAPTER SIXTEEN

@TwitterGirl
Super Bowl Sunday! Go Giants! Will Becker is a guest on the pre-game show!

It's a party atmosphere on this late Sunday afternoon as we arrive at the campaign headquarters, because it's a Super Bowl party. I've been looking forward to this day for two very important reasons.

– I want to see the Giants beat the hell out of the Patriots. (Known as "the evil empire" in New York.)

– We're all allowed one guest, so I brought Sam, who will be meeting Will Becker for the first time.

And I'm very nervous about what his take will be. Because things have been going very well and I don't want to hear anything bad.

Have I reached the rose colored glasses stage? No. Okay, maybe they have a slight tint because I'm a little bit smitten. But I'm still a reporter at heart and have to cover all bases.

The past few days have been a whirlwind since our relationship went public. We've been out to dinner a few times, which turned into photo ops during the appetizers. I'm being cheerful and pleasant with the media, knowing they have a job to do since I've been on the other side and know what it's like. But I know how to dodge them when I need a break.

Will Becker is seated in his office, dressed in a blue Giants sweater with their embroidered logo on the chest. Frank is looking over his shoulder. Both look to be in a good mood. Frank spots me and waves us in.

I head into the office along with Sam and handle the introductions. Becker gets up, shakes his hand and says, "Sam, I've heard so much about you."

"Same here," says my brother, studying the Senator's face.

"So," I ask, "what are you guys doing in here? The game's about to start."

"Looking at the latest polls," says Frank. "Your approval numbers are incredible."

"*I* have approval numbers?"

Frank nods. "One of the Washington newspapers did a poll on you. You've got an eighty-seven percent favorability rating."

"Mine's fifty-nine," says Becker. He turns to Frank. "Maybe she should be running for President."

I fold my arms and stick out one foot. "If elected, I will not serve."

Ripley appears as planned in the doorway and grabs my arm, "Hey, Cassidy, some people want to meet you."

"Sure. You boys get acquainted."

I leave Sam in the office, hoping that he'll like what he sees. Please like him, Sam. Please.

***

Ten minutes into the game I've had enough of meet-and-greet and I'm missing the damn Super Bowl. I look around the room and see Tyler sitting on the end of a couch talking to Sam, who is parked next to it. I quickly moved toward them and wave Tyler toward the middle of the sofa. "Scoot over. Wanna sit between my two best guys."

154

"Rose between two thorns," says Tyler.

"Think you got it backwards," I say, as I plop down just as the game breaks for a commercial. "Damn, I've been grabbed more than a pass-around girl at a frat party."

"Interesting visual," says Sam.

"So, what are you boys talking about?"

"You," they answer in unison.

"Oh, really? What about me?"

Tyler leans forward and looks at Sam. "Looks like we'll have to go to the men's room to continue our discussion."

"Fine, talk about me behind my back."

"Trust me, it's all good," says Sam. "So, everyone wants to meet my sister."

I shake my head. "No, everyone wants to meet *Senator Becker's girlfriend*. Big difference."

Tyler grabs the last nacho from his plate, then turns to me. "Aren't you having any of the goodies? Or did I miss your afternoon feeding?"

"Very funny. No, I haven't had a chance, so load me up a plate, big boy. You know what I like."

Tyler gets up and heads for the spread of food that fills a long table at the end of the room.

"You got him well trained," says Sam.

"No, he's just polite that way. Old fashioned guy. Tyler's a lot like you."

"Well, we do both have something in common."

"I didn't mean your challenges. I meant your personality. He's sweet. Protective. A gentleman. Total package."

***

Sam pulls the car out of the parking lot and we head home, once again fat and happy after the Giants win.

I always ride in the back seat of his van so I can stretch out my legs. I cannot wait a minute longer. "Well?"

"Great game," says Sam, keeping his eyes on the road.

Oh, shit. This isn't gonna be good.

"C'mon, spill," says Ripley, sitting next to him. "We want the full review."

Sam bites his lower lip and locks eyes with me in the rear view mirror.

"Uh-oh. I know that look. You didn't like him."

"I didn't say that," says Sam. "I didn't *dislike* him."

"But?" we say in stereo.

Sam shakes his head. "He's, I don't know, different. I guess cause he's a politician. I mean, he's friendly and all that but I get the feeling that the whole thing is an act. That's he's been packaged like a product. There's something about the guy... I can't really put my finger on it. But something's not right."

"Is that *something* bad enough that I shouldn't date him?"

"I don't know. But be careful, dear sister. And if I were you, I'd keep investigating that mystery you've kinda forgotten about the last two weeks. Get the stars out of your eyes and get back to being a reporter. If you don't find anything, fine. But you need to know if anything is there. Because I think something is."

"I've got stars in my eyes?"

Sam looks to his right. "Ripley?"

She turns around to face me. "Honey, you've got a whole constellation. Look, Sam and I both have the same weird feeling about the guy. Please do yourself a favor and check it out."

"But he's been a perfect gentleman so far."

"Just be careful, my friend. Listen to your brother. He's always right."

Yeah. That's what I'm afraid of.

***

I can't sleep.

Sam's assessment of Will Becker has my mind in overdrive, weaving a slalom around possible red flags that have no meaning.

So far.

Be he's right. And if he sees the same thing Ripley does, I have to put the infatuation aside. I can't go into this with blinders on. I know too many girls who did that and ended up in divorce court.

And the last thing I want to be known as is the President's ex-wife.

It's one in the morning as I head downstairs, passing Sam's bedroom on the way. I hear him snoring as usual as I quietly walk into my office, turn on a light, close the door and open my laptop.

I grab a yellow legal pad, adjust my reporting hat and start writing down the information and questions I already have. Which isn't much.

2005.
Missing time?
Missing money?
A twelve digit number.
A dead wife who took something to the grave.
"You have resources I do not."

Not much to go on, but in my reporting career I've started with less. However, at this hour, the only thing I can start to work on is missing time.

I do a search for Will Becker and click on "news" then use the drop down menu to put items in chronological order.

The search turns up thousands of articles on Becker, dating back to when he held a local office in New York. I set the search to filter out all the stories in the year 2005 when he served as a Congressman.

More than three hundred items.

I don't want to read them all, just find the "missing time" David

Gold talked about. I start scrolling through the results. Plenty of items in January and February. A smaller amount in March. Five in the first week of April.

Then nothing for the rest of the month. Nothing in May or June.

The stories pick up slowly in mid-July, then go back to their normal rate in August when he announced his candidacy for the Senate seat which would be open in 2006.

I note the dates the stories disappeared and resumed on the pad, then log onto the Congressional Record website, navigate my way through a typical confusing government website, then arrive at my destination.

Congressional voting records for 2005.

A quick search for Becker shows he didn't miss a single vote during the "missing time" period. He had a perfect attendance record.

So he wasn't physically missing, but for whatever reason he wasn't making any news. No print articles, no video clips from television interviews. Was he simply preparing for the Senate run and keeping everything close to the vest before an announcement? That doesn't make sense. If you're going to run for a higher office, especially one that was as wide open as this one was, you want a higher profile and as much face time as possible on the networks. And he'd gotten plenty of that before he went off the media grid.

Or was he involved in something that had him flying under the radar for a few months?

If David Gold was onto something, this was only a small piece of the puzzle. But I could no longer dismiss the man. He said there was missing time and there was to some extent. The bigger piece of the puzzle would have to come later, as I would take advice from my favorite movie, *All the President's Men*.

Follow the money.

Which means I'll need to let one of my closest friends in on my search.

***

@TwitterGirl
Happy Valentines Day! Give Senator Becker some love with your votes today...

They say timing is everything. But in this case, it's anything but.

The most romantic day of the year falls on Tuesday, which means that I will not be out on a date with Will Becker but spending the evening with Frank as the returns come in from a couple of primaries. The Senator is doing puddle jumps all day in the private jet and won't be back till later this evening.

Of course that hasn't stopped the tabloids from speculating about what should happen between us since Cupid's arrow is trained on us like a heat seeking missile.

Some of the graphics have gone over the top. Since the media now has a batch of photos from our few dinners in public, they've gone wild. There are dozens of shots with me holding a dozen roses and a box of candy, stuff like that. My favorite digital creation has Becker with a pair of wings shooting an arrow at me, while I'm looking up and clutching my chest as little cartoon hearts float around my head.

Which, if you must know, isn't too far from the truth.

Meanwhile, a tabloid that absolutely hates the President features a cartoon of him, fat as a tick, dressed as Cupid wearing Depends, frowning as an arrow sticks out of his ass. The caption reads, "Americans are falling out of love with President Turner."

And though Becker is going a mile a minute today, he told me to be at the ballroom tonight when he returns to talk to his supporters. I know he's got something planned and Frank won't tell me a damn thing, so I'm acting like a lovesick schoolgirl as we watch the returns. I'm looking at the clock every five minutes because I know the Senator will be back at eight.

Of course I haven't forgotten my own Valentine's obligation.

Even though the girl is supposed to get the flowers and candy, I've always gotten something for any guy I happened to be dating. So I picked up some cool cuff links made out of New York subway tokens, since Becker often rides the rails to get around Manhattan instead of tying up traffic with an entourage like so many politicians do.

I'm sure everything that happens will be scrutinized and some people might think my gift is strange, but I don't care.

It's Valentines Day, and love is in the air.

A huge cheer goes up as Will Becker emerges from behind a curtain and makes his way to the front of the ballroom wearing a big smile. With two major wins tonight in his back pocket, it really is beginning to look like he's a slam dunk for the nomination. But as Frank says, there's a long way to go and there could be land mines which could explode.

Becker moves to a podium that has been set up on stage as the cheers continue. I'm off to the side with Frank and the rest of the staff. The Senator makes a gesture with his hands for the crowd to sit down as he says, "Thank you" several times. They finally take their seats and I steal a look at the monitors that have been set up backstage which tells me we're live on every network.

Becker spends a few minutes thanking the voters and his staff, makes a few political remarks, and then I see a sly smile grow. "Well, this has been a busy day but I haven't forgotten it's a special day that has nothing to do with politics." He puts up one finger. "Hang on, I'll be right back."

Murmurs from the crowd float through the room as Becker goes backstage for a moment, then emerges with a huge bouquet of roses. The crowd cheers as he heads back to the podium and motions for me to join him. I head toward him wearing a big smile, taking the roses from him as we meet at the podium. "Thank you," I say, though I'm not sure he can hear me over the cheers from the crowd. I reach into my pocket, pull out a small jewelry box and hand it to him. He looks puzzled for a moment, obviously not expecting anything, then turns to the crowd. "Ooooh, I got something too." He opens the box and smiles, then holds it up so the camera can pick it up and send it to the giant screen behind him. "I don't know if you can see these, but they're seriously cool. Cuff links made from antique New York City subway tokens."

The crowd applauds and he asks them to quiet down. "Hang on, I'm not done. Since I met Cassidy Shea I've noticed she has a real sweet tooth. So, this being Valentine's Day… she'll need something to go along with those flowers." He turns to the side of the stage. "Guys…"

I look over as two men wheel out what has to be a six foot box of chocolates in the shape of a red heart. "The people at Cadbury tell me this is the biggest box of Valentine chocolate they've ever made." He turns to me with a soulful look. "A big heart for a girl with a big heart."

The crowd gives us a collective "Awwwww" as Becker opens his arms, waiting for a hug. But I walk right past him, pull the ribbon wrapped around the box, lift the lid and start tearing into the candy. The crowd laughs hysterically. I give them a thumbs up while I'm eating.

"She likes chocolate more than me," says Becker.

The crowd laughs as I move back toward him.

They start clinking their glasses with spoons like people do at weddings when they want the bride and groom to kiss. We lock eyes for a moment and know what we have to do. He leans over and gives me a quick peck on the cheek. I shake one finger at him like a parent saying no and point to my lips. The crowd cheers.

He takes my shoulders and gives me a kiss.

Hundreds of flashes go off, and as I look into his eyes we become the only two people in the room.

***

While most women who'd received a six foot box of chocolates, several dozen roses and an incredible kiss from an unbelievably attractive man on national television would be in the sack with said man, this is, as you've no doubt learned by now, not a typical relationship.

Becker is making the rounds of the cable shows and I'm back in my hotel room, alone, though on a sugar high I've never experienced.

Or maybe it's a different kind of high.

And I wanna share it with the people I care about. But my brother is surely asleep and Ripley's on a red-eye flight back from the west coast.

Tyler.

I send him a quick text, asking if he's in the mood to chat.

My iPad chimes a few seconds later and I lean back in bed, connect and see Tyler's face.

"What, you ate all the chocolates already?"

"Smart ass. I've saved you plenty. But you'd better claim them tomorrow because they'll be gone by the weekend."

"Well, I wanted you to have a good supply when I ordered the thing."

"Excuse me?

"Oops. Sorry, it was supposed to be a secret."

I furrow my brow. "The whole thing was your idea?"

"Guilty as charged. I come up with a good one every once in awhile. Viper was real busy and asked me to arrange something special for you. And, you know, there is this love affair you have with food."

"Wait a minute… *Frank* asked you to buy me a Valentine present?"

"Well, Top Dog delegated it to him and Frank is about as romantic as Dick Cheney, so he gave it to me. I didn't mind and it makes me happy that I came up with something you enjoyed so much."

"Oh. Well, you know the way to my heart."

"Glad you appreciated it, because it took a ton of phone calls to make it happen."

"Did you also come up with the *big heart for a girl with a big heart* line?"

"I plead no contest. Anyway, you looked really happy tonight, T.G."

"It was a unique experience."

"You also look like you're enjoying the attention."

"Well, I gotta admit, the whole thing is exciting. And having everyone in the country root for you is something no girl has ever experienced."

"They're not *all* rooting for you. You've only got an eighty-seven percent approval rating, so thirteen percent want you guys to crash and burn like Brad Pitt and Jennifer Aniston. Don't get cocky and let your poll numbers go to your head."

"Ha, very funny."

"But seriously, I can imagine having someone like Will Becker interested in you is every girl's dream."

We talk for another twenty minutes, mostly about a science fiction series we're both following and the upcoming baseball season, then I hit the wall and realize I'm about to crash. "Well, I guess I'll see you tomorrow Tyler."

"Sure thing, T.G. Look forward to it."

"And thanks again for your great idea about the chocolates and whatever you did to make it happen."

"I'm glad you enjoyed it." He looks away for a moment. "I'm, uh, happy for ya." He looks back and offers a slight smile. His eyes are a little droopy and I can tell he's tired. We end the call and I tuck myself in.

So the giant box of chocolates was Tyler's doing. And so was the line that went with it. But hey, Will Becker's a real busy guy and he doesn't have time for things like coming up with an idea for a Valentine gift while running for President.

Yeah, let's go with that.

CHAPTER SEVENTEEN

@TwitterGirl
#ChicagoDebate
Just said hello to some of President Turner's more loyal supporters. And then I left the cemetery.

While that dead voter thing has reared its ugly head again in the Windy City (the mother ship of political tricks) I've got something on my calendar that has absolutely nothing to do with the election and everything to do with me.

I'm having lunch with my old mentor Dale Carlin in one of Chicago's most famous pizza joints. Partly because I love their deep dish pies, partly because I've missed the guy.

And partly because I need his help solving the puzzle hanging over my head.

Dale smiles as he walks toward our table at the back of the loud, crowded restaurant and I give him a strong hug. "Damn, I miss working with you," I say.

"The network's not the same without you," he says as he slides onto a chair opposite me. "And I've heard rumblings from management that they think they made a mistake letting you go."

"Nice to hear."

"I know you miss the people, but do you miss the job?"

"You know, I thought I would. But the campaign has been soooo exciting."

"The campaign has been exciting or your love life has been exciting?"

"Fine. A little of both. Okay, a lot of one and a little of the other."

He reaches over and pats my hand. "You're actually glowing, Cassidy. I don't think I've ever seen you this happy and relaxed. It's a good look for you."

"I love what I'm doing and, well…"

"Not ready to say the L-word yet?"

"You know me too well. Though I *can* use the term *smitten*. Honestly, I don't ever think I've been so attracted to a guy. And the feeling seems to be mutual."

"Well, what guy *wouldn't* be interested in you? I hope it all works out. You deserve someone good and you two look good together."

"Thank you. I get that a lot."

A half hour's worth of catching up later, our lunch arrives. I eagerly dig out a slice and take a bite of the hot, steaming pizza, savoring the combination of cheese, thick sauce, pepperoni and sausage. "Oh my God, that's better than sex."

Dale laughs as he dishes out a slice. "Well, I can see nothing's changed as far as your eating habits go."

"I'll always be obsessed with food." I look around, see that for once no one is paying attention to me, then turn back to him. "Dale, I need a huge favor."

"Sure, anything for you. What is it?"

"It's something that will raise a red flag if I go looking for it, but since you're covering the President no one will notice."

"Okay."

"I need Will Becker's tax returns for 2005. And I'll need any documentation of large money transfers."

He furrows his brow. "What, you checking on his net worth? It's pretty common knowledge that he's got millions from his father's business."

"No, not that. I got a tip that there might be something… well, that something unusual happened during that year, and I want to check it out."

"What exactly are you looking for?"

"Not sure. Missing money, large transfers, weird expenses, crazy tax deductions, could be anything. But I'll know it if I see it."

"Where did you get this tip?"

"From a guy who used to be Becker's best friend who says he is not who he seems to be."

Dale grows a worried look. "Cassidy, this doesn't sound like something from a girl in love. Don't you trust the guy?"

"I do, and I seriously doubt I'll find anything. But Becker's former friend gave me another tip that actually checked out. And sometimes, as you know, where there's smoke, there's fire." I look down and exhale. "And then there's Sam."

"Uh-oh. Sam doesn't approve?"

"When he met Becker his bullshit detector went off. Big time. Like a friggin' red alert on the Enterprise. And it's usually spot on."

"True."

"If that's not bad enough, Ripley's not sure about Becker either."

He slowly nods. "She's a good judge of character as well. So what was the tip that checked out?"

"Becker basically was off the news grid for about three months in 2005, right before he announced his candidacy for the Senate. He had a perfect voting record during that time, but I could not find one single news item."

"Damn, that does sound strange, especially for a guy who loves the camera. You didn't find anything?"

"Not one sound bite, not one quote in a newspaper, not a single photo. Then, poof, he magically returns with the Senate campaign and is everywhere."

"Hmmm. Well, I can get the returns for you. Shouldn't be a problem. I've got a friend at the IRS and if anyone asks I'll say the

President's campaign was saying something about it."

"Thanks, Dale, I owe you."

"You don't owe me nothing, kid. You've always been the daughter I never had."

"And you're the dad I lost. I'm lucky to have so many people who look out for me."

"Cassidy, you owe it to yourself to be happy, and to be one hundred percent sure about the guy."

"Right now he's got a ninety-nine percent approval rating with me. It's the one percent I'm worried about."

***

The wonderful aroma hits me in the face as I walk in the front door. I drop my suitcase and run to the kitchen, knowing Sam's got one of my favorite dinners going.

He looks up from the cooking island and smiles. "Hey, how was Chicago?"

"Friggin' cold." I lean down and give him a hug. "Yay! You're making hot as hell shrimp!"

"Haven't had it in awhile and I found some royal reds I'd forgotten about in the freezer."

Sam is cooking a dish that's actually called shrimp diablo, a blazing concoction made with olive oil, cayenne pepper, diced tomatoes, a ton of chopped garlic and these wonderful seasonal shrimp from the Gulf of Mexico called royal reds. It's spicy as hell but delicious, and warms you like nothing else on a cold day. "Looks almost done."

"Five more minutes."

"Great timing."

"I checked on your flight arrival on the Internet, did the math and figured out when you'd be home. Rather have dinner ready than have you go on a hunger rampage through the pantry."

"That's what makes you the best brother in the world."

"Speaking of food, did you get your Chicago pizza?"

"I did. I had lunch with Dale yesterday. This will make you happy. He's gonna check on Will's financial stuff for me."

"Good." He looks up and me and notes I'm not smiling. "Caz, we're just being careful. You know I'm rooting for you. I always do."

"I know. But I also know you're always right."

"Maybe I'm due for a swing and a miss. The streak has to end sometime."

"I sure hope so."

"Oh, by the way, your new household name status has had a spillover effect. Some reporter from *The Post* called me and wants to do a story. I mean, it must really be a slow news day if they wanna do sidebar stories on me."

"What, you don't want to do it?"

"What's the point? They want to profile me as the possible brother-in-law to the president and they think it's interesting that we share a home."

"It could be a good thing, Sam. You could be a real inspiration to people with challenges."

"They did that story years ago after the accident."

"Yeah, but that's ancient history and it was a local story. This would get picked up by the wires and go national. I'm telling you, it would have a positive effect. Remember how down you were when you first learned you couldn't walk, and how all those other people in wheelchairs supported you, showed you how much you could accomplish? Maybe your story inspires someone who's in the same situation you were in. You'd be paying it forward."

"I hadn't thought of it that way."

"And it will give your famous sister the chance to brag on you and tell millions of single women why you'd be such a catch."

Sam sees the water is boiling and throws the pasta in. "I don't need millions, just one."

And I know which one he wants. "I know, but it wouldn't hurt to have a nice selection from which to choose. Besides, America needs to know why I turned out so normal."

"I think you have our parents to thank for that."

"I guess you forgot I was kind of a party girl before I moved back here. Haven't been to a club since. You settled me down, made me finally grow up. People need to meet my big brother."

"Uh, I'm ten years younger in case you forgot."

"Sweetie, it's not about age. You look after me, protect me, take care of me. I'd be nothing without you and God knows how I would have ended up if you weren't around. You'll always be my big brother, and it has nothing to do with a birth certificate. I want to marry a guy just like you."

***

I've never been to the opera, though I do like the music. So on my first trip I'm decked out in an elegant turquoise gown.

Will Becker, looking perfect in a tux, could easily be cast as the world's most famous secret agent.

"You look like James Bond tonight," I say, as the Lincoln town car whisks us through Manhattan Friday night traffic.

He turns to me and raises one eyebrow. "The name's Becker. Will Becker." He pulls out his cell phone as I laugh. "Moneypenny, I'll be tied up all night, so hold my calls."

"Very funny. At least I don't have one of those famous suggestive names all Bond girls have."

"Yeah, some of those were hilarious. Holly Goodhead was my favorite."

"Hmmm, I wonder why?" I reach over and take his hand as he blushes a bit. "I'm glad you could finally carve out some time for just us, away from the campaign."

"Hey, you're important to me and I haven't been able to give you as much attention as I'd like. I hope you've noticed I'm crazy

170

about you."

"Yeah, I kinda picked that up, and the feeling's mutual. But really, Will, I understand your time constraints. It's a unique situation."

"It will slow down after November. I promise."

"You think the White House will have a slower pace?"

"No, I mean all the travel and campaigning. That's what wears you out. When I'm in Washington just being a Senator not running for anything it's not exhausting like this."

The car pulls up at the Metropolitan Opera an hour before the performance as he wanted to do a meet-and-greet with high rollers. I see about a half dozen photographers and a few TV cameras waiting at the curb. Word obviously got out that America's lovebirds have tickets. The TV lights turn on. I reach for the door handle but he takes my arm. "Wait a minute," says Becker, who gets out of his side of the car, walks around to my side and opens the door for me. I step out into the bright lights and give my best smile for the cameras and for a moment I'm at the Academy Awards on the red carpet. Reporters shout a few questions but Becker puts up his hand. "No sound bites tonight, guys. Just wanted a nice evening with Cassidy." They grumble a bit but follow us like the Pied Piper as we walk into the building.

We're instantly surrounded by a well-heeled crowd, resplendent in black tie and evening gowns.

Most of the people want to meet me, not the next President.

I feel like royalty.

We're still glad-handing a half hour later when Becker's cell rings.

"Geez, I forgot to turn this off," he says. "Can you imagine if the thing rang during the opera?" He pulls the phone from his pocket and looks at it. "Hang on, gotta take this."

"Sure, we've got plenty of time." I continue to smile and shake hands as the crowd files past us.

Will's smile vanishes and he suddenly shakes his head. "Fine. I'll be right there." He ends the call and takes my shoulders. "Cassidy,

171

I'm so sorry. That was Frank and there's something I need to respond to right now."

"It can't wait a couple of hours?"

"He already booked me on two of the cable shows. I am so sorry." He hands me the tickets. "Go enjoy the show. I'll have another car come and get you." He leans in and gives me a quick kiss. "Gotta run. We'll talk tomorrow, okay?"

"Sure, Will. Good luck."

He turns and quickly heads out of the building. I see him heading for a waiting car with Frank standing next to it holding the door. They both get in and the car leaves skid marks as it peels off.

I'm left by myself holding two tickets.

And I really don't want to go in alone and sit next to an empty seat. It's not what Kate Middleton would do. The woman would never go to a place like this unescorted.

I'm ready to head home when it hits me that someone I know lives two blocks away.

Tyler.

I pull my cell from my evening bag and call.

He answers on the first ring. "Hey, T.G. What's up?"

"You like opera?"

"I love opera. Why, you calling to rub it in from the Met?"

"No, Becker got called away and I'm here needing a nice man on my arm. How soon can you throw on a suit and get your ass down here?"

"Still dressed from work since I had dinner with my sister-in-law. On my way."

I take Tyler's arm as we walk out into the night after being cornered by a society reporter. "So, T.G., that was your first opera?" he asks.

"Yeah. Won't be my last. That was terrific."

"That's why I've got season tickets."

"Really? Never figured you for an opera buff."

"When I'm not hitting Star Trek conventions, I'm over here.

I'm a man of very eclectic tastes."

"Well, then call me eclectic 'cause we like the same stuff." I take a quick look at my watch. "You tired?"

"Not really, why?"

"I was wondering if I could pay you back for saving me with some coffee and a piece of cheesecake."

He shakes his head and smiles. "I actually think you were wondering if you could disguise your desire for food with a thank you."

"Fine, I'm hungry, so sue me. You wanna eat, or what?"

"Sure."

"Yay!" I squeeze his arm. "Besides, a slice of cheesecake doesn't begin to thank you for what you did tonight. It was really nice of you to come over on short notice."

"It's my job."

"It's not your job to take care of me."

"Didn't you know? I'm actually a superhero, keeping the streets safe for women and children while rescuing smoking hot redheads who get stood up."

"Ah, I see. So what's your superhero name?"

"Haven't come up with one yet."

"I'll have to work on it then. By the way, you don't have to keep calling me smoking hot. I'm not."

"You are to me. And tonight, in that gown, under the moon-light, you are simply beyond smoking hot. You are devastatingly beautiful."

I'm shocked as I look at my watch and see we've been sitting in the coffee shop for an hour and a half. "Wow, didn't realize it was that late."

Tyler shrugs. "Tomorrow's Saturday, you can sleep in."

"I know, but I still gotta get home, and the ferry schedule at this hour is about once an hour."

"Oh, I was going to drive you home anyway."

"All the way to Staten Island?"

"Geez, you say it like it's halfway across the country. It's not a big deal."

"Don't be ridiculous, Tyler. I can take a cab."

"Sorry, it's not open for discussion. I'm not sending a woman home alone at this hour and you're a bit overdressed for a boat ride. Besides, there could be ne'er-do-wells lurking on the ferry."

"Part of your duties as a superhero?"

"Absolutely. A complete rescue of a smoking hot redhead requires me to see her safely to her front door."

"Hey, I thought I was devastatingly beautiful!"

"I have to rescue the women who fit that description as well. Thankfully, only one exists."

His parade of compliments makes me blush. "God, you are sweet to me. Tell you what, if you're hell bent on taking me home, you're staying in our guest room. I don't want you driving back at two in the morning. It's already been a long day for you. So swing by your place and get a change of clothes."

He nods. "Okay, I'll take you up on it. But I warn you, I sleep really late after a work day."

"After what you did for me tonight, you can stay all weekend if you like, Tyler."

CHAPTER EIGHTEEN

@TwitterGirl
Enjoyed the opera last night, now waiting for the fat lady to sing for a few candidates…

It's nearly noon and I'm starting to think about lunch. Sam and I have been up for a few hours, but we haven't seen Tyler yet.

"You might wanna go check on him," says Sam. "He's got that condition, right?"

"Yeah. I'm sure he's exhausted, but you're right."

I head up the stairs to the guest room which is next to mine, put my ear to the door, don't hear any snoring, and gently tap on it. "Tyler, you decent?"

"Yeah. Come on in."

I open the door and what I see takes me back a bit.

Tyler, still in bed, looking pale.

I rush to the side of the bed and take his hand as I sit on the edge. "Geez, are you feeling okay?"

"Sorry, I should have warned you about how I sometimes look on a recovery day."

"But are you okay?"

"I'll be fine. Just have to stay in bed a while longer and take things slow today. Yesterday was a really long one."

"God, now I feel guilty about dragging you to the opera and out for cheesecake. And then I let you drive me home. You should have told me it would wipe you out."

He offers a smile. "You're worth it. And I got you home safe."

"You certainly did. Anyway, you stay put and I'll bring you something to eat. My turn to rescue the superhero. You hungry?"

He nods. "Yeah."

"Okay, be right back." I grab a remote from the dresser and hand it to him. "Find something on the tube and I'll keep you company."

Fifteen minutes later I return with some soup and a grilled cheese sandwich on a bed tray, hand it to Tyler, and sit on the other side of the bed to watch television with him.

Three hours later I'm on one side of the bed, head propped up on a pillow while he's still under the covers on the other side. The cheesy 1950s sci-fi movie ends and I look over at Tyler, whose eyes are a bit droopy. "You look like you're fading."

He covers a yawn with his hand. "I'm sorry. I could use a short nap. Maybe an hour or so and then I'll be back to normal."

"No hurry, sleep as long as you like."

"I'm sorry I'm putting you out."

"Don't be ridiculous."

"No, it's Saturday and you probably had plans tonight."

"Uh, Becker's in Washington, remember? It's just dinner and cards with my brother and Ripley. You play cards?"

"Love to."

"Good, we can have teams." I slide off the bed, lean over and kiss him on top of the head. "Get your rest, superhero, and I'll come get you when dinner's ready."

By the time dinner's over and we head for the card table, Tyler's recovery is complete. He's his normal self, or at least the guy I'm used to seeing. What he goes through on his "recovery days" has both surprised me and increased my admiration for him. Like my

176

brother Sam, he deals with the challenges life has thrown at him with grace and good humor.

Speaking of the latter, I don't think I've laughed as much at dinner in years. Tyler and Sam are on the same page when it comes to wit, and they've been in tune all night, like they've been friends for years. They've really connected in a short amount of time. I can tell they enjoy each other's company and will become good friends.

"So," says Sam, arriving at the card table, "is it gonna be boys against the girls tonight? Or does my sister think she and her new partner can actually defeat the unbeaten team of Sam and Ripley?"

"Bring it," I say, as I sit down next to him and crack my knuckles. Ripley takes the seat opposite Sam while Tyler sits down directly across from me. I'm excited because we're playing pinochle, which we haven't done in a long time because few people know how to play it and you need a fourth. Luckily Tyler is familiar with the game and I hope he's a good player, because my brother and best friend are like mind readers when they team up for this game.

"So, Sam, what were these two like growing up?" asks Tyler.

"He was too young to remember," I say.

Sam starts to deal. "That's what my sister thinks. The guest room used to be my bedroom and I would lie on the floor next to the vent and hear what was going on in her room."

My eyes widen as I turn to my brother. "Excuse me? I never heard about this."

"Yeah, it was like a soap opera when Ripley would come over and you guys would talk about boys."

Ripley narrows her eyes at Sam. "You little sneak."

Sam shoots a quick smile at her, then turns to Tyler. "Anyway, during their senior year in high school they both had a thing for the quarterback on the football team—"

I reach over and grab Sam's arm. "Tyler doesn't need to hear this."

"Yeah, but I want to," says Tyler.

"Dear Lord," says Ripley, who buries her head in her hands.

"Anyway," says Sam, "they both had no interest in cheerleading but joined the squad to get close to the guy. They weren't getting anywhere so they borrowed my mom's sewing machine and did some, shall we say, *alterations* to their uniforms."

My jaw hangs open. "You know about that?"

"The results were hard to miss. So this one day I hear the sewing machine going all day in Cassidy's room but it's loud and I can't hear what they're saying. But I know something's up with these two. Anyway, when they're done this one starts walking around with her skirt hemmed up to her ass to show off her legs while this one is practically spilling out of her top."

Tyler looks at me as I'm turning beet red.

"I need more wine," says Ripley, as she gets up and heads for the kitchen.

"Make it a double for me," I say.

"So what happened?" asks Tyler. "Did either one ever get a date with the quarterback?"

"Nope," says Sam, who finishes dealing. "He was already sleeping with another girl. But the whole episode did make for an interesting yearbook photo of the cheerleading squad."

Tyler turns to me and smiles. "I'd love to see that—"

I grab my brother's arm again. "Don't you dare, Sam."

"You know," says Tyler, "a photo of the Senator's girlfriend in a cheerleader outfit could be worth a lot of votes."

I glare at him.

"Kidding," he says. "You couldn't possibly look better than you did last night anyway."

The next four hours are a mash up of stories, wine and laughs. And amazingly, my new partner and I have managed to defeat the previously unbeaten team of Sam and Ripley. We're on the same page, like we've been playing as partners for years.

Tyler looks at his watch. "Guys, this has been great but I probably need to get going."

"Somewhere you gotta be at midnight?" I ask. "What, you gonna turn into a pumpkin?"

"I don't want to overstay—"

"Nonsense," I say. "The guest room is still available and you don't want to miss one of our wonderful Sunday brunches." I turn to my brother. "Sam, deal the cards."

***

I hear the boys laughing as I plod down the stairs on a bright Sunday morning and smell something new coming from the kitchen. The coffee pot is gurgling as I enter and I head straight for it. "What is that wonderful aroma?"

"You'll see," says Tyler. "Thought you guys might want to try some of my specialties. I think you'll be hooked."

"If it's edible, she'll be hooked," says Sam.

"Hush, dear brother." I pour a cup of coffee and take a seat at the kitchen table, then study Tyler's face. "You look well rested."

"Long as I get my recovery days, I'll always be back to normal."

"Good. I heard you two laughing, what the hell are you guys talking about?"

"You," they say in unison.

"Oh, here we go again. Sam, you didn't show him the yearbook photo, did you?"

He shakes his head. "Nah. I tortured you enough last night. But I've hidden it so I can keep it as blackmail."

The oven dings and Tyler grabs a potholder. "Okay, get ready for something wonderful." He opens the over and pulls out a cookie sheet filled with what look like some sort of biscuits.

"What are those?"

"Cranberry walnut scones. I have a friend in London who sent me the recipe."

179

"Oooh, they look fantastic."

He slides the cookie sheet on the island and I get up to grab one, but he playfully slaps my hand. "Gotta let them cool a bit and then you eat them with clotted cream and jam."

I lean on the island and stare at them. "Tyler, how about you move into that guest room permanently?"

Tyler grabs his coat as he heads for the door. "Guys, I can't thank you enough for the hospitality."

"Great having you," says Sam. "Please come back and stay another weekend. We had a blast."

"Really," I say, taking his shoulders in my hands. "And thank you again for what you did Friday night."

"Hey, this turned out to be the best weekend I've had in years. Anyway, I'll see you tomorrow."

"Okay," I say, as I open the door and he heads out toward his car. I smile as I watch him make his way through the snow. He turns and sees me as he puts the key in the door. "What, you gonna heat the whole neighborhood?"

"Just making sure you get to your car and don't fall on the ice."

He waves, gets in his car and drives off.

I shut the door and find Sam smiling at me. "What?"

"I don't think I've seen you this happy in a long time, that's all. It's a good look on you."

"Hey, all is right with the universe. I live in a great house with my amazing brother, I have wonderful friends, I'm healthy, I have a really cool job, and we just had a terrific weekend doing simple stuff."

"Yeah, you have nothing to complain about. A far cry from those days right before Christmas."

"Really. Amazing how things work out. And I even have a terrific guy who's crazy about me."

"Yep," says Sam. "You sure do."

CHAPTER NINETEEN

@TwitterGirl
It's so cold today in Washington the President has his hands in
his own pockets.

Remember I mentioned that a society page reporter talked to
me after the opera? I'd forgotten about it but now there are two
photos splashed across *Page Six*. One showing me arriving on
Will Becker's arm and the other has me leaving with Tyler. And a
story about how I switched escorts in the middle of the evening.

WHY WASN'T TWITTER GIRL DANCIN' WITH THE
ONE WHO BRUNG HER?

By Jane Freelich

Patrons of the arts were thrilled Friday night when America's
favorite couple, Senator Will Becker and Cassidy Shea, showed
up for a performance at the Metropolitan Opera.

Yet when the spunky redhead also known as Twitter Girl left the
Met, she was on the arm of another man.

Trouble in paradise? Not likely, as the presidential candidate was called away on an emergency and chief campaign strategist Tyler Garrity was brought in to pinch-hit. "I was left with an extra ticket and knew Tyler lived around the corner, so I called him," said Ms. Shea. "He was nice enough to be my escort for the evening."

When asked if she was hurt by the Senator's quick exit, she shook her head. "Look, right now the American people are his first priority, and I understand that trying to date someone who is running for President isn't going to be easy. We'll be fine. And he's worth waiting for."

No argument here. Shea, who was dressed in a spectacular turquoise gown, towered over her second date, who looked absolutely thrilled to have the beauty on his arm even though he barely came up to her nose.

I quickly head toward Tyler's office and find him reading the newspaper while holding a pair of scissors. "Hey, Tyler. Look, I'm sorry—"

"Hey, T.G.! Did you see our picture in the paper?"

"Yeah, and about that—"

"It will have an honored place in my scrapbook." He starts cutting the article out of the paper.

"You're not upset?"

"About what?"

"The article."

"Why would I be upset? It's a great picture of you and me."

"Yeah, it is. I meant, you know, the story that went with the photo."

He shrugs. "I thought you handled it well. Good line about the American people being more important than a date."

"I meant what it said about *you*."

"Hey, I *was* absolutely thrilled to have you on my arm." He studies my face and then he gets it. "Oh, that. Look, I can't help it if you're going to keep wearing those platform shoes. But legs like yours should never be in flats." He shoots me a smile that warms my heart.

"Tyler, you are an amazing man."

The smile fades a bit. "Yeah, that's what women keep telling me."

***

I head up the stairs to the plane as the engines start roaring. We'll be taking off in a few minutes as Will Becker will be making a few campaign speeches in Virginia and Philly before Super Tuesday, the biggest primary day of the season. Jessica greets me with her usual cheerful smile and closes the door as I make my way back to my regular seat next to Frank.

I still haven't seen or talked to Becker since he was pulled away Friday night.

It occurs to me he told me he would call me on Saturday. But I forgot. Guess he forgot too.

"Hey," says Frank, "Becker wants to talk to you once we're airborne. He's back in the office."

"Sure thing."

"Great sound bite you gave at the opera."

"Thanks. Just trying to do my part."

"You're doing much more than your part, Cassidy."

The plane taxis down the runway and quickly takes off, not having to wait in line for an hour like every other flight at a New York airport. Rank has its privileges. We reach a cruising altitude quickly and Jessica turns off the seat belt light. A few seconds later the door behind me opens. Will Becker sticks his head out and smiles at me. "Hey, come on in."

I get up, quickly move into his office and lean against the wall as he closes the door behind me. "Cassidy, I wanted to apologize for the other night—"

"No apology necessary, Will. I understand."

"And I'm sorry I forgot to call you this weekend."

"Well, you know. Men always say they'll call but they never do." He looks worried for a moment until I give him a warm smile.

"Oh, you were kidding. I really need to spend more time with you or get some sort of Cassidy Shea humor decoder."

"I'll have one on your desk tomorrow." I run one finger inside his lapel. "But you'll have more fun if you discover things along the way. What good is a treasure hunt if you already have the whole map? It's like what we women say about shopping: it's not the treasure but the hunt."

"You really are a treasure." He moves closer and gently takes my shoulders. "As for your comment about the American people being more important than you, that's not true." He looks right into my soul. "Right now you're as important as anything in my life."

His words make me melt as he pushes me against the wall and gives me a long, passionate kiss while sliding his hands down my sides until they meet at the small of my back. I take his head in my hands and run my fingers through his thick hair.

The plane hits a bit of turbulence and makes us lose our footing for an instant and break the embrace. "Why, Senator, I'm not that kind of girl. But I'll make an exception in your case."

"I've been saving that since Friday night."

"So, when's our next opportunity for private time, since, as you say, you've been saving yourself for me?"

"Don't know, but I'll figure something out."

***

@TwitterGirl
My younger brother and hero, Sam Shea, is profiled in today's

edition of The Post!

MEET CASSIDY SHEA'S LIVE-IN GUY

Senator Will Becker's girlfriend has been living with a man for the past ten years. But there's no way the presidential hopeful will be jealous.

Because it's Cassidy Shea's kid brother Sam.

The two have shared a Staten Island home since a car accident took the lives of their parents and left Sam unable to walk. Cassidy, ten years older and his only sibling, put her television news career on hold and moved back home to take care of her fifteen year old brother, who needed both a legal guardian and extensive rehab. A decade later, Sam is completely self-sufficient, but his sister doesn't have the desire to get her own place.

"Sam is my emotional rock. When I first moved back we weren't even that close because of the age difference. But Sam is an old soul, and incredibly mature. Our relationship is amazing. He takes good care of me like a big brother and I couldn't even imagine living without him."

Sam Shea, now a handsome, fit young man of twenty-five, still has to use a wheelchair due to the extensive damage to his legs. He's not paralyzed but is unable to walk. "Maybe someday, as I understand there's some stem cell research that might help," he says. "But I don't even think about it anymore. I have a normal life and my chair is simply a vehicle that allows me to do everything I want to do. I'm not confined to a wheelchair, I'm liberated by it."

Sam, who works as an advertising copywriter, gets high marks

from Cassidy's best friend Ripley DeAngelo, who spends a lot of time at the Shea house. "Thank goodness Sam can cook, 'cause Cassidy could burn a salad. The guy is incredible. He drives like a Manhattan cabbie, does all the grocery shopping, has a great job and is one of the kindest people you'll ever meet. He's sweet, protective, funny, incredibly smart and a real old-fashioned gentleman. And he's cute as hell. Honestly, if you were going to build a perfect man from scratch, you'd end up with Sam. He's everything a girl could want."

I walk through the door and find Sam sitting at the kitchen table, sipping coffee, staring into space. The newspaper article in front of him.

I was afraid of this.

Ripley's quote.

"Not feeling well today?" I ask, knowing he's physically fine. I rest one hand on his shoulder.

He looks up at me, eyes a bit misty. "I didn't want to do the article, but you made me."

I crouch down and wrap one arm around him while stroking his hair with my free hand, then lean my head against his. "I know it hurts sometime. But maybe this article will lead to someone who really *is* perfect for you."

"*Ripley's* perfect for me. I know it, you know it. Why the hell doesn't she know it?"

"Ten years is a big age difference, Sam."

"It doesn't seem to be a problem with us."

Damn, he's got a point.

"Caz, maybe I need to tell her how I feel."

Dammit, she already knows. I shake my head. "No, no way. You'd lose her as a friend. And I know you don't want that."

He drops his head and sighs. "No. You're right, I sure don't. Not having Ripley in my life would hurt even worse. I always want her to be around. Even if she'll never feel the same way about me

186

that I do about her."

I look at the clock. "Well, get yourself together because she's coming over for dinner and I rented a movie. I'll order a couple pizzas, I know you're not in the mood to cook." I playfully mess up his hair, then kiss him on the top of the head. "I know this doesn't mean as much coming from your sister, but you really are everything a girl could want."

"Thank you, but I get tired of hearing that. Just go find me the girl."

The romantic comedy I rented is hilarious but Sam has barely cracked a smile. Ripley and I are on opposite ends of the couch sipping wine, as two empty pizza boxes take up most of the coffee table. Of course she showed up looking spectacular in the red dress with the cut-out shoulders that's his favorite, making things worse. I'm kicking myself for not warning her about his mood.

The movie ends and I mute the sound during the credit roll. "Well, that was a keeper."

"Yeah, hysterical," says Ripley. She turns to Sam and studies his face. "Didn't you like it?"

"It was okay. Not wild about the actress who played the lead. She doesn't do anything for me."

"Yeah, I guess she's an acquired taste." Ripley refills her wine glass. "By the way, young man, great article about you in the paper today. Very inspirational."

He nods slightly. "Yeah. I guess."

She turns to me with a gleam in her eye. "You know what I found interesting, Cassidy?"

"No, what?"

"I'd never been quoted before so it was strange reading my own words in print. Makes you look at things from another perspective. You see yourself in a different light."

"Yeah, I know what you mean. When I started on TV I had the same feeling."

"Well, I'm sure glad I wasn't misquoted. That reporter got it right, verbatim. I would want anything I said taken out of context about Sam."

He gives her a soft smile despite the sad eyes. "That was really nice what you said about me, Ripley. Thank you."

Damn, he looks like he's about to lose it.

Or worse, tell her how he feels.

"I meant every word. Boy, that reporter was thorough. She was asking me how you get around in that chair, how you drive, stuff like that." Ripley gets up and walks toward him, carrying her wine. "I was telling her how the armrests of the chair come off and you can slide into the van, onto the couch, in and out of bed." Ripley reaches down with her free hand and removes one of the armrests and puts it on the coffee table.

Sam looks up at her, then turns to me. I have no idea what she's up to and shrug as she removes the other armrest.

"Ripley, what are you doing?" he asks.

She sits on his lap and wraps one arm around his neck. "Just wanna be comfortable and the armrests get in the way."

Sam's eyes widen. "Uh, how much wine have you had?"

"This is my third glass. Not enough to make me do anything I don't want to do. But enough to make me totally honest." She turns to me. "Hey, Cassidy, remember that list I had in our dorm room about the perfect guy?"

I'm still clueless as to where she's going with this, and Sam's beginning to look like a nervous schoolboy who is having a *letters to Penthouse* fantasy come true. "What?"

"The list. You know, the thing I had in college. You remember it?"

"Yeah, I couldn't miss it. You hung it on the back of the door which intimidated the hell out of your dates. You titled it *the five qualities of Ripley's perfect man*."

"Right, that's what I called it. What were those five things?"

"*You* don't remember? Hell, it's burned into my brain."

"Enlighten me, dear friend."

188

"Fine." I envision the hand written sign she had on the door. "Number one was that he had to be very smart."

She nods. "That's right. I wanted a guy with a really good head on his shoulders." She looks at Sam and taps his head with a knuckle. "Check." Then back to me. "Next?"

"Number two, he had to be an old-fashioned gentleman. A guy who opens doors for you, compliments you, puts you first, treats you like a queen."

"Right. It's all coming back to me. A guy who knows how to treat a woman." She looks back at Sam and runs her hand down the side of his face. "Check." Back to me. "Three?"

"Third, he had to be a sweetheart. Sentimental. Romantic. A flowers and candy kind of guy who doesn't forget your birthday and gives you a gift without needing an occasion."

"A romantic, sentimental sweetheart." She looks at Sam and nods. "Check, check and check. Annndddd… fourth?"

"He had to be ambitious, have a good career and respect the fact that you had your own and not stand in your way. Treat you as an equal."

Back to Sam. "Yep. I'd say that's a check." Back to me. "Finally?"

"He had to be full of life and extremely cute, because classically handsome doesn't do anything for you. Boy next door type with a sense of fun."

"A fun, extremely cute boy next door, right, I remember." She runs her fingers through his hair. "Oh, that's a major check."

Finally Sam speaks. "Ripley—"

She puts one finger on his lips. "Shhhh. Ripley is talking and she has something very important to say. By the way, young man, when there's a girl on your lap you should support her back with your free hand. The other goes under my legs or around my waist."

Sam is still in shock and sitting there with his arms hanging down at his sides. "Uh-huh."

"Hands. Use 'em. Ripley needs to be held."

"Right." He wraps his arms around her waist and she leans

189

against him.

"Ah, yes, very nice. You comfortable?"

"Uhhhh…."

"I'll take that as a yes. Anyway, Sam… remember Christmas Eve when you told us that we both had *tells* when it comes to men? That, in my case, my eyebrows do this little jump when I see a man who turns me on. Remember that?"

"Uh-huh."

"Well, I was watching a video of us from a few years ago, someone's birthday party. Lotta people, lotta fun. And in the video there's one shot where I look at you. And you know what happened?"

"What?"

"My *tell*. Just like you said. Amazing. My eyebrows did that little jump. When I was looking at you. And I remember having three glasses of wine that night, just like tonight. Which makes me honest." She turns to me. "Anyway, Cassidy, it's just like seeing my words in the paper. Or, like you said, seeing yourself on television. So I'm watching this video and all of a sudden I'm thinking, *who is this girl? And why can't she see what the camera sees? Why doesn't she believe her own words when the newspaper prints them?* Sometimes you really don't know who you are unless you can see yourself through different eyes, another point of view. And then it hit me." She turns back to Sam, gently takes his chin in her hand and tilts it toward her face. "It hit me that you make my eyebrows jump like no one else. That I love how you look at me in that soulful way and make me feel like the most beautiful girl in the world. I love how you cook for me and always make my favorite things when I come over. I love how you don't let any obstacle stand in your way. I love how you treat your sister like a precious gem. I love the fact that your hair has never, ever been combed but always looks great. I love how you're protective, how you stood up and defended my honor like a white knight that time in the bar. I love that you'll spend hours playing gin rummy with me like we're

190

an old retired couple in Florida. I love that you love the same TV shows I do. I love how every time I'm feeling down I can put on this red dress because I know I'll get a compliment that will cheer me up and a look that will make me feel special. I love how when you're in Connecticut you stop at that old-fashioned candy store and get me a bag of licorice that I can't find anywhere else. I love how you've always respected me, the way you respect all women. Samuel Shea, I hope you can forgive me because I have been a complete idiot. The best guy in the world has been right in front of my nose and I couldn't see him. You are the perfect man on the list in my dorm room and I am terribly sorry it took me so damn long to realize it."

Sam's eyes are wide as his jaw hangs open.

I have the same look.

Ripley raises her wine glass. "Hold this a minute. Ripley is done with the verbal portion of her apology." Sam takes the glass. Ripley takes his head with both hands and kisses him, long and hard.

I'm in absolute shock and what I'm looking at brings a lump in my throat like never before. A single tear rolls down my cheek as I see the two people I love most making the ultimate connection.

After what seems like a beautiful moment frozen in time, their lips slowly part and she leans back. "So, am I forgiven?"

"Whuh?" says Sam, still stunned that his dream girl is sitting on his lap and has just planted a big one on him.

"For being an idiot. Am I forgiven? By my perfect man." She puts out her lower lip in a pout and bats her eyelashes. "Please don't make poor little Ripley get on her knees and beg."

"Apology accepted." Sam turns to me and we lock misty eyes, but he says nothing. I smile and nod, giving him the non-verbal go-ahead, then he turns back to Ripley. "Any chance you could apologize to me again?"

"I've got lots of apologies for you," she says. "Several years worth. Now, since I have deemed you ready to *drive off the lot*, why don't you roll us both over to your bedroom?"

I'm greeted with the wonderful aroma of frying bacon as I head down the stairs shortly after nine. I see heavy snow falling through the front window and know this will be a good day to be a couch potato.

I walk into the kitchen expecting to see Sam but instead find Ripley mixing pancake batter while bacon fries on a griddle.

"Morning!" she says, with a huge smile.

(It should be noted that Ripley is the antithesis of a morning person. In college she would get up at the crack of noon and anyone who gave her a cheerful greeting would receive "bite me" as a response.)

"My, aren't we up early, and ambitious." I walk around the kitchen island and see the only thing she's wearing is one of Sam's long-sleeved blue oxford shirts, unbuttoned halfway down, showing off her perfect boobs. "Well, that's a new look for you. Is this from the Hooters restaurant spring collection?"

"Couldn't cook in the red dress. And Sam seems to like this outfit."

"Gee, what a surprise. And since when do you do get up early to cook breakfast?"

"My growling stomach woke me up."

"After all that pizza?"

She gives me a sly smile. "Burned a lot of calories last night."

"Hey! That's my brother you… you know…"

She shrugs and turns back to preparing breakfast. "Hey, you know that fettuccine dish Sam cooks with the shrimp and scallops and the cajun spices?"

"You mean better-than-sex pasta?"

"Well, you need to change the name. Because it's not."

My jaw slowly drops.

She leans toward me and whispers in my ear. "Best. Sex. Ever."

"Ripley! Stop it!"

She leans back and smiles. "But you should know—"

I put up my hand. "I don't wanna know!" I put my hands over my ears. "La, la, la, la, la—"

"Okay, I'll stop!" she yells.

I drop my hands, then fold my arms. "Mind explaining what happened last night?"

"Just like I said. The newspaper article led me to the video and it all led me to the realization that what I was looking for was right under my nose."

"I hope you're sure about this. You know how Sam feels about you and if you broke his heart—."

"You have nothing to worry about, dear friend. I would never toy with his emotions. He has my heart and I'd be an idiot to look elsewhere. As you say in your poker games, I'm *all in* because I know I've got a winning hand. He's the perfect man and he worships the ground I walk on. About time I worshiped him."

"Then I'm beyond happy for you guys."

"And boy, did I worship him last night."

I roll my eyes, knowing any attempt to shut her up will be pointless. I hear Sam's bedroom door open and see him heading in our direction. "I smell something good." He shoots me a look of pure joy as he passes, then comes to a stop next to Ripley and his eyes widen since he's at the perfect level to look inside her shirt.

I shake my head. "You two give new meaning to the phrase *My eyes are up here.*"

Sam blushes as he looks up at her. "You need some help?"

"Nope," she says, running one hand through his hair, "for once I'm waiting on you. However…"

"Yes?"

She scratches her chin. "Well, the cooktop is a bit low. I need a better vantage point." She grabs the giant measuring cup filled with pancake batter, sits on his lap and begins pouring the batter on the griddle. "There. That's perfect." She turns to him and gives him her wide-eyed little girl look along with the innocent bimbo voice. "You have to keep a close eye on things if you want perfect pancakes. You don't want things to get too... hot."

Sam gulps. "Damn," he says, as he wraps his arms around her waist. "I could get used to this."

I can't help but smile. "Let me get some coffee, cause this is better than late night cable."

An hour later we all lean back, seriously satisfied after a delicious breakfast helped out a bit by that real maple syrup I brought back from New Hampshire. "Ripley, you've outdone yourself today," I say.

"Really, it was delicious," says Sam. "Loved the chopped pecans in the pancakes."

"Glad you enjoyed it," she says, giving him a kiss on the cheek as she gets up and starts clearing the table. "Wait till you see what I'm making you for lunch."

"I thought you had that weekend shoot with your client today," I say.

She points out the window. "Uh, the blizzard outside canceled it."

I glance out at the giant flakes piling up. "Oh, right."

"Just stay the whole weekend," says Sam, with a gleam in his eye.

I get up to help her with the dishes. "Really, you don't need to be out driving in this stuff. I'll get you some clothes."

"That's okay," she says, tracing his jawline with one long red fingernail. "Don't think I'll need any."

CHAPTER TWENTY

@TwitterGirl
It's Super Tuesday! President Turner puts "bring out your dead" scene from Monty Python movie on his website.

This is the big one.

Eleven primaries in one day, all across the country. I don't know how many frequent flyer miles we'll be logging, but I need to be at the top of my game. This is pretty much the make or break day for the candidates, as tomorrow we'll see some of the also-rans sent packing.

It might also be the day when Will Becker can lock up the nomination, or get pretty damn close.

By the way, the "top of my game" does not refer to Twitter, though I'll be tweeting all day.

Will wants me to accompany him to each and every stop. After the Valentine's Day scene turned into such a hit, the campaign higher-ups have been clamoring for this. I'll be by his side, doing the Tammy Wynette "stand by your man" thing in front of millions. And while it's nice that party leaders consider me to be an asset to the campaign, it's much more important that he considers me an asset to him personally.

Some are calling me "The New Jackie" in reference to JFK's

wife, who often got more attention than President Kennedy when they traveled together.

While I don't own a pillbox hat, I can't help but be flattered. Jackie Kennedy was an icon, and I don't remotely deserve the comparison. But I'm not turning it down. Besides, Will started calling me "Jackie" the other day with a Boston accent, and when he says it things seem perfect.

The party chairman wanted to buy me a whole new wardrobe but I know people who donate to a campaign don't want their money spent on clothes for a candidate's girlfriend, especially after that flak Sarah Palin got years ago about the cost of her wardrobe. Besides, I've got tons of great outfits the network bought me and don't want to appear like some diva. So I have two green outfits packed for today along with the emerald green dress I'm wearing. And it worked out well since the campaign logo is in Kelly green and that's my best color anyway.

The plane touches down in our first stop, Virginia Beach. I look out the window and see a cheering crowd waiting on the runway, waving Becker campaign signs.

And one I don't expect.

I heart Cassidy.

"They love you more than me, you know," says Will, leaning over my shoulder and looking out the window. "You and your damn approval ratings."

"I really don't get it."

"A good friend once told me you can't judge yourself. You need to look at yourself from other points of view. Cassidy, if you could see yourself the way I see you, the way the American people see you, you'd understand."

The engines cut off and Jessica opens the door of the plane.

Will extends his hand and does a Kennedy impression. "C'mon, Jackie. Your, ah, fan club awaits with, ah, great vigah."

I take his hand and we head down the aisle.

As soon as we hit the top of the stairs, the cheering begins.

And Will raises my hand with his own.

He starts waving and flashing that famous smile, so I follow suit as we make our way down the steps and over to a podium that has been set up. Will moves to the microphone as I stand next to him, still holding his hand. He gestures for the crowd to quiet down, then steals a line from JFK's Paris trip.

"Good morning. I do not think it entirely inappropriate to introduce myself to the audience. I am the man who has accompanied Cassidy Shea to Virginia."

The crowd roars and then they start chanting my name like a sports star. "Cass-i-dy! Cass-i-dy!"

The whirlwind has begun.

The returns are in. Will didn't run the table but won eight of the eleven primaries, coming in second in the other three. He still needs a few more delegates to lock up the nomination. So the race continues.

As for the returns on me, Frank says it was a clean sweep.

I've never felt such warmth and adoration as I have today, all of it undeserved. All because I'm dating a guy running for President.

The name chanting became a popular greeting as the day went on. I felt like a baseball player after a game-winning home run.

I received flowers everywhere we stopped, sampled food at probably a dozen restaurants and shops (no complaints on that), got a kiss from Will after every one of his speeches, and generally felt like royalty. I smiled so much today I think my face is now frozen like those women who use so much Botox it's impossible to tell if they're mad.

I'm also physically exhausted, and so is Will.

We had originally planned to fly back to New York tonight but he's doing live interviews for the West Coast so Frank pushed it back till tomorrow morning. Wheels up at eight.

Despite the wonderful day, I find myself once again alone in my hotel room, so wired I can't possibly go to sleep.

I need my FaceTime buddy.

I text Tyler on my cell. *"You still up and wanna talk?"*

I sit there at the desk in my room, drumming my fingers on the top, waiting for his usual lightning fast response.

Nothing happens.

I check my phone to make sure the text went out. I see that it did, just as Tyler responds.

"Just for a little while, okay?"

"Yay!" I quickly grab my iPad and hit the button to connect.

Tyler's face fills the screen, but it's not the smiling upbeat look I've gotten used to. He looks drawn, eyes sad.

"Hey, Tyler, you okay?"

"Just dealing with some personal stuff, that's all. Kind of a depressing day."

"I'm sorry. Anything I can do to help?"

"Not really."

"Well, I'll take you to lunch tomorrow. It's my job as a superhero to feed you and cheer you up."

"You're a *superheroine*. A female superhero is a superheroine."

"Whatever. In any event I patrol the streets keeping seriously cute men safe from depression with my snarky personality and food obsession."

I get a little smile. "Ah, so I'm seriously cute?"

"If the shoe fits, Tyler. So, what'd you think of the results tonight?"

"I'm happy. Would have been nice to wrap the thing up, but eight out of eleven is still terrific. How are you doing?"

"Exhausted but excited, if that makes any sense."

"Yeah, I could tell from the coverage. You looked great today with all the different outfits. Of course you'd look good in anything."

"Thank you, Tyler. I felt like a queen today."

"And you deserve to be treated like one. Well, glad you had a good time. Your tweets were hilarious as well. Listen, I'm gonna turn in. I'll see you tomorrow when you get back."

"Oh, okay. See you then. G'night."

"Night, T.G."

The screen goes dark and I see the conversation lasted a little longer than one minute. Usually we talk for more than an hour.

I can tell from his look something's wrong.

***

"No! Absolutely not! I don't give a damn if you are the head of the party, I'm not going to authorize that and neither will Frank. She'll be hurt, not to mention it will offend millions of Americans. I personally find it in really poor taste. And don't even *think* about having one of your secret political action committees doing it, because I'll find out and there will be hell to pay. You don't want what I know about you getting out." Tyler slams the phone down and looks up to find me standing in the doorway with my mouth hanging open. "Oh, sorry. Didn't know you were standing there. Now you know I have a dark side."

"Actually, nice to know you can get pissed off. What was that all about?"

He waves it away. "Nothing. Just a fire I had to put out."

"Nothing my ass. You said *she'll* be hurt. Unless Becker's had a sex change, I assume you were talking about me."

His face tightens and he exhales audibly as he leans back in his chair. "Fine. Close the door."

I do so, then take a seat next to him as I slide a gift basket on the table. "What's wrong, Tyler?"

"That was James Hennison, head of the party. He wanted to do something I thought was in seriously bad taste."

"Concerning me?"

He nods.

"What?"

199

"He suggested we do a poll on you and Becker."

"I thought some newspaper already did that."

"Not the same thing. He wanted a poll on... how far your relationship should go. Specifically, if conservative voters would be turned off if you two...you know..."

"What?"

"Had sex before getting married."

I sit up straight and my eyes widen. "You gotta be kidding me!"

"Nope. Someone high up in the party is worried that pre-marital sex would cost votes. I believe the term was *living in sin*."

I fold my arms as my eyes narrow. "Whose idea was this?"

"Don't know."

"C'mon, Tyler. You know everything. Spill."

"I'm being honest. I would never lie to you. If I knew who it was I'd kick their ass. In any event, I killed it."

"What's to prevent someone going rogue and doing it anyway?"

"Trust me, T.G., no one wants to deal with me if I'm pissed off. And I'd be really pissed off if someone hurt you. The idea is dead and buried."

"What was that you said?... *you don't want what I know about you getting out*... you've got blackmail material on Hennison?"

"No, but he doesn't know that. Look, everyone in politics has skeletons, but they don't know what I might have. I use that line on everyone so they assume I have something since they *all* have something to hide. Works every time."

"Pretty slick, Tyler."

"You probably shouldn't play poker with me."

"No, I guess not." I exhale some tension and relax a bit, then rest one hand on his shoulder. "Well, once again you saved me, superhero. I've really gotta get a nickname for you."

He finally notices I placed a huge basket of food on the table. "That your lunch box?"

"Very funny." I slide it in front of him. "Nope, this is for you. Yesterday I was really wishing you were along for the trip and I missed you, so I picked up a little something at every stop."

His face brightens as he pokes through the goodies in the basket. "Raspberry preserves, chocolates, nuts, cookies, a cupcake—"

"Well, there were, uh, two cupcakes."

He rolls his eyes.

"Kidding!"

His eyes light up as he continues looking at the contents. "This is really nice. You didn't have to go through all this trouble."

"Like you don't go out of your way for me. And after the way you looked last night, I'm glad I did. I hope this cheers you up a little."

"It does. Thank you, it's very thoughtful. No one's ever done anything like this for me."

"Well, I know you have a hard time traveling but I wanted you to feel like you're along for the ride."

His eyes start getting misty and he bites his lower lip.

I put my arm around his shoulders and give him a hug. "You sure you don't wanna talk about it?"

He shakes his head. "I can't."

"Well, whatever is bugging you, Tyler, just know I'm here to help if you need me. I'll always be there for you the way you are for me."

***

Kristin Becker stands up and smiles as I weave my way through the tables in the crowded restaurant. I hear my name whispered by several people who recognize me, some probably from TV, most from *Page Six*. The Senator's daughter shakes my hand as I arrive and take off my coat.

"Thanks for doing this, Cassidy," she says, as we both sit down.

"My pleasure. I'm flattered that you'd rather talk to me than hit a beach on spring break."

"My sister and I aren't much for partying and no one needs to see a candidate's daughter hammered on South Padre Island. We're more concerned about our careers, so any help you can provide is great."

"Well, I've always liked helping the interns at the network, and you need to know where all the minefields are if you're going into the business."

"Minefields?"

"Politics is worse, but TV news is another backstabbing industry. And, as I mentioned, people are already going to dislike you because they think you have an unfair advantage."

"Are you already telling me not to go into the business?"

"I'm just warning you what to expect in the real world. In college you have these rose colored glasses and view that you'll be able to change the world with a story, then you get your first job and realize the beancounters that run the place don't give a damn about anything but the bottom line."

She nods as she picks up the menu. "So it really is just like politics."

Kristin is a pleasant young lady, but not what I expected. Her dislike of politics seems to go beyond a simple distaste for the process. I can tell she's not wild about her father running for president and the possibility of being part of the nation's first family.

In any event, the topic of my dating her father has not come up, which makes me wonder if she approves. And I really need to know because I don't want to be one of those second wives who comes between a guy and his children.

"Kristin, I wanted to talk about what happened with me and your dad, and that photo—"

She smiles and waves her hand. "No big deal, Cassidy. We knew he had the hots for you and it was only a matter of time before he started dating again. I mean, he's not *that* old."

"Well, I was worried that seeing the photo before he had a

chance to talk to you would make you guys upset."

"No, it's fine. You seem like a good person and he really raved about you. And Cassidy, if your relationship becomes really serious, you don't have to worry about us being those types of kids who hate the second wife."

I exhale some tension. "Thank you, that's good to hear." I pause a moment, take a sip of water. "I lost my parents pretty young. Not as young as you two, but it still hurts."

"We were really close to mom. She home-schooled us, you know, so we were around her constantly. And with my father away so much it was almost like being raised by a single parent."

"Probably why you hate politics so much."

"That's a big part of it. I mean, my father loved mom and was great to us, he just wasn't around much. But when she lost the baby, it really changed her. She was never the same."

I sit up straight. "Oh, I didn't know."

"It's not common knowledge as it's very painful for my father to revisit and he doesn't ever talk about it. We had a little brother for a couple of days, but he was born with a lot of physical problems and died before he ever came home. Mom was devastated. Didn't even go to the funeral. Neither did we. Dad didn't want us to experience that."

"He was obviously trying to protect you."

"I guess. We tried our best to comfort her, but it was like part of her had died, like she had this hole in her heart that could never be filled. It had been one of those rough pregnancies where she had to stay in bed almost the whole nine months. Hardly anyone even knew she was pregnant. She was really shy, opposite of dad, and she didn't tell anyone because if she miscarried she didn't want to have to answer questions that were bound to make her cry. Anyway, we were little kids, we didn't know what to say. Dad stayed home for three months but it still didn't help. I mean, he was pretty depressed as well. I remember he had a priest come over just about every day after the baby died for a couple of weeks.

They would talk in his office for hours. Mom never looked at Dad the same after that, like she blamed him. We always felt there was something she wasn't telling us, but we could tell their relationship had gotten cold after that."

"I'm sorry to hear that. I almost lost my brother in a car accident that killed my parents, so I can relate."

"I read about him. That was a nice story. Sounds like you have a relationship like I have with my sister."

"Yeah, Sam's great. Couldn't live without him."

"I often wonder what our brother would have been like. If he'd take after mom or dad, or be a combination of both. But I guess it's a blessing that God took him. We'll meet him eventually. His name was Brian."

"So when did this happen?"

"Spring in 2005. He was born April thirteenth to be exact."

Missing time… off the grid.

This explains a lot.

Except… his perfect voting record.

CHAPTER TWENTY-ONE

@TwitterGirl
Gavin Turner making plans for his Presidential library. Already signed Crayola as a sponsor.

Finally, Will and I are going to go out tomorrow on an actual Saturday night date and spend the weekend together. His daughters are supposed to be in town and he managed to score four tickets to the hottest Broadway musical that has been sold out forever. It will be the first time we're all out together and I'm interested to see how the girls react. I'm planning to be very low key, with no public displays of affection beyond hand holding while they're around.

And when they're not around? Who knows. At least there's not a poll on that thanks to Tyler. But the whole staff has Monday off as we're pretty much fried from the whole Super Tuesday thing and Frank thinks we need a break. Will is looking tired and the public needs to see the energetic Senator who will revitalize the White House. Though the party nomination is close to being sewed up, we've still got seven months to go. It should be a knock down drag out affair against the President and he needs to pace himself.

So I'm walking with a spring in my step as I head into Will Becker's office.

And the spring pops when I see his face.

"Fine," he says, exhaling obvious disgust as he shakes his head. "I know I *have* to be there. At some point the public needs to know I'm doing my job as a Senator and they're not paying me to campaign all year. See you tonight." He ends the call and looks up at me. "Well, so much for our long weekend."

"What happened?"

"Special session of the Senate. It's a major vote that I cannot possibly miss, and the debate will probably go on all weekend with a vote on Tuesday or Wednesday."

"Well, as I heard you say, it *is* your job. I'll take your daughters to the play if they don't mind. It can be a girls' night out."

"Oh, and it turns out I screwed up on the dates when I got these tickets months ago. They have exams starting Monday and won't be here." He reaches in his desk, pulls out an envelope and hands it to me. "Take some of your friends."

"You can hand them out to the staff if you want to give out some rewards."

"Nah, you take 'em. I know much you wanted to see that show." He gets up and puts on his suit jacket. "Got a plane to catch. See you next week. I hope." He gives me a quick hug and kiss and heads out.

I open the envelope, look at the four tickets, and know immediately who to take. I head across the office to the war room and poke my head inside. "Hey, Tyler, you like Broadway musicals?"

"Love 'em. Why?"

"Becker can't go and I can't think of a better escort. Be my date tomorrow night?"

***

We pull out of the parking lot after the play, which was terrific. Sam maneuvers his van deftly through the Manhattan traffic and hops onto a bridge. "I've discovered a new place for cheesecake.

It's decadent. They've got a dozen flavors."

I'm hungry again so that's good news. I turn to Tyler who is sharing the back seat with me. "You hungry?"

"I never turn down cheesecake."

Ripley turns around and looks at us. "Neither does she."

I slap the back of her seat. "Stop it!" Everyone laughs as she turns back, facing front.

"That was a great musical, thanks for asking me," says Tyler.

"Hey, you're my go-to guy when I need a cute escort."

The cheesecake was sadly disappointing, and now I know why I never heard of this place just a mile from our home. I still have a sweet tooth as I climb back into the van at midnight.

Then it hits me.

"Sam, you forgot Tyler lives in Manhattan."

He slaps his forehead. "Oh, dammit. Sorry, Tyler, I'm so used to driving back to the island."

"That's okay. Just drop me off at the ferry," says Tyler.

"You won't get home till one or two," says Sam.

"Well, you're not driving me. Then *you'll* get home at two."

I see Sam's eyes light up in the rear view mirror. "Hey, why don't you stay with us again?"

"You sure?"

"Loved having you the last time."

Tyler looks at me, sort of asking for permission.

"Yeah, stay with us," I say. "Of course, there is a charge. You'll have to do some baking for Sunday brunch."

"If that's the only condition, I'd love to stay."

"Scones!" I yell.

"I'm just a source of food for you," says Tyler. "But…"

"But what?"

"I don't have a change of clothes with me."

Ripley turns around. "Hey Cassidy, didn't your old boyfriend leave some clothes behind? That guy you dated about three years ago? He was about Tyler's size."

"Yeah, you're right, they're in the basement. I never got around to bringing them to Goodwill." I reach over and pat Tyler's hand. "You're covered. And since we're off Monday, you can stay a couple of days."

"You sure?"

"Hey, how much fun was the last weekend you spent with us?"

"Okay. Oh, speaking of Monday, it's opening day and I've got Mets tickets. You guys wanna go?"

"I can't take the day off," says Ripley.

"Me neither," says Sam. "Not all of us get long weekends on a whim."

"Hey, we've been working our asses off," I say.

"Yeah, flying on a private jet and changing outfits is tough," says Ripley. "Cue the violins."

"Hey, you don't see all the behind-the-scenes stuff." I say, then turn to my escort. "Looks like you and me, Tyler. Play ball."

***

We make our way in the bright sunshine down the aisle toward the dugout. It's a perfect day for a baseball game as spring is definitely in full bloom, about seventy degrees with a light breeze. I've got my hair up under a baseball hat along with sunglasses which will hopefully let me go unrecognized. Bottom line, I'm a jeans and sweatshirt kind of girl, and it's nice to put the Jackie Kennedy thing aside for a day.

We continue as the usher leads us farther down and I realize we've got really terrific seats. "Geez, Tyler, how'd you get such great seats for opening day?"

"Friends in high places," he says with a smile, as we arrive at our seats in the first row next to the dugout.

"Wow, I've never sat so close before. Beats the hell out of the press box."

"You want anything? These seats actually come with a waiter."

"You mean if I want a hot dog you're not gonna go get it for me?"

"Nope. I figured with your appetite I'd miss the whole game."

"Okay, very funny. I'll wait till the game starts before I begin my feeding frenzy."

I glance out at the beautifully manicured field as the Mets take batting practice and run in the outfield. They finish up and head for the dugout.

One of their star players I instantly recognize looks directly at Tyler and smiles, then jogs toward us and stops in front of the rail, extending his hand. "Hey, Tyler, glad you could get away from the campaign."

Tyler shakes his hand. "How could I miss opening day with you pitching?"

"You two know each other?" I ask.

The player smiles, turns around and points to the name on the back of his uniform.

Garrity.

"Meet my brother Sean," says Tyler. "Sean, this is—"

"Twitter Girl, yeah, I know. Hi, Cassidy."

"Hi." I turn to Tyler. "You didn't tell me your brother played for the Mets."

"You didn't ask."

"He keeps me under wraps because I'm the underachiever in the family," says his brother, a strapping athlete with eyes that match Tyler's. Sean Garrity is baseball's version of Tim Tebow, a squeaky clean guy. "He got the brains, I got the curve ball."

"Well, it's nice to meet you, Sean."

"I feel like I know you already," he says. "You met my wife Rachel at the Giants playoff game."

"Oh, that was her? She's terrific. And that's why you were in Florida. Spring training."

"Yep. But Tyler takes good care of her when I'm away," he says.

"He takes good care of me, too."

"Well, it's nice to finally meet you. I've heard so much about you."

I turn to Tyler. "Really. So you've been talking about me?"

"You're *all* he talks about," says the ballplayer. "Well, gotta go warm up if I'm gonna start this game." He tips his cap to me. "Nice meeting you, Twitter Girl. Now take good care of my brother."

"Again, I think it's the other way around."

Sean turns and jogs toward the bullpen.

"So, that explains the great seats."

Tyler nods. "Well, in addition to being his brother I do act as his agent. I negotiated his last contract and all of his endorsement deals. Part of the deal with the Mets was great season tickets."

"Tyler, you never cease to amaze me. Meanwhile, I'm *all* you talk about?"

"He's exaggerating. I may have mentioned you a time or two."

* * *

I open the door Tuesday night and find Dale Carlin carrying several very fat manila envelopes. "That's what you got from the IRS?"

He nods as he enters our home. "You wanted his tax returns and financial statements. When you're worth millions, you generate a lot of paperwork."

We walk to the kitchen and he puts the envelopes down on the table. "Remember, a lot of this is caused by single transactions. Every time there's one over ten thousand dollars, it gets flagged by Internal Revenue. I'm sure most of these are things like stock transactions, that sort of thing. But if we're going to find a large amount of missing money, it's going to be in this pile."

Sam comes over to the table. "You guys look like you could use some help."

I sit down, grab one of the envelopes and slide it over to him.

"We've gotta do this the old fashioned way. If you see anything with our magic number, that's what we're looking for."

I write the number in bold magic marker on a sheet of paper and tape it to the back of the only empty chair so we can all see it. Dale sits down and grabs an envelope while I do the same.

"This reminds me of that scene in *All the President's Men*," he says. "Where Redford and Hoffman are in the Library of Congress going through that mountain of slips."

"So this is old fashioned legwork," says Sam, as he begins going through the stack of papers.

"Technology can be wonderful, but you can't google a great story," says Dale.

An hour later we're about halfway through. At this point we've all got the magic number memorized, so things are moving a little faster.

"Damn, this guy's got a lotta money," says Sam.

"Dad founded Becker Industries," says Dale. "And Will inherited fifty percent when the guy passed away."

My eyes are bugging out at some of the amounts on the papers. "I knew he was loaded, but this is unreal."

"Careful," says Dale, "or people will start calling you a gold digger."

"I wouldn't care if he was broke."

Suddenly Sam sits up straight. "Hey, I got something."

Dale and I both get up and look over his shoulder. The number matches, and the figure next to it is large enough to raise a big red flag.

Two million dollars.

Transferred in May of 2005, which falls in that "missing time" period.

But there are also letters in front of the number.

EIN.

"Well, that's a big chunk of change," says Dale.

"What the hell is EIN?" I ask.

"No clue," says Dale.

Sam pulls his tablet from a pouch on the side of his chair. "I'll look it up." He turns it on and does a quick search typing in the three letters. "Well, that was easy. It's an employer identification number used by the IRS. Basically like a social security number for any business entity."

Dale looks at me. "So he transferred two million to a business."

"Sam, type in our magic number with EIN in front of it."

My brother does so but gets no results. "Nothing. Apparently they're also as private as social security numbers."

"I'll have to get back to my contact at the IRS," says Dale.

"So, what do you think it is?" I ask.

Dale shrugs. "Could be something as innocent as a subsidiary of Becker Industries. Maybe a venture capital deal. Or, with him being a politician, could be some sort of bribe or payoff."

I really don't want to believe that. "That last part doesn't sound like Will."

"I'm sure it isn't, but let me call my contact and find out. I'm sure once we can put a name with that number all the pieces of the puzzle will fall into place. Let's go through the rest of the papers to see if we find something else."

We return to our chairs and begin sorting through the remainder of the papers.

Dale stops suddenly. "Oh, speaking of puzzle pieces, I do have an answer about his perfect record in Congress while he was supposedly at home. It's called *ghost voting*."

"What's that?"

"That's when a member of Congress knows he's going to be absent and gets another member to vote for him. Apparently it's against the rules but as we all know the rules don't really apply to anyone in Congress. I don't know who voted for Becker while he was gone, but I did confirm that he was not in Washington for three months."

CHAPTER TWENTY-TWO

@TwitterGirl
Price of gasoline is so high Congress to explore drilling rights to President Turner's head.

I stick my head in Tyler's office. "Hey, what are you doing for dinner?"

"Hadn't thought about it, why?"

"I was wondering if you'd like to join me."

"Top Dog get called away again?"

I move into the office. "No, it has nothing to do with him. I feel like having dinner with *you*, okay? And there's this great new Mexican place uptown that I recently discovered. C'mon, my treat."

"I love Mexican. You sure I'm not keeping you from your main squeeze?"

"We're not joined at the hip, Tyler. I'll see plenty of him on the long road trip later this week and I won't see you. So I need my Tyler fix before I leave."

"Oh, so you're addicted to me?"

"Can't I simply take a good friend out to dinner without an interrogation?"

We arrive at the subway platform, which is about ten degrees warmer than it is outdoors while the air is stagnant. It's crowded as usual, filled with what I call the "commuting undead." People who are so fried from work they look like zombies on the train. Amazingly, no one recognizes me, or, if they do, they're too tired to even shoot me a look of recognition.

"We could have taken a cab," says Tyler, who I know is not fond of the subway.

"Too much traffic, and I already made a reservation." Suddenly the hot platform has made me thirsty. "Hey, you want a soda?"

"I'm good."

"Be right back."

I head to the little stand selling newspapers, drinks and snacks, my mouth watering for something cold. I grab a bottle of Dr. Browns root beer—.

"Oh my God!"

I whip my head around toward the source of the woman's scream and see two things.

A little girl, maybe five years old, on the subway tracks, dangerously close to the third rail that would electrocute her.

And a train heading straight for her.

A transit cop is already running toward the child, but he's at the far end of the platform and I don't think he'll make it.

The train is getting closer. Its brakes put out an ear-piercing squeal as the motorman has obviously noticed the child.

And then Tyler jumps onto the tracks.

"Tyler!"

The soda drops from my hand, crashing to the platform. I start running toward Tyler, who has reached the child.

The train is bearing down on them.

I can see the motorman's face, filled with dread.

He knows he can't stop the train in time.

The commuting undead are paralyzed, staring at the scene.

Tyler picks up the child and runs back to the platform. I reach the spot at the same time as the transit cop and kneel down at the edge of the platform.

My eyes lock with Tyler's for a split second. I somehow know what he's going to do, so I open my arms wide and he tosses the little girl toward me.

I catch her and fall backward.

The transit cop reaches out for Tyler, grabs both his hands and yanks him off the tracks a split second before the train roars by.

The crowd starts to surround us. The hysterical mother grabs the child from me and hugs her for dear life as I brush myself off and start to get up. "My God, Tyler, you could have been—"

He's not moving.

"He hit his head on the pole," says the transit cop, who grabs his radio. "Need paramedics right now on the northbound subway platform…"

His words fade and all goes silent. I crawl toward Tyler as blood runs fast down his forehead. I need something to apply pressure and stop the bleeding. I reach up for my scarf but I've forgotten it on my desk.

The blood is flowing faster.

I need something.

I rip off some fabric from the hem of my dress and apply pressure with it as I lift his head off the ground and rest it in my lap. The cop takes his pulse. "You his wife?"

"Good friend."

"What's his name?"

"Tyler Garrity."

The cop gently pats Tyler's face. "Hey Tyler, wake up. C'mon buddy, wake up."

But he doesn't.

My arms are wrapped around my waist as I pace in the cold waiting room that smells of antiseptic. People have been staring at me, not from recognition but from the fact I'm walking around with a bloody ripped dress. It's been two hours, and the longer I wait the more I worry. Tyler was still unconscious when they brought him in. The paramedics told me it was obviously a concussion, but the cop told me he hit his head really hard, which makes me wonder if it's something more serious. I couldn't get in touch with Will but did talk to Frank, who's on his way from Jersey.

The waiting room is about half full. Some are watching the television mounted on the wall. The sound on the TV is low, but loud enough for people to hear. I glance up as the newscast is starting, and see a grainy black and white surveillance video from the subway platform.

Tyler's heroism is the lead story.

I walk toward the TV to get a closer look. Everyone in the waiting room watches in amazement as the video shows the child falling onto the tracks and Tyler jumping in a few seconds later. The video runs normal speed, then goes slow motion as the transit cop pulls Tyler out just as the subway car rolls by. He had inches to spare.

The bright red graphic across the bottom of the screen describes it perfectly.

Subway Hero.

"Garrity?"

The doctor's voice breaks my concentration and I move quickly toward him. "I'm with Tyler Garrity." My words are thick in my throat. "Is he—"

"He's stable, but he's in a coma."

My hands go to my face. "Oh my God…"

The doctor takes my shoulders. "Look, it's a bad concussion and he'll probably be fine. We just have to wait for him to wake up?"

"How long do you think that will be?"

"No way of knowing. Five minutes, five days. The body is healing itself, and when it's done he'll wake up. But he's out of immediate danger and we've transferred him to a private room."

"Can I see him?"

"Are you related?"

"Do I need to be?"

The doctor rolls his eyes, then notices the blood on my dress. "Okay, *Mrs. Garrity*. Go ahead. Room 225 down the hall."

Tyler's breathing is steady. I'm sitting in a chair close to the bed so I can hold his hand. The EKG machine emits a steady low beep. My head rests on the mattress, as I'm emotionally drained.

I hear a gentle tap on the door and look up to see Sam and Ripley, who is wheeling a carry-on bag. "How's he doing?" she asks.

"Still in a coma."

"The video was incredible," says Sam, as they move to the other side the bed. "I mean, talk about brave. Tyler's got some brass ones."

"Does he have family here?" she asks.

"Only his brother the ballplayer, who's on the way. The others live in California. Flying out on the red eye."

"Have you been here all by yourself?"

"No. Most of the campaign people came by. Frank just went down to the coffee shop and will be right back. The woman whose daughter he saved was here. Bunch of reporters talked to me about what happened." I look at the carry-on. "Ripley, you going somewhere?"

"No, but we figured you weren't and I saw your dress on the video. Brought you some fresh clothes and a bunch of snacks."

"You know me too well. I don't want him waking up alone."

"Why don't you take a shower and change out of that bloody thing and we'll keep a close eye on him."

"Not right now, Ripley."

"Sure, sweetie. Whenever you're ready."

A nurse wanders in carrying a clipboard and looks at me. "I'm sorry Miss, but we don't have any cots available. You can spend the night in one of our empty rooms if you like."

I shake my head. "No, I'll stay in here with him. This chair will be fine."

"You're a good friend," she says, as she leaves.

I lay my head back on the mattress and stare at Tyler, watch

217

his chest go up and down as he breathes.

C'mon, dammit, wake up.

Two hours later Sam and Ripley are gone and Tyler's brother is sleeping in the room across the hall after offering to take over the watch. My back starts barking from the stiff chair. I'm not sure I can get any sleep in this thing.

But I'm not leaving him alone.

I'm not leaving him, period.

Fortunately he's in a decent sized bed. I move to the other side and lay down next to him, taking his hand. I lean over and kiss the top of his head, stroke his hair, then whisper in his ear. "Wake up, Tyler. I can't lose you. Follow my voice. Focus. Take my hand and follow my voice. Concentrate."

I squeeze his hand, my fingers entwined with his, hoping for a response. But nothing happens. I lay my head on the pillow. The emotion of the day catches up to me and I'm out cold in a matter of seconds.

***

"Cassidy?"

I crack open one eye and see Frank a few feet from the bed. "Oh, hey Frank. What time is it?"

"Nine. You stayed here all night?"

"Yeah." I quickly turn, hoping to see Tyler has woken up, but he's still got his eyes closed. I gently pat his face. "Tyler? C'mon, wake up."

"I'm sure he'll come around soon," says Frank, trying his best to look convincing. "The doctor said he should be okay."

I sit up and get out of the bed. "I sure hope you're right, but I'm worried you're not. Where's Will? He never called back last night."

"Full schedule today. Couple of speeches, big fundraiser, then

218

off to the west coast."

"He's not coming by?"

"Don't think he can make it."

"*You* made it, Frank."

He looks down at the ground. "Will sent flowers."

"*You* made it, Frank. Twice. And so did everyone else in the campaign."

"Listen, about the road trip—"

"I'm not going anywhere till Tyler wakes up. And if the fact that Jackie Kennedy isn't along for the ride upsets some people in the party, I don't give a damn."

"That's fine, Cassidy. I was going to say you could do your Twitter Girl thing from here, but if you don't feel like it don't worry about it."

"Thank you. I don't exactly feel snarky today. But don't plan on my being back at the campaign office till Tyler's better."

"Not a problem, Cassidy. It was really nice of you to stay. You want me to go get you some coffee and something to eat before I have to go?"

"That would be nice. Thanks, Frank."

"Okay, be right back. And remember, please call me the minute he wakes up."

"Will do, Frank."

The phone in the room rings as soon as he leaves so I answer it. "Tyler Garrity's room."

"Hi, this is James Hennison. Who's this?"

"Cassidy Shea."

"Oh, hi. Looking forward to meeting you soon."

"Yeah, same here." And I'm gonna give you a piece of my mind when I do.

"How's Tyler?"

"Stable but still in a coma. So nothing new to report."

"Well, I'm sure he'll come around. Tell him I called when he wakes up. We're all praying for him."

"Sure, James." What the hell, I've got the guy on the line and time to let him know he can't push me around. "Hey, before you go... can I ask you something?"

"Shoot."

"Why did you think it was a good idea to do the *sex before marriage* poll?"

Dead silence.

"James, you there?" (Damn, wish this was via FaceTime so I could see the bastard sweat.)

"You, uh, weren't supposed to know about that."

"Well, I happened to walk in Tyler's office when he reamed you a new one."

"Look, when the candidate wants to do something, I try to go along. Will really wanted to know how the voters would react if you two... you know."

My jaw drops and my eyes become saucers.

You gotta be kidding me.

It was Will's idea.

More dead silence, this time from my end as I'm trying to process information I never expected.

"Cassidy?"

"Uh, yeah, James. Listen, you need to know something about me. I will not be used in this campaign. You wanna parade me around as his girlfriend, fine, but you do not have the right to control my personal life because of some poll. Are we clear?"

"Sure, Cassidy. I'm sorry you found out about it."

"Don't let it happen again."

I slam down the phone.

I'd give Will a piece of my mind as well, but he's not here.

And I'm beginning to think Sam was right again.

***

"I don't think I've ever seen you without an appetite."

Ripley gives me a soulful look as I nibble at my sandwich while keeping an eye on Tyler. "I'm just sick about this. And it's my fault."

"How the hell is it your fault?"

"I was the one who invited him to dinner. He wanted to take a cab but I made us take the subway. If I had just listened to him—"

I feel my eyes well up as I bite my lower lip. Ripley comes over and starts rubbing my shoulders. "And if you hadn't taken the subway, a little girl would be dead. God needed you to be there."

"Stop using logic on me."

"Things happen for a reason, Cassidy. I *know* Tyler's going to be all right. Have you watched TV today?"

"No."

"You should see the newscasts. The whole city is praying for their newest hero to wake up. They had a special vigil at Saint Pat's. God's got a whole lot of people bending his ear. He wouldn't take Tyler away from us. Or away from you."

"I guess."

"So, was Will upset that you're not going on the trip?"

I shrug. "If he showed up I'd ask him."

She furrows her brow. "You're kidding me… he hasn't been by?"

I shake my head. "Nope. Apparently he's too busy at ten thousand dollar a plate fundraisers. Everyone else at the campaign managed to visit, every single person, even the interns. All I got was a voice mail message from Will. Tried to call him back to tell him to get his ass down here but no luck. And that's not the worst part."

"What?"

I shake my head, still in disbelief. "He's the one who wanted to do the poll on whether we should have sex before marriage."

She sits up straight as her eyes widen. "Excuse me? He was the one?"

"Yep. Hard to believe, huh?"

"Have you talked to him about it?"

"No. And I'll do that face to face."

"Geez, Cassidy, that's really insensitive of him, don't you think?"

"At this point I don't know what to think."

She folds her arms. "Well, *I* do, but I'm sure you don't wanna hear it."

"Not now, Ripley. My emotions have too much on their plate right now. And right now Tyler's the only one I'm thinking about."

There are still no cots available, and even if there were I doubt I'd sleep in one. One of the doctors said it's important for people in comas to have audio and physical stimulation, so I've been talking to him all day and holding his hand. Reading all the great newspaper stories about him. Hoping he can hear me, follow my voice. Can feel my touch and let me lead him out of the darkness.

As I crawl into bed next to him, I realize I lied to Ripley.

Tyler's not the only one I'm thinking about.

As I fall asleep, I'm wondering who the hell Will Becker really is.

***

"I must be dreaming. There's a smoking hot redhead in my bed."

My eyes flicker open and I see Tyler looking at me, sleepy eyes open about halfway. "Oh my God, you're awake!"

"So this isn't a dream?"

I quickly wrap my arms around him and give him a strong hug. "God, Tyler, I thought I'd lost you."

"Water."

"Huh?"

"Water. Now. I'm dying of thirst."

"Right." I grab the pitcher that is sitting on the table next to the bed, pour him a glass and hand it to him. He starts to guzzle it but I grab his hand. "Take your time."

He slows down, drains the glass, then holds it out. "More."

"Sure." I refill it and he takes a few more sips.

"What the hell happened?"

"When the transit cop pulled you off the tracks you hit your head on a pole and it knocked you out. You've been in a coma."

"A coma? How long?"

"Two days. How are you feeling?"

"A little dizzy and very hungry."

"Hang on, let me go get a doctor." I lean forward and kiss him on top of the head. "Great to have you back, Tyler."

***

@Twitter Girl
New York's subway superhero Tyler Garrity is awake! Thanks for your prayers but keep 'em coming! He'll be home in a few days!

Tyler props himself up with two pillows. "So, let me get this straight. I have to be here two more days for observation, so you're going to stay here and observe me?"

"Yep. Gonna watch you like a cranky sex-starved nun in Catholic school."

"Are there any other kind?"

"Not really."

"You should really catch up with the campaign. Viper will arrange a plane—"

"Already told Frank I'm not going anywhere till you get discharged. He's okay with it. I can do my Twitter Girl thing from here if I feel like it, and right now I feel like observing you."

"Becker looks better with you at his side."

The thought actually makes me cringe. "Right now you need me at *your* side. You gonna push the nurse's call button if you slip back into a coma? No, of course not. Because, duh, you'll be *unconscious*. So shut up and commence being observed." I do that

223

I'm watching you thing cops on TV do with their fingers.

"Yes, Nurse Ratched."

"Well, I can tell from that comment you're getting better."

"So what's for dinner? If it's hospital food, just shoot me now."

"Hell no. You'll never get well eating that cardboard mystery meat. I put in an order for shrimp scampi pizza."

"You're going out to Staten Island to get me a pizza?"

"They're bringing it here. Tyler, you're like a real life Batman to this city. People want to do things for you. The guys at the pizza place were thrilled when I called and told them who it was for."

A gentle tap on the door grabs our attention. I figure it's the pizza but turn and see the little girl Tyler saved along with her mom.

"We heard you were up," says the mother, a slender, thirtyish brunette who leads her daughter over to the bed. "I'm Jeannine Frazier. And this little bundle of trouble is Samantha."

"Hi there," says Tyler.

Tears roll down the woman's cheeks and her voice cracks. "I know I can't thank you enough for saving my daughter's life. And risking your own."

"Doctor says I'll be fine."

"Thank you for saving me," says the little blonde girl. Which of course, makes everyone's eyes well up.

The mother runs her hand over the girl's head. "It happened so fast. My other daughter got away from me and when I turned to grab her this one fell on the tracks. Thank God you were there. Oh, Samantha has a favor to ask of you. Go ahead, honey." She pushes her daughter toward Tyler.

The little girl is carrying one of New York's tabloids and hands it to Tyler. "Can I have your autograph? Sign your picture for me?"

"Sure, sweetie."

"I've got a pen," I say, as I grab my purse and pull one out. I hand it to Tyler and as I do I see the front page of the paper.

A photo of me and Tyler. He still unconscious in the hospital bed, me in the chair wearing a torn dress covered with blood, leaning forward with my chin on the mattress, eyes locked on him while holding his hand.

The headline says it all.

Vigil for a Hero

***

Tyler is starting to yawn even though it's only ten o'clock. Despite being in a hospital bed, he's had a busy day between the visits from media people, friends and family. Sam and Ripley showed up after work and we played cards for an hour.

President Turner, probably sensing Will Becker had missed a photo op that was an absolute no-brainer, flew up from Washington with the entire White House press corps and told Tyler that he will be invited to the Oval Office when he's well.

Turner shook his hand while posing for pictures and called him "a real American hero."

Governor Schilling, seeing this, also dropped by with a basket of goodies from the Garden State which included a huge box of delicious salt water taffy. (Okay, so I sampled a few pieces.)

The Mayor of New York visited and told Tyler he would be getting the key to the city and have a day in his honor. Tyler's brother Sean brought a bunch of his teammates, while a few of the New York Giants dropped by with an autographed football.

Everyone but Will Becker.

That photo on the cover of the tabloid has gone viral and I have a new nickname. Jackie Kennedy has been replaced with Florence Nightingale.

Meanwhile, some media people are privately wondering why Will Becker never showed up to visit one of the main guys in his campaign who has known him for years.

They're not the only ones.

But again, Tyler is my priority right now.

"You look like you're fading," I say, sitting on the cot that was finally delivered.

"Yeah, I'm about ready to crash. And you probably need to sleep in your own bed. Seriously, you can go home. You've done too much for me already."

"We already discussed this, Tyler. They don't make rounds as often in the middle of the night and I want to be here just in case."

"Well, okay. I do love your company."

I grab one of the newspapers with Tyler's photo on the front page. "Hey, how about a bedtime story?"

"Huh?"

"You haven't read any of these yet. Don't you wanna know what people are saying about you?"

He shrugs. "I'll read them eventually."

"Well, let me read one." I get up and walk toward the bed, then sit on the corner and look at the newspaper. "Once upon a time, there was a very brave, seriously cute guy named Tyler…"

"That's not in the paper."

"Kidding. Okay, here it is for real." I open the paper and start to read.

I close the newspaper and place it on the table next to the bed. "Now, when was the last time someone read you a bedtime story with a happy ending like that?"

"Thank you, that was really nice. Can I go to sleep now?"

"Sure. I'll get the lights."

I get up, move to the door and close it almost all the way, then turn out the lights. Moonlight spills into the room through the large window, so I can still see where I'm going. I head into the bathroom and change into a long sleep shirt, then go back to the cot.

"You sure you're gonna be able to sleep on that thing?" he asks. "It doesn't look very comfortable."

"I'm not going home, Tyler, so stop asking me or I'll hit you

226

with a ruler."

He smiles at me. "Okay, T.G. Pleasant dreams."

"You too." I lay back on the cot, which is actually very soft. "Wow, it's a pillow top cot. I didn't know such things existed."

"So it's comfortable?"

"Very. Much nicer than what you're sleeping on."

"Yeah, this mattress is kinda hard."

I lay on my side facing Tyler and see he is still looking at me. "What?"

"I'm just really lucky to know someone like you, that's all. You're really special to me. And you look like an angel in this light."

I get a lump in my throat as he smiles and locks eyes with me for a moment.

And for a moment… I feel something I've never felt and cannot explain.

He closes his eyes and turns his head to the side.

I throw back the blanket, get up, walk to the bed, get in, and lay down on my side facing him.

He opens his eyes. "I thought you had a good mattress," he says.

"The cot has a very nice mattress. But I need to be *comfortable*." I slide closer and rest my chin on his chest. "And like I said, I need to keep close watch on you." I place one hand over his heart and look up at him. "I'm nurse Cassidy and I'll be monitoring your heartbeat this evening. Think of me as a human EKG machine. Goodnight, superhero."

Our eyes connect again in the moonlight for a moment, then I lay my head on his chest.

Tyler wraps one arm around my shoulders and pulls me close.

This time I'm not thinking of Will Becker as I fall asleep.

CHAPTER TWENTY-THREE

@TwitterGirl
Tyler Garrity goes home today! And all is right with the universe…

After a huge news conference for Tyler in which he works the crowd like a pro, I take him home, then head down to the campaign headquarters. It's manned by a skeleton crew today, since most of the staff is on the road trip. Frank said there was no point in my flying all the way to California to meet them since everyone would be back soon, but that he needed me to do my Twitter Girl thing during tonight's debate.

So I find myself with a lot of free time this afternoon.

And a lot of questions.

As my cell rings and I see who's calling, I'm thinking one of them is about to be answered. "Hi Dale."

"Hey, Cassidy. How's your hero friend?"

"Just released from the hospital. He'll be back to normal in no time."

"Good to hear. That was an incredible piece of video."

"Yeah, no kidding."

"But that's not why I called. My contact found out what the number belongs to. It's not a business."

228

"I thought those EIN numbers were for businesses."

"In most cases they are. In this case, it's for a private trust."

"What, you mean like those things rich people set up for their kids?"

"Yeah."

"So is it something his daughters tap into when they turn twenty-one?"

"I don't know what it's for, Cassidy, because it's a private trust and all I got was the name. But it doesn't sound like it is set up for his two girls."

"Why not?"

"It's called the Brian Fillorio Trust."

"Who the hell is Brian Fillorio?"

"No clue, but I don't have time to look as Air Hump One is about to take off. Good luck with this, Cassidy."

"Thanks so much, Dale, I appreciate it."

I end the call and with the afternoon off I put my reporter's hat back on.

And it feels damn good.

***

After an Internet search and a visit to the campaign archives, I have no new information. There is no connection between Will Becker and someone named Brian Fillorio. There's not a single person in the entire country with that name, and only a few people with the surname.

Sam is busy cooking as I head into the kitchen and give him a big hug.

"Well, look who finally came home."

"I'm fried. Very stressful week."

"But at least it had a happy ending." Sam covers the pot as she turns to me. "I almost hate to ask, but did Becker ever show up?"

I shake my head and look down. "Nope. Too busy raising money on the west coast. And there's something else, Sam. Something really bad. He was the one who wanted the poll on whether or not we should have sex."

Sam's face tightens. "Caz, I know you don't wanna hear it, but that's a bunch of big red flags."

"Yeah, I know. Ripley implied as much."

Sam turns his attention back to the stove and stirs the contents of a small saucepan. "What you did for Tyler was amazing."

"Hell, what *he* did was amazing."

"True enough. He get home okay?"

"Yeah, dropped him off after his news conference and his family is gonna stay with him. I don't think that guy's ever gonna have to pay for a drink in a bar for the rest of his life. President Turner came by. The Mayor visited and said he'll be getting a key to the city."

"That's nice. Tyler's a great guy."

"Yeah, he is. Meanwhile, in a related story, Dale found out the identity of the magic number. It's not a business, but a private trust for someone named Brian Fillorio."

"Who's that?"

"Haven't been able to find out. It's a real dead end. Can't even find someone with that name."

"That makes no sense," says Sam.

And then it hits me.

"I often wonder what our brother would have been like. If he'd take after mom or dad, or be a combination of both. But I guess it's a blessing that God took him. We'll meet him eventually. His name was Brian."

The pieces of the puzzle can't possibly fit together that way, can they? Missing time, a baby only lived two days, no funeral, a priest at the house…

I know it but cannot prove it.
You have resources I do not.

And suddenly I think I know who my anonymous source is.

I stand bolt upright, my eyes wide. "Oh my God..."

"What?"

"I think I figured it out. When I had lunch with Becker's daughter, she told me her mother had a baby with a lot of health problems that only lived two days and his name was Brian."

"I never heard that story. Is it in his bio?"

"It's nowhere to be found."

"How does the media not know this?"

"Becker kept it quiet. You can do that when you're filthy rich. His daughter said her mom had a difficult pregnancy and was in bed for nine months. That her parents didn't tell anyone in case she miscarried so she wouldn't have to answer painful questions. And when the baby died Becker's wife and kids didn't go to the funeral because it would have been too depressing. She said for weeks afterward there was a priest at the house and her mother was angry at Becker after that and never got over it."

"Cassidy, you've lost me. What does this have to do with a trust?"

"Hang on a minute. Gotta check something. Dear God, please let my network access code still work."

I run to my laptop, turn it on and hit the bookmark that takes me to the network's information site. I type in my user name and password, hit enter, and cross my fingers. "C'mon, please—"

Welcome, Cassidy Shea

Thankfully, the lazy slug in the network's IT department hasn't deleted my account. I navigate to the section that can search personal information and start to fill in the blanks.

Name: Brian Becker

Date range: April, 2005

I hit enter and drum my fingers on the table as the little hour-glass spins.

The information I need pops up.

"Okay, that part checks. He was born on April thirteenth."

"But you knew that already, right?" asks Sam.

"Right. Now for the part I need to clear up." I navigate to death records and fill in the blanks. And wait.

The little hourglass spins, and when the screen clears my blood runs cold.

Your search has returned no results.

"Dear God, Sam…"

"What does this mean?"

"It means there's no death certificate, which means Becker has a son out there. Somewhere."

"That doesn't make any sense. Why would his daughter tell you the baby died?"

"Because that's what her father told *her*." I lean back in my chair as I try to process everything. "Okay, so we've got a three month leave of absence from Congress, two million dollars in a trust fund for a person who apparently doesn't exist, a dead baby with no death certificate and a wife who suddenly hates her seemingly perfect husband. Then, as soon as Becker goes back to Congress he announces his candidacy for the Senate."

"You said the baby had a lot of health problems? And that his wife was in bed for nine months?"

"Yeah, that's what his daughter told me."

"So, let's say the baby needed constant care and his wife was recovering from a tough pregnancy. And they had two small daughters at the time. Would he have been able to run for the Senate?"

I don't want to believe it, but the reporter in me is saying it all makes sense. "Becker would have had to wait six years for the next Senate election, and he would have been running against an incumbent instead of for an open seat. And how would it look for him to have a child with serious health problems and him immediately going on the campaign trail for a year dumping the kid off on his sick wife or a nurse? People would think he was heartless and he couldn't win. The only way to win was to get rid of the one thing holding him back. He obviously put the baby up for adoption. That has to be it." My jaw clenches as my eyes narrow. "The kid was too much of an inconvenience. He threw the child away, Sam."

Sam reaches over and rubs my shoulder. I feel my eyes well up as I grab his hand. "Hey, you said there was a priest at the house?"

"Yeah, why?"

"Then you know we have to call Uncle Steve."

You have resources I do not.

I nod and grab my cell phone so I can call our uncle the priest, who works for Catholic Social Services.

In the adoption agency.

***

My mom's younger brother is known as Father Steven to most, but Sam and I have never called him that. He's simply our uncle who happens to wear a collar, and is a superhero in his own right. He may be fifty, bald and paunchy, but he's got an invisible cape.

He finds homes for children who otherwise wouldn't have one.

And if anyone found a home for Becker's son through his agency, he would know.

But could he tell?

My uncle greets me with a hug as I enter his office. "Cassidy, it's been too long."

"Really, Uncle Steve."

"You've certainly made a name for yourself lately."

"For some of the wrong reasons."

"And some of the right ones. I've read what you did for the subway hero."

"Just being a good Catholic."

"There's a switch. When's the last time you went to Mass?"

I bless myself. "Bless me Father, for I have not been to church in awhile."

"You've done plenty of good deeds and I absolve you." He makes the sign of the cross in front of me, then kisses me on the head. "Anyway, I've been conflicted about calling you."

"Really? Why?"

"Well, as you know adoptions are supposed to be private and I'd be breaking a rule in this case. However, I was worried my niece was ending up in a serious relationship with a man she really didn't know. So I prayed about it."

"And?"

"C'mon. Let's take a ride."

***

I hear steps moving toward the front door. My uncle takes my hand as he's done so many times. "Remember, she doesn't know who the parents are, so don't mention Becker."

"Got it."

The door opens and we're greeted by a slender woman around forty with jet black hair and a huge smile. "Father Steven, come on in."

"Hi Marilyn. Want you to meet my niece, Cassidy."

She takes my hand and shakes it. "Right, you said you were bringing one of your volunteers. I didn't know it was a relative.

Nice to meet you, Cassidy."

"Same here." Thankfully, she doesn't have the look I usually get from being recognized.

My uncle closes the door. "I thought it would be good if she met one of our most special children."

Her dark eyes beam at the compliment and turns to me. "Well, you've come to the right place. Brian is coloring in the kitchen." She leads us through the modest home and into the kitchen, where I see a boy about ten at a small round table, head down, gently holding a crayon as he slowly colors a picture on some pale construction paper. "Brian, look who came to visit!"

He looks up and his face knocks the air out of me.

He's a dead ringer for Will Becker.

"Father Steven!" he says, in a distorted voice that sounds like it's underwater. He gets up and moves toward him, one leg swinging out wide while the other goes straight, wraps his arms around my uncle's waist and gives him a strong hug.

My uncle hugs him back and strokes his hair. "Hello, Brian! Good to see you, buddy." He holds on for a moment, the gently pushes the child back and turns him toward me. "Brian, I want you to meet my niece, Cassidy."

The kid looks at me and his eyes light up. He comes to me and gives me the same treatment, a strong hug. "Hello, Cassidy!"

My eyes well up and I hug him back. "Great to meet you, Brian." I turn to his mother. "Quite a welcome."

"That's his standard greeting," she says. "Brian loves everyone. I always say if all people were like him there would be no wars. He doesn't know the meaning of hate."

The child looks up at me. "Do you like to color?"

"I love to color, Brian."

"Let's draw a picture."

"Okay, sure."

He takes my hand and leads me to the table where we both sit down. He grabs a fresh piece of construction paper, then grabs a bunch of crayons and holds them out toward me. "Pick one, but don't take red."

"Okay." I scratch my head. "Let me see, which one do I want... how about green?" I take the green crayon from his hand and he sets about drawing.

"He brings such joy to our home," says his mom, looking at me. She lowers her voice. "It boggles the mind that someone didn't want him, but he's been a blessing to us. Our other two children love him like you wouldn't believe. And if my husband were home you'd see the incredible bond they have."

I quickly glance at Brian who is totally focused on his drawing. "Did you have any qualms about adopting—"

"A special child? No, not at all. Look, he takes a ton of care and has a lot of medical problems, but I wouldn't trade him for anything. He has such an innocence, such a purity of heart that you never see in so-called normal people. Like I said, he makes anyone who meets him feel better."

"I can see that."

"Sometimes I think special children are angels sent by God to remind the rest of us to be thankful for what we have."

"That's a beautiful way of looking at it."

Brian grabs my arm. "Green. Your turn. Two dots."

I glance at the drawing which doesn't look like anything yet. "Okay, where do you want the two dots?"

He points. "There and there."

I dab the crayon on the paper. "Is that all you want me to do?"

"Yep." He goes back to the drawing.

"Well, that wasn't too hard." I turn back to his mother. "So, what's the prognosis?'

"You're looking at it. This is as far as he'll ever progress, which is fine. And we have enough money for his medical care since the birth parents were apparently wealthy and set up a trust." Her smile fades. "Amazing that some people threw money at what they perceived to be a problem to make it go away. What kind of person does that?"

"Really."

She shakes her head. "I wonder how those people can live with themselves." She looks back at Brian. "But to us he's a gift, not a problem."

My uncle puts his hand on Marilyn's shoulder. "Cassidy, this is why we placed Brian here. I've known Marilyn and Jack for years from my parish. We knew he'd be loved and well taken care of."

Brian grabs my arm. "Finished." He hands me the sheet of paper.

I look at the crude drawing of a tall red haired woman, a smile that looks like a slice of watermelon, the two dots I placed with my crayon now her green eyes.

"Picture of you," Brian says, with a huge smile.

My emotions well up as I look at him. "Thank you, Brian, it's beautiful. It's the best picture of me I've ever seen."

"His point of view is always positive," says Marilyn. "And he seems drawn to people who have a good heart." She suddenly gets the familiar look of recognition and her eyes widen. "Now I know where I've seen you."

I start to answer but she interrupts.

"You're the subway hero's girlfriend."

CHAPTER TWENTY-FOUR

@TwitterGirl
Subway hero Tyler Garrity fully recovered and back to work!

"Welcome back," I say, as I stick my head in Tyler's office.

"Thanks. Feels good to get out of bed."

"No after affects?"

He shakes his head. "Nope."

"Hey, I've got a hypothetical question for you."

"Shoot."

I close the door and take a seat next to him. He studies my face. "Okay, what's bothering you?"

"It's that obvious?"

"Yeah."

"This is hard for me, Tyler, but you're the only one who will understand."

He reaches out and takes my hands. "Just tell me."

"Okay, here goes. Let's say you found out something about Becker, something horrible. Something that told you he wasn't fit to be President. What would you do?"

He furrows his brow. "Is there some reason you're asking me this?"

"Just tell me what you'd do. And don't forget, it would cost you your job and the jobs of everyone else in the campaign."

"Why are you—"

"I'll tell you in a minute. What would you do?"

"Well, first of all, all political campaign jobs are temp jobs, as they are in every campaign. I personally don't need this job and I know the rest of the staff would easily catch on somewhere else. But that's not the important part of the question. The important part is one of ethics."

"I see why people say you're so smart."

"If I found out something horrible, I'd first need to know what the fallout would be if I leaked the story. Who else would get hurt? I would have to consider that part. But if the collateral damage was minimal, I couldn't live with myself helping someone get elected President who had covered up something horrible."

"Makes sense."

He slowly nods. "You've got something on him, don't you?"

I look down at the floor and don't answer.

"You gonna tell me what it is, or should I just begin cleaning out my desk now?"

I look up at him and we lock eyes.

I have to tell him everything.

My words come pouring out, accompanied by emotions I cannot fully explain.

Tyler listens, not saying a word for five minutes, his look one of both shock and disgust.

"That it?" he asks.

I nod. "Yeah."

He shakes his head. "Good God, that's awful. I never would have guessed he would do something like that."

"So what should I do?"

"I know you'll do the right thing."

"But *how* do I do it?"

He folds his hands in his lap and leans back. "Okay, if you leak it to one of your media friends, it will be devastating to his

239

daughters. But here's the really bad part; you'll turn every camera on the adoptive family and Brian. I know you wouldn't want to do that."

"No, of course not."

"But, there is a way…"

I sit up straight. "Yeah?"

"You know the trick I used on the party chairman when he was gonna do that sex poll? The one I use on everyone?"

***

Will Becker is all smiles as he arrives shortly before noon, shaking hands as he makes his way through the campaign headquarters. I'm already in his office, blinds drawn, fists and jaw clenched, sitting across from his desk. His face lights up as he sees me. "Damn, you're a sight for sore eyes." He moves toward me, arms extended, waiting for an embrace.

I don't stand up and simply glare at him.

He studies my face. "Something wrong?"

"You got some 'splainin' to do, Senator. Shut the door. Have a seat."

He furrows his brow. "Cassidy, what's going on?"

"Shut the door and *sit down*. We need to talk."

He puts up his hands. "Okay, okay." He closes the door to his office, walks behind his desk and slides onto his chair. "Obviously I've made you upset."

I fold my arms. "Why didn't you stop by the hospital to see Tyler?"

"Oh, that." He exhales deeply and leans back. "Look, I thought Frank explained to you my schedule was packed solid. I couldn't get away."

"You're the candidate. You can do whatever the hell you want."

"A lot of people paid a lot of money to be at those fundraisers.

I couldn't stand them up. Besides, you were already there representing the campaign."

His words launch me out of the chair. "I wasn't *representing* the campaign. I was there because Tyler's my friend. Is he simply a staffer to you? For God's sake, Will, you've known him for years. He almost died. Did you happen to notice the President of the United States even came by?"

"Well, I'm sorry. I'll go speak to Tyler."

"It's too late and that's not the point."

"Okay, fine. How can we—"

"I'm not done." I rest my hands on his desk and lean forward. "Mind telling me why you wanted to do a poll on whether or not we should sleep together?"

He looks down. "You, uh, weren't supposed to know about that."

"Well, uh, I do. So, did you also commission a poll on whether you should kiss me? Whether I was suitable enough to be your girlfriend? Maybe you should have put my picture next to Ripley's and let the voters decide. Oh, wait, you didn't need to do that because I already had approval numbers. You were behind that, weren't you?"

"I'm sorry, Cassidy. The sex poll was a bad idea, and I know Tyler killed it. Frank didn't know about it and was furious that I'd even suggested it to the party chairman." He looks up at me. "Please forgive me, Cassidy. We can get past this. You have to understand—"

"Understand what? That anything is fair game in politics? What, you pick a girlfriend like you pick a Vice President? You're supposed to be the candidate that's an actual human being, that's why you're winning. And you treat me as if I'm one of your talking points? Was there some focus group behind one-way glass when we had dinner?"

"Again, I'm sorry. I should have considered your feelings." He stands up and extends his arms. "Let me make it up to you."

"How? By putting two million dollars in a trust account? I've

241

got two words for you, Will. Brian Fillorio."

The color instantly drains from his face as his knees buckle and he plops down into his chair. "Oh, dear God." He stares at his desk and says nothing for a few seconds, unable to look at me. "How did you find out?"

"You've been dating an Emmy Award winning reporter, or were you so obsessed with using me as a campaign prop that you forgot?"

"I never used you." He looks up. "I could never use you because I love you, Cassidy."

The words I once hoped to hear now make me feel sick. "Don't you *dare* say that to me. But I really don't care what you did to me, I'm more concerned about what you did to your wife and kids. Was that little boy so much of an inconvenience that you would throw him away? You broke your wife's heart, Will. Just so you could run for the Senate. You threw away a human being, your own flesh and blood, for political gain. Because he was getting in the way of your own ambition. What kind of person does something like that?"

He doesn't say anything for awhile, then looks up, eyes moist. "So where does this leave us?"

"Us? You gotta be kidding me! There is no *us*. I seriously doubt there ever was. Do you really think I could love someone like you after this? Did you happen to notice I have a brother in a wheelchair and I'm close friends with Tyler? Did it ever occur to you that I'm not the type of girl to throw people away because they're not physically perfect? I put my career on hold when Sam got hurt and it was the best thing I ever did. It made me a much better person. But you did just the opposite. Because you're selfish."

"So I guess you're also leaving the campaign?"

"*That's* what you're taking from all of this? But hey, why am I not surprised since all you care about is your political career. Yes, I'm leaving the campaign and I'm leaving skid marks. Right now. And guess what, Will? So are you."

"Excuse me?"

"I'll give you till Friday to drop out of the race. Make up whatever excuse you want. Personal reasons, illness, I don't give a damn. Because if you don't I'll leak this story about your secret son and your campaign will be dead anyway. Bow out gracefully and the media doesn't ever hear about this. The story stays buried. But if you ever run for a political office again, I leak the story. And considering your propensity to throw people away, if anything mysterious happens to me, the story is in a secure location and automatically triggered to go to all the networks and every newspaper in New York."

"You're blackmailing me?"

"No, Will, I'm saving the country I love from someone who is unfit to be President. Because now, more than ever, this country needs someone with a soul." I grab my purse and head for the door. "Friday, Will. Tick tock. I'm a reporter and I have never missed a deadline."

"Cassidy, isn't there anyway we can resolve this? I can lose the Presidency but I can't lose you. We can make this work. I know you love me as much as I love you."

"Goodbye, Will. And if you want someone to love, look in the mirror."

He says nothing, looks down at his desk.

"Oh, one more thing, Senator. The same deadline applies to your daughters. If you don't tell them the truth, I will."

***

I push my Kung Pao chicken around the plate as I watch the coverage with Sam and Ripley. Seeing Will Becker wrap up his speech is killing my appetite and the food has no taste though it should be blazing hot. His face is drawn, his eyes bloodshot. The vibrant man who was the country's most eligible bachelor looks defeated. "Finally, I am releasing my committed delegates, and I do not want my name placed in nomination at the convention. I realize this will create an open convention but hope the party can unite behind the best candidate to defeat the President and take back the White House. Thank you all for your support in the past, and God bless America."

Reporters bombard him with questions, but Becker simply turns and walks away.

Sam turns down the sound on the television. "Well, Tyler's strategy worked. He didn't call your bluff."

"Which proves he doesn't know me at all. He should know I would never release a story that would cause such pain to his children and Brian's family."

Ripley reaches over and pats my hand. "You did the right thing, we're proud of you."

"So why do I feel like crap right now?"

Sam takes my hand, his fingers entwine with mine. "Because you got used, and because you were thinking with the wrong head, like a man."

"Huh?"

"He's right," says Ripley. "It was high school all over again. Only this time the quarterback was the country's most eligible bachelor. But sweetie, any girl would have done the same thing. I mean, they turned you into Jackie Kennedy for a few weeks and you were dating an incredibly hot guy who seemed to be everything you were looking for. Plus, you got caught up in being America's favorite couple. Don't beat yourself up."

"Why didn't I see it?"

"Because while love is blind, infatuation is just plain stupid," she says.

I feel my eyes welling up. "I really thought he cared for me. And I hate to say this, but I think I was falling in love with him."

She wraps an arm around my shoulders. "No, you weren't. You were in love with *being* in love with him, if that makes any sense. You would have become Mrs. Will Becker and the First

Lady, but Cassidy would have disappeared into the shadows. His identity would have destroyed yours. And I know that's not what you wanted."

"I never should have taken the damn job."

"Then you wouldn't have fallen in love," says Ripley.

"You just said I wasn't really in love."

Sam reaches over to the coffee table, grabs a stack of newspapers and tosses them in my lap. "You fell in love, Cassidy, but not with Will Becker."

I look at the front page of the tabloid, the now famous photo of Tyler and me at the hospital.

My brother taps the paper. "If that's not the look of love on your face, then I don't know what is."

"He's right," says Ripley. "You had the title of Becker's girlfriend, but you were dating Tyler. Sometimes we have to see ourselves from someone else's point of view. Remember?" She turns the page on the newspaper and points to a quote the paper has pulled and put in bold black letters. "Read what you said. Aloud."

I wipe my eyes and focus on my own words. "Tyler Garrity is just about the finest man I know. He's incredibly kind, an old-fashioned gentleman that every girl wants." My voice cracks, overcome with emotion. "And right now when I look at him, I see my hero." I feel the waterworks about to blow.

"Cassidy," says Sam, "those two weekends Tyler spent here… I don't think I've ever seen you happier. You two are a perfect match. He's your soul mate. And he's head over heels in love with you."

"He is?"

Ripley grabs my shoulders. "Good God, are you blind? He treats you like Sam treats me."

"If he's in love with me, why didn't he ever say something? Why didn't he ask me out?"

"He wanted to the first day he met you, but thought he couldn't compete with Becker," says Sam.

"How do you know this?"

"We talked about it that time we were making breakfast before you woke up."

"Well," says Ripley, "*I* didn't have to talk to him about it. I could see it plain as day. And I could see you were in love with him." She flips the newspaper back to the front page. "Picture's worth a thousand words, right?"

I stare at the photo, looking at myself.

"I think the light bulb is turning on," says Ripley.

"Give it time," says Sam. "In her case it's on a dimmer switch."

I flip the newspaper open and read my words again.

Ripley takes my chin and turns my head to face her. "You and Tyler went to a Broadway show, an opera, a Mets game, a Giants game. You spent two weekends together. You have everything in common. You're so in tune you kicked our ass in pinochle the first time you played as a team. You miss him terribly when he's not around. He's the first guy you called when you were on the road and you talk so much the battery runs out on your both your phone and your iPad. You spent four nights in a hospital room with him, sleeping next to him in a bloody dress and holding his hand, and I know you would have been devastated if he had died. You told a newspaper reporter he was your hero. The last time you had a good night's sleep was with him in the hospital. Sure sounds like someone you love to me." She reaches into her pocket, pulls out her cell phone and taps it a few times. "Watch."

I see myself and Tyler, playing gin rummy during one of our weekends together, laughing and having a good time. Ripley taps the phone again, and I watch the two of us sitting next to each other enjoying breakfast, kidding around.

"Look what you're doing with your hand," she says.

I'm twirling my hair as I look at Tyler.

"It's your *tell*."

I look up at Ripley, see her soft smile. "Why did you tape this stuff?"

"You needed another point of view, just like I did. Sometimes

246

we girls miss the obvious." She looks over at Sam and takes his hand. "Sometimes the right guy is right in front of us."

I then turn to Sam.

"You should know by now I'm never wrong," he says. "But I wouldn't wait too long, he's New York's most eligible superhero. Oh, and as a reminder, you recently said you wanted to marry a man just like me. Well, there he is."

I suddenly get up, put the newspapers on the coffee table, grab my purse and head for the door. "I have to go."

"Feel free to use my script," says Ripley. "And I don't think you'll need a teleprompter."

CHAPTER TWENTY-FIVE

@TwitterGirl
The campaign was fun while it lasted. I'll be in touch...

Tyler opens the door and smiles. "Hey, I didn't know you were coming by."

"I didn't either."

"Well, come on in." I enter and see an ironing board is unfolded next to a basket full of clothes. "You're ironing shirts on a Friday night?"

"Well, the Disney bluebirds didn't show up to do my laundry. They're incredibly unreliable." He studies my face and drops his voice. "You watched his speech, didn't you."

"Yeah."

"I told you not to do it."

"In case you hadn't noticed, Tyler, I'm a little bit stubborn."

He takes my arms in his hands. "I can tell it upset you. I'm sorry you got hurt."

"I'm more mad at myself than anything."

"Hey, he fooled me for nine years. He fooled everyone." Tyler gives me a hug and strokes my hair for a moment, then pulls back. "So, anything I can do to make you feel better?"

"Just seeing you makes me feel better. But Tyler, I need to ask you some stuff. Important things I need to know and I want you to be totally honest with me."

"Sure, fire away."

"Okay. You like me a lot, right?"

"Geez, for a network reporter you sure start off with a stupid question. Of course I like you a lot. I'm surprised you have to ask."

"How long have you liked me a lot?"

"From the first day I met you. You asked me to be honest, I'm being honest."

"And do you know that I like you a lot?"

"Well, yeah, sure. I mean, you just spent the better part of a week with me in the hospital. But that day I met you I could tell we had a connection and were on the same wavelength. You know how you click with some people? We've always been on the same page from the start."

"So, if you liked me a lot from the first day we met, and you knew I liked you, why didn't you ever ask me out on a date?"

"Why are you asking me this stuff?"

"Because I need to know. And I need to know right now, so please bear with me because I'll explain my reasoning shortly. Why didn't you ever ask me out?"

He shoves his hands in his pockets and looks down at the floor. "I, uh, well... I knew I couldn't compete with Becker and that you were interested in him."

"But I didn't really start dating him, if you even want to call it that, for a while. Why didn't you ever ask me out on an official date, Tyler? Before I started seeing Becker."

He looks up at me with sad eyes. "I figured you were, you know, out of my league."

"Excuse me?"

"Look in the mirror. You're gorgeous and smart and funny and have a big heart. The kind of girl who could have any guy she wants. Girls like you don't usually go out with guys like me."

"What do you mean, *girls like me?*"

249

"Like I said, you're the total package. You can have any guy you want, and you wanted the Senator. I picked that up right away. And I knew I couldn't measure up to him."

"Tyler, you're ten times the man he is."

"Thank you, that's very kind of you to say."

"So, did you *want* to ask me out? Before I started seeing Becker?"

"Of course, but I didn't want to get shot down."

"Why would you assume that I'd say no?"

"Again, you're everything a guy could want. A dream girl. And since you have this affinity for platform heels, I assumed you'd want a guy built like Becker."

"You really didn't ask me out because I'm a few inches taller than you?"

He shrugs. "That's part of it."

"Did you happen to notice that when you stayed at my house I had clothes that fit you from an old boyfriend? Didn't that tell you I don't mind dating guys who are shorter than I am?"

"Yeah, but by then you were doing your Jackie Kennedy thing with Becker. I'm not sure any man could compete with that."

"Final question. After my so-called Jackie Kennedy tour, is that why you were down when I called you that night? Be honest."

He looks down again. "I'm embarrassed to say I was really jealous. It hurt to see you with him because I wanted you. That's why I didn't feel like talking. I wanted to be happy for you but I couldn't. I hope that doesn't sound selfish but you asked me to be honest. I figured you only wanted me as a friend and I had to accept that. And it hurt. It really hurt."

I slowly nod and take his hand.

It's time for Ripley's script.

"Let's sit down a minute, there's something you need to hear."

"Sure." I lead him over to the couch and gesture toward it. He sits down and I climb onto his lap, curling one arm around his neck. His eyes widen. "Uh…what—"

"Shhhh." I put one finger over his lips. "Cassidy is talking and she has something very important to say. By the way, young man, when there's a girl on your lap you need to hold her. And Cassidy really needs to be held right now. Hands, use 'em." He wraps his hands around my waist. "Very nice. Now, do I have your undivided attention?"

He nods and mutters, with the same look Sam had when Ripley sat on his lap. "Uh-huh."

"Good. Tyler, it hit me when we were in the hospital and I got in bed next to you. I have never, ever felt so comfortable with a man in my life. It hit me when I read what I said about you in the newspaper when you were in the coma. It hit me when I saw how I looked at you in the front page photo when I thought you might die, how I never looked at a man that way, even the guys I've loved. It hit me when I saw video of the two of us and I was twirling my hair, which is my *tell* when I'm really attracted to a guy. So I'm thinking, *who is this girl, and why doesn't she see what the camera sees? Why doesn't she believe her own words in the newspaper?* Sometimes you really don't know yourself without a different point of view. And then it hit me. I love the way you and I have been so in tune since the first day we met. I love how you watched me walk to my car the night I brought you a pizza to make sure I was safe. I love how we can talk on the phone for hours about any subject. I love how you like the same movies and sports that I do. I love how you rescued me in the deli from Wheeler the Dealer. I love your sense of humor, how you're always bright and cheerful. I love how you threatened to kick the party chairman's ass and killed that poll because it would have hurt my feelings. I love your clever little nicknames for people. I love that you were the one who arranged for me to get a six-foot box of chocolates and wrote the line that came with it. I love that you know how to cook and can make the most incredible scones. I love the look on your face in our photo that made *Page Six* after the opera. I love how you tease me about my ridiculous appetite. I love how you call me *smoking hot* even though I'm not even close. And I love how you risked your own life to save that little girl, which means you would take a bullet for me and will always protect me. Tyler Garrity, I hope you can forgive me because I have been a complete idiot. The best man in the world has been right in front of my nose and I didn't see him. You are absolutely the perfect man for me and I am sorry it took me so long to realize it."

He's in shock, his jaw hanging open while those incredible eyes of his lock with mine.

"Cassidy is now done with the verbal part of her apology." I take his head in hands and kiss him, soft at first, then harder as the electricity I feel is off the charts, much more than I ever felt with Will Becker. His hands run up my back, into my hair. Suddenly I feel a hunger for a man I've never felt before, and I can't stop kissing him. Finally our lips part. Tyler's look of shock has morphed into a slight smile. "So, am I forgiven?"

"Excuse me?"

"Am I forgiven for being an idiot? By the man who is absolutely perfect for me. Or does poor little Cassidy have to get down on her knees and beg?"

He shrugs. "Depends."

"Depends? On what?"

"On what you do when you're on your knees."

"Why Tyler Garrity, you have a dirty mind."

"There's a smoking hot redhead on my lap who just gave me a tonsillectomy, what did you expect?"

"So, are you gonna make it official and ask me out on a date?"

"Absolutely. T.G., would you—"

"No, no more initials. I want you to say my name."

"Fine." He gets a gleam in his eyes. "Would you like to have dinner with me, Twitter Girl?"

I hug him hard as the emotions I've been holding in finally explode and tears roll down my cheeks. Only they're tears of joy. "I'd love to have lots of dinners with you. Lots and lots of dinners. But the next meal we have together is going to be breakfast."

"Oh, I get it." He leans back. "You just want me for my scones."

"Well, you are the total package and you know I need a man who can cook. By the way, when a guy is perfect, Ripley says he's ready *to drive off the lot*. So why don't you give me a ride to your bedroom?"

***

"I must be dreaming. There's a smoking hot redhead in my bed."

I crack open one eye and see Tyler lying on his side, smiling at me. "I'm the one who's dreaming. There's a smoking cute guy in my bed."

"Oh, is that my new nickname? *Smoking cute*?"

I pry open both eyes and prop myself up on one elbow. "No, I still haven't come up with a nickname. I'm simply stating a fact. You are smoking cute."

"I've never heard the term."

"I just made it up. It means you're the ultimate in cute."

"Isn't it better to be hot than cute?"

"Cute lasts forever. You'll always have that boyish thing about you, even when you're old. And you're a smoking cute guy." I yawn and lay my head back on the pillow. "What time is it?"

"A little after noon. It's my recovery day, so I sleep late, remember?"

"After what you did to me last night I'm the one who needs a recovery day. God, Tyler, you were amazing."

"You were pretty incredible yourself. You hungry?"

I roll my eyes. "Seriously?"

"Sorry, stupid question. I'll go make something."

"We can go out if you want, my treat."

He throws back the covers. "Nah, I like waiting on you."

I grab his arm before he gets out of bed. "Hey, I wanted to ask you something."

253

"Again with the questions? *Now* what?"

"Okay… my bother told me you guys talked about me that time you spent the weekend at our house. Specifically that you had a crush on me."

He blushes a bit. "Yeah, but it was a lot more than a crush. What about it?"

"What exactly did my brother say?"

"Well, first off, he couldn't stand Becker. Thought he was a huge phony. I told him he was wrong but he really didn't want you to end up with him. He said you'd figure it out and eventually break up with the guy. That I should be patient, that in time I'd have my chance with you. And I told him I was worried that even with Becker out of the picture I'd get shot down. But he said he was one hundred percent sure you'd go out with me if I asked."

"And after that you were still scared to ask me out?"

"Like I said, you're a dream girl. Haven't you ever had guys scared to ask you out before?"

"Well, yeah. Sure. Every girl has. But I mean, you and I were already close friends."

"Well, thankfully you made the first move."

"If I hadn't, would you?"

He smiles and nods. "I was in the process of working up my confidence, but I was still scared. Ripley has been calling me constantly, encouraging me ever since you dumped Becker. She told me you were in love with me but just didn't know it."

"She was right. So, when were you gonna pop the date question?"

"I was going to make you a batch of scones and bring them by on Sunday, then ask you to go for a ride. I was gonna take you down to the Jersey shore and then hit a really nice restaurant I know overlooking the ocean when we were coming back. Then ask you when we got home. I've been rehearsing what I was going to say."

"How about we do that anyway?"

"I already asked you out last night."

"I know. But it sounds so romantic I want to hear your original

254

words. And if you rehearsed it I wouldn't want it to go to waste. Besides, you already know the answer." I run one finger down his chest. "Please? If you do it there will be a reward."

***

After a hot shower I'm greeted by the sound of sizzling as something has hit a frying pan. I walk toward the kitchen running a towel through my hair as I go and see Tyler pouring batter onto a griddle. "Yay, pancakes! Make a lot of 'em, cause I'm starving. And, as you know, I'm a growing girl."

"I know, you missed your morning feeding," he says, as he holds up a jug of syrup. "And by sheer coincidence, someone thoughtfully brought this back from New Hampshire."

I pat my belly as I arrive in the kitchen. "Great, I need something to fill me up. I mean, you know, besides you."

He blushes and then his eyes widen as he takes in my outfit, which consists of one of his white oxford button down shirts and nothing else. "Damn."

"You like?"

"You have redefined the term *smoking hot*."

"Sam really likes Ripley in this outfit, so I thought I'd try it on you. Of course, she leaves the top unbuttoned, and, as you discovered last night, I'm not half as well equipped up there as she is."

"Doesn't matter, I'm a leg man. I take back what I said before, yours even look great without heels."

"You're sweet. But y'know, I don't see why *you* shouldn't leave a few buttons open for *me*." I rest one hand on his back, pop a few buttons with the other and slide it inside his shirt, running it across his stomach. "Right now I can't keep my hands off you. By the way, I was pleasantly surprised to discover you're ripped. Quite the six-pack, young man. And here I was expecting skin and bones."

"Well, I work out during my normal days. I may look thin but I'm wiry and stronger than I look."

"I'll say. You carried me to the bedroom like I weighed nothing." I slide one finger inside the waistband of his shorts and steal his breath.

"I'm really enjoying what you're doing, but you keep this up and I'll burn the pancakes."

I take my hand away. "Well, my body does need fuel after last night." I wrap my other arm around his shoulders and give him a quick kiss on the cheek. It's the first time I've been barefoot around Tyler and notice he's a little taller than I originally thought. I pull him close, shoulder to shoulder and he turns to face me. "See, you were worried about nothing. I'm just a little bit taller than you, maybe two inches. Not a big deal."

"Yeah, until you put on the gold stilettos, the red ones with the straps or the stacked heel boots you wear with the jeans. Then it's half a foot."

I fold my arms. "Well, well, well, a man who notices a girl's footwear. And I thought only women had the shoe chromosome. I'm impressed."

"Again, leg man. Goes with the territory. Killer legs should always be accessorized with proper footwear."

"When did you see me in boots and jeans?"

"Giants game. And I might add that no one fills out a pair of skinny jeans like you. We were walking to our seats and I saw every guy checking you out as we passed. When I turned around you had left a wake of hanging jaws behind you." He turns back to the pancakes.

I wrap my arms around his waist from behind. "Keep up the compliments and I won't care if the pancakes are burned. So, does my leg man have a favorite pair of shoes?"

"They all have their good points, but I guess the red ones are the best."

"Those are the highest heels I've got. So, you like me as tall as possible."

"I've always had a thing for six-foot-four snarky redheads, but they're so damn hard to find."

"Guess what, Tyler? No matter how high the heels I will always look up to you."

He looks over his shoulder. "Now you're the sweet one. By the way, are you staying here today?"

"Where else would I go?"

"Didn't know if you had stuff to do. I'd offer you some clothes from an old girlfriend but I don't have any."

I rest my head on his shoulder. "That's okay, I don't think I'll need any."

***

"Well, look who finally came home."

Sam smiles at me from the kitchen as Tyler and I walk in shortly after ten on Sunday morning.

"Sam, she obviously was too tired to drive home and Tyler was nice enough to offer her his guest room," says Ripley with a wicked grin as she sets the table for brunch.

I see Tyler blush a bit. "I had to bring her home. I ran out of food."

I say nothing but cannot hold back a smile as I move toward Ripley while Tyler brings a grocery bag of goodies into the kitchen. She whispers in my ear as I give her a strong hug. "Party girl."

I whisper back. "Best. Sex. Ever."

She leans back and looks at me wide-eyed.

I lick my lips. "Four times."

"You *cheap* party girl."

"I'm a *very happy* cheap party girl." I slide my hands down her arms and take her hands while giving her a soulful look. "I can't thank you enough."

257

"Hey, it took me years to realize I loved Sam. At least you only took a few months."

***

I lean back, fat and happy.

And in love.

I take in the scene around me. My brother and best friend in a solid relationship. A terrific guy for me.

Even thought I'm now unemployed again, it hits me.

I have a perfect life.

Tyler walks around the table topping off everyone's coffee cup as Sam turns to Ripley. "I guess now's a good a time as any."

Ripley nods. "Yeah, it's safe to tell them."

"Tell us what?" asks Tyler as he sits down.

My brother gets a sheepish look and I can tell he's been up to something. "We have a confession to make."

"We've been playing matchmaker with you two," says Ripley.

I'm puzzled. "How did you play matchmaker?"

Sam picks up the ball. "Remember the Broadway show we all went to? And how I brought you back to the island for cheesecake?"

"Yeah, and it was lousy cheesecake," I say. "Can't believe you picked that place."

"It wasn't about the cheesecake. We needed a place we've never been on the island and that was the only one," says Ripley.

"Is there a point anywhere in our near future?" I ask.

Sam smiles. "Remember how much fun you had when Tyler spent the weekend here the first time?"

"Yeah…"

"We wanted you to experience that again. So I pretended to forget Tyler lived in Manhattan and made sure it was so late he'd have to stay with us. If I'd picked one of our regular places you'd have known it was too far for Tyler to get home, so I just said

258

I found a new place and wanted to surprise you guys. You got distracted talking to him in the back seat and before you know it we were on the island."

I turn to Tyler. "Did you know about this?"

He shakes his head. "No, but I'm glad they did it. And I like the way they think."

I look at Ripley. "Now I know my brother isn't this devious, this had to be your plan."

She holds out her wrists like a criminal waiting to be hand-cuffed. "Guilty as charged. But since it worked I'm hoping for a suspended sentence."

***

I'm like a kid on Christmas morning, waiting to open that special package under the tree. We stroll up the walk to my house after a wonderful day. A ride along the Jersey shore, a long walk on a secluded beach, dinner alfresco at a great seafood restaurant overlooking the ocean. My fingers are entwined with his as we reach the front door.

This is it.

The man I love is going to ask me on a first date.

I turn to face him. "Thank you for a great day, Tyler. This has been a fabulous weekend."

"I figured you needed it after the rough week you had."

"Hey, that was nothing after what you've been through."

"Speaking of which, I wanted to tell you something about what it was like those first days in the hospital. You know, before I woke up."

"You remember stuff? I figured you were dreaming."

He shakes his head. "I thought so too. Anyway, when I was in the coma I kept having this recurring dream. You were back at the television network, anchoring the news. But every story you read was about me saving the little girl. One of the nurses said you read a lot of newspaper stories to me while I was out. So I wasn't really dreaming, I could actually hear you."

"That's what I was hoping for, Tyler."

"Anyway, every time you ended a story, you said the same thing. *Follow my voice.* And then you would reach out with your hand. Each time I would try to grab it but it would slip away. Finally I kept hold of it and you pulled me out of the coma. The nurse told me you were sleeping with me, holding my hand. So what I thought was a dream was real."

I get a lump in my throat as I bite my lower lip.

He moves closer to me, places his hands lightly on my waist and looks up at me. "I was hoping you might follow that little voice in your own head, the one that is hopefully telling you to give me a chance. The one that says Tyler's not what any girl dreams of, but he's a good guy who thinks you're the best girl in the world and will always protect you. I realize that I might be jeopardizing our friendship but I have to know if there's even the slightest chance you might have feelings for me. And I realize you're the kind of girl who can have any guy she wants, but I'm hoping you'll follow the little voice in your head that tells you to give me a shot. I followed your voice, so I hope you'll do the same."

My eyes well up and the little voice confirms I've found my true soul mate. "Well, since you think I can have any guy I want, I'll have to agree with you, because the guy I want is you. And, you know, I already had you."

We kiss under the porch light and the stars, one with the universe.

When our lips part I open the front door, take his hand and pull him inside. "Too late for you to drive home. You're staying here."

"So, the guest room is available?"

"My little voice tells me it's too messy, so you'll have to sleep with me. I did promise you a reward, after all."

CHAPTER TWENTY-SIX

@TwitterGirl
As President Turner would say, "Vote early, vote often."
Please vote for Dan Kirkland!

SIX MONTHS LATER, AMERICA'S CAMELOT
COUPLE ON SEPARATE PATHS

"It was a unique experience, and I ended up with the man of my dreams. What more could a girl ask for?"

Had we taken a time machine from the spring to present day and seen that quote, we could have assumed the woman known as Twitter Girl and America's most eligible bachelor were headed for a life of wedded bliss in the White House.

Instead, on the day of the Presidential election, former Senator Will Becker has turned into a recluse and the man of Cassidy Shea's dreams is none other than New York's subway superhero, Tyler Garrity.

How we got to this point is somewhat of a mystery, and one that may never be solved, as the parties involved offer little in the way of clues. But there is a focal point in the story, and everything indicates it is the day Garrity saved a little girl's life. That event seems to have set the dominoes falling.

On the morning of that spring day, Senator Becker was seen a slam dunk to be the next President of the United States. Cassidy Shea was his girlfriend and frequent companion on campaign tours while maintaining her duties as Twitter Girl, firing snarky barbs at the competition. Tyler Garrity, known as the Stephen Hawking of politics, was serving as Becker's chief strategist.

And then a little girl fell on the tracks.

While she survived, a campaign and love story derailed.

Becker and Shea seemed like the perfect couple and looked hopelessly in love. The public followed the romance like the Brits rooted for Prince William and Kate Middleton. Garrity was often Shea's escort on a few occasions when Becker's campaign duties took priority and the two had become good friends.

"Tyler and I spent a lot of time working together in the campaign office and had become close," said Ms. Shea. "When I was on the road we'd talk on the phone for hours. But I didn't cheat on Becker and Tyler never hit on me while the Senator and I were dating. He was a perfect gentleman when he escorted me."

Becker, reached by phone, had nothing but kind words about his former girlfriend. "I have tremendous respect for Cassidy Shea and wish her the best. She's an incredible woman who taught me a lot. But our relationship was like a Roman candle. It burned hot and fizzled out. That's the best way to explain things."

Again, the subway incident is the focal point of said fizzling.

Ms. Shea was about to leave for a long campaign trip with Becker and asked Garrity to join her for a meal uptown before she left. While they were waiting for the subway, five year old Samantha Frazier fell onto the tracks dangerously close to the third rail. Garrity jumped in and saved her, then was pulled out by a transit cop seconds before a train roared by. But while being yanked to safety he hit his head on a pole and fell into a coma.

And for the next four days, Cassidy Shea never left his side in the hospital.

"Usually you only see that kind of devotion from a family member," said a nurse working at that time. "But that woman was with him every minute, holding his hand, talking to him, playing music, reading the newspaper out loud, trying anything to get him out of the coma. When he finally came to, she stayed another two days just in case he slipped back into a comatose state. By the time they left, you could see there was something special between them. That photo in the newspaper says it all."

That now famous photo of Shea resting her head on the mattress looking desperate in a torn bloody dress while holding Garrity's hand went viral. Everyone who saw the look on her face knew she had romantic feelings for him.

Except Ms. Shea.

Meanwhile, Senator Becker never showed up to check on the man who had been working for him for nearly a decade. It did not go unnoticed by a media that was fawning over the candidate, but was never reported.

A campaign staffer, speaking on condition of anonymity, said Shea was furious with Becker for attending a ten thousand dollar a plate fundraiser instead of coming by the hospital before he left on the west coast campaign swing. "You could tell the woman was livid. I mean, every single person on the staff except Becker went to see Tyler. Anyway, she had fire in her eyes and was waiting in the Senator's office when he got back. The door closed and about five minutes later she stormed out looking like she wanted to strangle someone and never came back. Becker looked devastated and had tears in his eyes. It was obvious she broke it off instead of the other way around. But I figured there had to be something more, something really bad that set her off… I mean, what woman dumps Will Becker?"

Of course a few days after that there was another bombshell, as Becker suddenly dropped out of the race and resigned his Senate seat for "personal reasons" which have never been explained.

"Sometimes a relationship just ends," said Ms. Shea in an emotionless tone without a tinge of regret. Her eyes went cold when asked to elaborate. She also declined to say anything else about the Senator, even after being read his comments about her. While she hasn't seen Will Becker or spoken to him since that day, she maintains a relationship with his oldest daughter Kristin. "She wants to be a television reporter and is graduating next summer. I'm trying to mentor her and put her on the right path. Kristin is a terrific young lady and she's got her head on straight."

Those same green eyes brighten when asked about her current love, Tyler Garrity. "I didn't realize what I had in Tyler until after my relationship with the Senator ended. But if you look at that photo of us when he was in the hospital, you can see the look of love on my face, so I guess subconsciously I was falling for him then. I didn't realize how much I cared until I almost lost him. Looking back, I can see I was simply infatuated with the

264

Senator and got caught up in the whole First Lady thing. Tyler is an incredible guy, treats me like a queen. We have everything in common. I respect him like no man I've ever known with the exception of my brother Sam and my late father. And the guy's a superhero... there was a real life white knight in New York City. Who knew? He did more than save little Samantha, he saved me."

Garrity, who hooked on with eventual candidate Dan Kirkland's campaign after the party's open convention, sounds like he can't believe he ended up with his dream girl. "It was love at first sight when I met her, but like every other woman on the campaign she had eyes for the Senator. Then she became Becker's girl, so I had to settle for being a good friend. And honestly, it was pure torture when she spent those days with me in the hospital because I wanted her so badly. But I felt like I hit the romantic lottery when she said she had feelings for me. I'm completely blown away that such an amazing woman would choose me over someone who looks like Will Becker. She is so kind... I've never known a finer person with such a big heart. She's the perfect woman for me and I can't imagine being with anyone else."

Both Shea and Garrity are tight lipped when asked about future wedding bells but you can tell from the way they look at each other they're in this relationship for the duration. While he's been busy with the new campaign, she's turned her Twitter Girl fame into a business, hiring herself out to anyone who wants to use sarcasm as a promotional tool. Dan Kirkland was her first client, but she has no desire to work in the White House.

As for Becker, he wouldn't even reveal his location when we contacted him by phone. He plans to run his father's company and stay out of the public eye.

So America's dream of a second Camelot was not to be. But like most fairy tales, this one has a happy ending… at least for two of the three people involved.

***

Tyler pops a bottle of champagne as the final returns come in confirming that Dan Kirkland has enough electoral votes to be declared the winner of the Presidential election.

I can't help but wonder how close I came to making a huge mistake as I watch him stroll to the podium.

"Well, the best man won," he says, pouring the bubbly for me, Sam and Ripley.

"Amazing how it worked out," says Sam. "You guys started out working for a guy you thought was squeaky clean and he turned out to be the biggest loser on the staff. Then you end up with a man who is legitimately squeaky clean."

"And Cassidy ends up with the guy who was meant for her all along," says Ripley.

I lock eyes with Tyler and smile as he sits down next to me and holds up his glass. "A toast!"

"To the next president?" asks Sam.

"Hell no. To the women we love!"

We all clink glasses and sip our champagne. I lean over and give Tyler a kiss while Ripley does the same with Sam.

"Well, I think I've had enough of politics for a lifetime," I say.

"Oh, come on," says Tyler. "We make a great team. Kirkland couldn't have won without you."

"Ask me again in four years. But right now, all I want is to spend time with you. We make a great team regardless of what we do."

My phone chirps telling me I have a text. And just when I think all the loose ends have been neatly tied up, I find one more that I had forgotten.

You proved that all was not as it seemed.
Wish to thank you in person.
O'Reilly's Grill, 501 East 43rd, noon, tomorrow.

***

I peek over the menu every time the front door opens, looking for… someone. Someone who will make eye contact with me and reveal the final piece in the puzzle. I'm waiting for my version of Watergate's Deep Throat, the person who tipped me off and saved me from what could have been a disastrous relationship that would have cost me the true love of my life.

I find it interesting that my secret source wants to thank me, when it should be the other way around.

A middle-aged businessman walks in, looks around and makes eye contact.

I start to get up but he heads for someone else, and I realize he simply recognized me.

And then the person I suspected all along walks in next.

I stand up and smile as she weaves her way through the tables. Kristin Becker picks up her pace and gives me a hug, then holds on for dear life.

Finally I pull back. "You okay?"

"Yeah."

"I had a feeling it was you."

She sits down. "Well, that's why I need you as a mentor. You're a great investigative reporter. You found the truth that we couldn't for years. After the right guy won the election last night, I figured it was time to tell you. You changed history."

I slide back onto my chair. "Well, if it weren't for you, I would have ended up with the wrong man."

"I'm happy for you, Cassidy. I read that story yesterday about you and Tyler. He's a great guy."

"Yeah, I'm really happier than I've ever been. And I'm glad you finally found the truth. Anyway, you're the final piece of the puzzle. I'd like to hear the story if it's not too painful to tell."

"No, you deserve to know. My sister and I always suspected something wasn't quite right with that whole situation, even though we were very young. There was one night when mom and dad got in a huge argument, and we could hear them upstairs. And she said one thing that stuck with us. *You took him from me.*"

"So you knew your brother was alive?"

"We asked mom about it and she wouldn't elaborate as to what she meant. She wouldn't even let us bring up the subject. But as we got older we started to put two and two together. The fact that there was never a funeral or an obituary in the paper was the main thing that raised a red flag. And the priest at the house with my father, day after day. I mean, we're Catholic but my father rarely made it to church and wasn't at all religious. So we started trying to check the possibility of adoption but as you know those are incredibly private. When you came aboard the campaign, we knew you might be able to help. Not only were you a reporter, but you had the one connection we needed. Your uncle the priest."

"How did you know my uncle worked for Catholic social services?"

"We were doing an Internet search on you, reading some articles, and we saw one about your family, how your uncle was a priest who spent a lot of time with you and your brother after your parents were killed. And there was a photo of the two of you from ten years ago, and we recognized him. We were like, oh my God, that's the priest who was at the house!"

I slowly nod. "See, you're gonna be a great reporter. What about the number you sent me?"

"We were in dad's office one day and found a slip of paper with that number on it next to Brian's name, so I copied it down. I figured it was something important."

"So, why the secret messages?"

"We figured if we simply contacted you face to face you'd think we were a bunch of rich brats who hated their parents. And my journalism teacher says all great reporters will investigate every lead, no matter how small. I knew you were that kind of reporter because I'd seen a video of a talk you gave to a college class."

"Yeah, I'm like a dog with a bone when it comes to a story. Every lead has to be investigated."

"But we were really getting worried when you and dad were getting romantic. Thank goodness you saw his true colors."

"Well, thank you for pointing me in the right direction and keeping me interested in finding the truth. It all worked out for the best. So, I hate to even ask but... what's your relationship with your father now?"

"We don't have one. We're both twenty-one now so we cleaned out our trust funds and are taking care of our own expenses. We haven't spoken to him since he told us the truth. We're legally changing our last names and taking our mother's maiden name. We don't want to even be associated with him. By the way, thank you for setting us up as volunteers for your uncle. It's actually very rewarding helping unwanted children find good homes."

"I thought it might help with the healing process. And it would be a back door way to meet Brian."

Her face brightens. "We love our little brother. Of course we can never tell him or his parents we're his sisters, but it's great getting to visit him once in a while."

"He's a beautiful child. The kid loves everyone."

"Yeah. Hard to believe his father only loved himself."

CHAPTER TWENTY-SEVEN

@TwitterGirl
Six shopping days left till Christmas. Seven till the exact same stuff is half price. Do the math and get twice the stuff.

Christmas is in the air as we finish our dinner exactly one year to the date that I got fired. The exclusive restaurant is beautifully decorated with a half dozen trees and twinkling lights wrapped around gold garland and red bows that run along the ceiling. Even with the holidays just around the corner, I can't help but think of the incredible events that transpired which led us to this point.

But this point, for tonight anyway, is aimed at Ripley, as Sam is going to propose. She has no idea and I know she's going to be blown away. The restaurant staff is in on it and I'm standing by with a camera.

"Excellent dinner," says Sam as the waiter hands him a dessert menu.

Suddenly the waiter looks down at the floor. "Sir, I believe you dropped something."

That's the cue.

Tyler gets up and moves to one side of Sam's wheelchair while the waiter stands on the other. They each grab him under one arm and help him get down on his knees as I pull out my camera.

Ripley's face tightens. "Hey, what's going on?"

"I dropped something," says Sam.

"Well geez, Sam, I'll get it," she says, as she tosses her napkin on the table.

Sam pretends to reach for the floor, then opens his hand in front of Ripley. "Oh, this must be yours."

Her eyes positively bug out as she sees the massive diamond ring my brother is holding. She clutches her chest with both hands. "Oh my God," she says, her voice barely audible.

Everything in the restaurant comes to a halt. All eyes are on our table.

My brother looks up into her eyes as Tyler and the waiter support him. "Ripley DeAngelo, I have known since I was eight years old that you were the perfect girl for me. It started as a crush, then became love when I understood the meaning of the word. You started out as a special friend and became something much more. You would make me the happiest man in the world if you would do me the honor of becoming my wife."

Ripley's still in shock but I see a smile slowly appear. "Oh, hell yeah!" She thrusts her left hand forward. "Ring me, baby!" Sam slides the ring onto her finger, then she kneels down next to him and gives him a big hug and kiss. The crowd applauds as she gets back up while Tyler and the waiter help Sam back into the chair.

"Champagne all around," says Tyler, as he sits down next to me.

"Very good, sir," says the waiter, who heads for the bar.

I'm getting misty taking in the scene in front of me. Sam and Ripley, holding hands, exchanging longing looks. "I am so happy for you two. Now lemme see the ring!"

Ripley smiles as she holds her hand across the table, displaying the rock that has to be at least three carats. "Eat your heart out, dear friend!"

"Damn, you're gonna be walking sideways with that thing. But it's gorgeous. C'mere." I get up and she does the same. We hug, long and hard, two best friends forever who have shared so much.

I move over to Sam and he gives me the strongest hug ever. When we break the embrace I have to brush a single tear from his cheek.

We sit back down as the waiter returns with the champagne and begins to fill our glasses. Sam and Ripley go back to being locked in, oblivious to what's going on around them. I rest my head on my palm and savor the scene. I realize I'm going to be losing my brother, sort of.

"You okay?" asks Tyler.

"Yeah. I get sentimental around stuff like this. Guys wouldn't understand."

"Try me."

"Well, every girl always dreams of the perfect guy getting down on one knee asking for her hand in marriage. Nice to watch it come true for my brother and my best friend."

"You look a little jealous." Tyler looks up at the waiter and tugs at his sleeve. "Excuse me, doesn't my girlfriend look a bit jealous?"

The old waiter studies my face. "Indeed she does, sir. I would surmise she might be envious of that rather sizable ring and the situation across the table."

I look up at the waiter. "Hey, I'm not jealous. That's my brother and my best friend. I'm happy for them. You're about to blow a big tip."

A middle-aged bald guy at the next table taps Tyler on the arm. "She looks jealous to me."

I whip my head around at him and give him the death stare. "Hey, who asked you?"

"Sir," says the waiter, pointing to the floor under Tyler's chair, "I believe you dropped something."

Tyler leans over and nods. "Yeah, you're right." He gets down on one knee, reaches under the chair, and comes up holding a diamond ring as big as Ripley's.

The air is knocked from my lungs as my jaw drops.

"Caz, you really do miss the obvious sometimes," says Sam. I look over and see him smiling at me while Ripley has a camera

272

pointed in our direction. Then I turn back to Tyler.

He looks up into my eyes as he takes my hand. Once again everyone in the restaurant hits the pause button.

"When I almost died it was you I heard in the darkness, telling me to follow your voice. Your touch was the only one I felt. Yours was the hand that guided me back to life. When you realized you loved me, it was the little voice in your head that told you to follow your heart. I am asking you now to follow my voice and my heart, to take my hand in marriage, to share everything for the rest of our lives. Twitter Girl, will you marry me?"

I don't hesitate for a second. "Tyler, both the little voice in my head and my heart agree, and my real voice has the answer. Oh, hell yeah! Ring me, baby!"

I stick out my left hand and he slides the ring on my finger.

It's a perfect fit, just like the man who is giving it to me.

I kneel down next to him and hug him for all he's worth, then give him a big kiss as the crowd applauds.

When we stand up I find Ripley next to me. We hug, tears in both our eyes.

"Lemme see that ring!" she says.

I show it to her and she nods, then whispers in my ear. I lean back and smile as we put our hands side-by-side, turn to our future husbands and say in unison, "Is her ring bigger than mine?" The crowd laughs as we both put our hands on our hips and give the guys disapproving looks.

"They're exactly the same," says Tyler. "It was buy one, get one free."

"So who got the free one?" asks Ripley. Her eyes narrow. "It better not be me!"

"It better not be me!" I add.

"You can't put a price on love," says Sam.

@TwitterGirl
Sorry, girls, America's most eligible bachelor is off the market.

I'm engaged to New York subway superhero Tyler Garrity!

***

Six months later…

@TwitterGirl
On honeymoon with the love of my life and new husband, Tyler Garrity. A white knight and superhero rolled into one.

A gentle breeze carrying salt air blows through the open door of the balcony, filling our cruise ship suite as we sail across the Atlantic toward jolly old London. After a whirlwind engagement and double wedding, we are relaxing on a three week honeymoon. We wanted to visit Europe and since air travel is such a hassle for our guys, we booked transatlantic crossings and are traveling the old fashioned way, which beats the hell out of the flying egg cartons known as commercial jets. It's incredibly relaxing, and besides, do you think this girl could survive an eight hour flight on a bag of airline pretzels? So, five days on the luxury ship, eleven days in the UK, then five days back.

When we return, I will find my perfect life all set up and ready to go. As will my brother and Ripley.

Ah, Sam. Leaving him was the one thing I feared would be my only regret.

But then we got a wild stroke of luck when the house next door went up for sale. Tyler and I quickly snapped it up, so we'll be a hundred feet or so from Sam and Ripley. She's moving in to our home since it made sense as it is already set up to accommodate Sam's chair. Meanwhile Tyler, who wanted Sam to be able to visit our new home, had a covered walkway built between the two houses and our new home remodeled. Now we'll be one big family, like the Ewings in *Dallas*, although a lot happier than those guys.

And Tyler said we didn't have to order monogrammed towels since he already had some and we had the same initials. Tyler Garrity. Twitter Girl.

Oh, as it turned out, Tyler and I are the same age but his birthday is one day after mine. Which means I'm older. So Ripley has been calling me "cougar" since we found out because I've been doing it to her.

Anyway, it's my first cruise and I must say it won't be my last. It's so relaxing, like the outside world doesn't exist. Meanwhile, you'd think those Disney cartoon bluebirds actually do exist. Leave your cabin for a few minutes and your bed is made. Drop a towel on the bathroom floor and it is magically replaced by one folded into a swan sitting on your bed. And, of course, there's the food. Twenty-four hour room service, a buffet on the Lido deck that never closes, a midnight buffet, a chocoholic buffet, two entrees at dinner if I feel like it. And, every afternoon, tea with… wait for it… scones! Even my brother is amazed at the food I'm packing away. But, hey, I'm a growing girl.

It's Tyler first cruise and he loves the flexibility of participating in the shipboard activities or just loafing. Sam is having a blast and really excited about his first trip to Europe and I know he's beaming because his new wife does nothing but turn heads on the ship when she goes to the pool. He wanted her to enter the bikini contest but she would hear nothing of it. Turned out there was a write-in vote for her anyway and she took home the trophy.

Right now I'm getting ready to tie up one final loose end which has been bothering me for months. No, it has nothing to do with the puzzle on he-who-must-not-be-named. Until last week I still hadn't come up with a nickname for Tyler's alter ego superhero. But thankfully it finally hit me and I have an appropriate present to give him in a minute, just in time for the ship's costume party tonight.

He enters the cabin, carrying a single sheet of paper. "I got the list of costumes they have available for tonight's party."

"Oh, I packed costumes for us."

"You did?"

"Yeah." I reach under the bed and pull out a gift wrapped box. "One final wedding present." I pat the bed next to me. "C'mon, open it."

He sits down and starts unwrapping the gift. "I hope you aren't making me dress up like a Chippendale again."

"Nope, that was just for my eyes only and will never leave our bedroom. Besides, I don't have any dollar bills."

He tosses the paper aside and opens the box, then smiles. "Superhero uniform."

"You're a real life superhero, you're my hero, so why not? Besides, I've been promising you that I'd come up with a name for your alter ego."

He pulls out a blue cape, tights and shirt, then holds them up. "Very nice. So what's my superhero name?"

I point at the logo on the shirt. "See the wings and halo? You're The Guardian. Y'know, like guardian angel. Since you've been protecting me and watching over me since we met."

"I like it, thank you." He leans over and gives me a kiss. "So what are you wearing?"

"Ah, that's a surprise. You're going to the party with Sam and then Ripley and I will follow a few minutes later."

"So you guys wanna make an entrance."

"The surprise will be a lot better that way, trust me."

"Original Star Trek uniform?"

"Nope."

"Hooters waitress?"

"No, but I'll file that request away for future reference."

"French maid?"

"You seem to have one thing on your mind, leg man. But trust me, you'll like it."

Ripley turns to face me. "How do we look?"

"You look spectacular. Me, I'm not so sure. I think I'm a little old for this."

"Pffft. Don't be ridiculous. It's a costume party. You supposed to let your hair down and we're the best looking things here. Tyler will trip over his tongue when he sees you in that."

"Okay. If you say so."

"Let's rock."

We turn the corner, head into the crowded ballroom and wander through the crowd, looking for our guys. We pass a lot of tame costumes, no doubt the ones handed out by the cruise ship, many of which are not age appropriate. (Sixty year old woman dressed like Dorothy from The Wizard of Oz.) But as usual, Ripley is right. The crowd parts like the Red Sea as we walk through it and get plenty of stares.

"Everyone's looking at us," I say.

"As previously mentioned, we're the best looking women on the ship." Ripley stops and points across the room. "They're at a table in the corner."

I see Sam and Tyler, deep in a conversation. They don't notice us until we arrive at the table, then both their jaws drop.

Sam's eyes bug out. "Oh. My. God."

"You weren't kidding," says Tyler, staring at my legs. "Unbelievable. As advertised. Better than advertised."

Sam is gawking at Ripley. "Rah. Rah."

"I'm thinking we get them both sewing machines for Christmas," says Tyler.

"Just remember," says Ripley, "you two married a couple of thirty-five year old hags who both easily fit into their high school cheerleader uniforms."

"And didn't need a pair of Spanx to do it." We both shake our pompoms.

"The yearbook photo doesn't do you justice," says Tyler. "And you two actually look better now."

"Of course we do," I say. "When you're married to the two best guys on the planet, you're gonna glow."

***

"I always wanted to date a cheerleader," says Tyler, as he wraps one arm around my waist. We look out at the waves from our balcony as the pure salt air fills my lungs.

"Well, now you've got one on retainer any time you want," I say, pulling him close. "You sure you want me to keep this outfit on?"

"Are you kidding? Talk about a fantasy come true. That costume gave me an idea… I think I have a new nickname for you."

"Really? What?"

"Legs."

"I like T.G. better."

"Okay. By the way, back in high school were you the head cheerleader?"

"No. That title went to the girl with the dirty knees."

"Very funny."

"The fantasy come true for me is marrying a superhero. I'm in love with The Guardian."

"I love you too, Cassidy."

"God, I love it when you say my real name. But keep it for special occasions. It makes me melt when I hear it. Like it did at the altar the first time you said it to me. I almost lost it when you were reading the vows."

He looks up at me and gently strokes my hair. "This is like that night in the hospital when you got in bed with me."

"Huh?"

"You know, when you were on the cot and the moonlight hit you just right."

278

The memory brings a lump to my throat. "You said I looked like an angel. That almost made me cry."

He points at the full moon. "But the moonlight here is brighter without all the light pollution from the city. You look even more angelic."

"Well, I guess The Guardian needs his own angel. Speaking of light, remember how you once told me a political wife spends her time in the shadows?"

"Yeah."

"You're my sunlight, Tyler." Our fingers entwine as we look out at the passing waves and another cruise ship far in the distance. The moon is low on the horizon, reflecting off the water. "You wanna hear something funny?"

"What?"

"This probably won't make sense to you, but I have a crush on my new husband."

"You're right, it doesn't make sense. You already have me. You've got it backwards."

"I know that, but it's the same feeling. You know how you feel when you want someone and they're unattainable? I have that feeling of longing combined with the comfort that I've gotten my wish. It's hard to describe. Sometimes I look across the room at you, or at the pool when you go to get drinks for us, and I desperately want you. And then it's pure joy knowing you're mine."

"I did enough longing during the campaign. Now I stick with the pure joy twenty-four seven."

We kiss, then I take his hand and lead him back into the cabin. Knowing he's mine.

He gets into bed and I slide in next to him, wrap my arms around him, throw one leg over his waist, bend it and curl it around his knees. I hug him tight as I rest my head on his chest.

He puts one arm around my shoulder and strokes my hair with his free hand. "You're holding on pretty tight tonight."

"The cheerleader with a crush has captured her superhero and doesn't want to lose him." I give him a squeeze. "You can't get away, so don't even try."

"You know damn well you're my Kryptonite and I'm powerless against you. Besides, why would I want to get away?"

I turn my head and look up at him. "Because you're one of those guys."

"What guys?"

"You know. *Those* guys. The total package. Smart and funny and sweet and smoking cute with a big heart. Incredibly brave. A hero. A dream guy. One of those guys who can have any girl he wants."

"And the only girl I want is you."

I squeeze him a little tighter. "That's because I'm a growing girl."

He furrows his brow. "You think I want you because you eat a lot?"

"Silly, of course not. I meant I'm growing *emotionally*. Took me awhile but I finally discovered what love is. In fact…" I reach for the nightstand and grab my cell. "I wanna tell the whole world."

"You're tweeting *now*?"

"Hey, it'll only take a minute, and Twitter Girl has some wisdom to impart on her adoring public." I quickly type a tweet, then turn the phone so Tyler can see it. "You like?"

@TwitterGirl
Love is not about finding someone you can live with, but someone you can't live without. I found my someone.